INTERVENTION

by

Mike Rothery

INTERVENTION
by
Mike Rothery

Copyright © 2015 Mike Rothery

3rd Edition Sept 2018

(Previously published as 'The Waiting Pool')

United Kingdom Licence Notes
The right of Mike Rothery to be identified as the Author of this work has been asserted by him in accordance with the Copyrights, Designs and Patents Act 1988

All rights reserved. Apart from any use permitted under UK copyright law no part of this publication may be reproduced, stored in a retrieval system, or transmitted, in any form or by any means, without the prior permission of the publisher.

This is a work of fiction. Names, characters, places, events and incidents are either the products of the author's imagination or used in a fictitious manner. Any resemblance to actual persons, living or dead, or actual events is purely coincidental.

~ Chapter One ~

> On the bank at Season's ending
> quietly sending blushing petals,
> blood red clouds of gentle blossom
> drifting down upon the winding waters,
> like sons and daughters off to who knows where?

The sound of distant thudding seeped into a consciousness that was neither asleep nor awake. Gradually the thudding grew louder, now accompanied by a faint whine, and the half-asleep brain tried to recall why the noise was vaguely familiar, and why it seemed so important.

The whine rose to a turbine shriek, the thumping to a rhythmic *chop-chop-chop*. Then it was overhead, and with a jolt, the brain came fully awake, sending light-speed emergency signals coursing through its network.

Patrick tore apart the reed matting in his panicked scramble out of the shelter, then lurched through the soft sand waving and shouting after the helicopter. When it had gone he slowed to a standstill and stood staring accusingly at the ridge where it had disappeared. Hope faded with the receding clip of blade tips; faded into a black void of disappointment.

Furthermore, his fire had gone out in the night – so there was nothing to light the beacon with; no way to recall the helicopter. He sank his knees deep into the dew-damp sand and wept. And now, exacerbated by his ever-present hunger, the aftereffects of adrenalin-rush kicked in, and he collapsed in a bout of feverish shakes.

When the fainting spell had passed he got to his feet and loped up the hill to watch the helicopter, now little more than a distant speck receding over a glittering sea. Impotent rage rose within him once more. He waved and shouted and cursed. He cursed the aircrew for their blindness; he cursed a world that was ignorant of his pitiful existence. Winding up to a frustrated passion he gave free rein to his emotions to roar at the unfairness of it all. He spun round in wretched fury, lost his balance and thumped painfully to one knee on the rocky ridge.

And as quickly as it had come upon him, the madness drained away. Crouching like a runner on the starting blocks, he stared at the dust mote suspended above the razor-sharp horizon. He lifted a hand to scratch his chin, long, filthy fingernails penetrating the matted beard. The object was no longer getting smaller, no longer going away from him. He continued to watch it; a crouching cat watching a mouse.

Then, a brief glint of reflected sunlight. His fingers froze in mid-scratch and he muttered, 'The blind bastard's turning.' Now it tracked east, heading towards the newly risen sun, and climbing. For untold minutes, like a snake poised to strike, he watched the helicopter climb and drift from left to right, until it merged with the glare under the sun's lower limb. Had his tortured mind imagined it getting closer?

Either way, he could no longer see it. He kept watching for it to reappear to the right of the sun, watching.

'Where the fuck…?'

Had it all been a cruel deception? A waking dream caused by the insanity of loneliness?

He sensed movement out of the corner of his eye, swivelled his head to the north and quickly brushed aside a clump of hair that had fallen over his eyes. Had the helicopter doubled back without him seeing it? He scanned the empty sky, and then dropped his gaze to the horizon. And saw it, not the helicopter, but a puff of white smoke, hanging motionless in the still morning air.

A ship?

His mind soared with renewed hope.

Then a distant *boom*, followed by a faint metallic scraping sound, rising in pitch and fading. Before the strange noise had faded away entirely the sequence repeated; a second puff of smoke, boom, scraping sound, now fading. And again, now three puffs of smoke.

'Patrick me old mate,' he murmured, 'if we're not mistaken, that's…'

With shocking suddenness the air was filled with a blast of sound like an approaching express train, and Patrick threw himself flat, clasping his hands over the back of his head.

The high explosive shell burst fifty yards away to his left and a wall of heat slammed into his side. Stones and splintered wood from a shattered tree rained down, peppering his naked back. Terrified, deafened and with his head ringing, he scrambled to his feet and hurled himself down the hill towards the beach. At the screaming rush of the second projectile he dived once more for the ground. He was now far enough down the hill from the fall of shot to escape the rain of debris. He ran onto the beach and crouched there, watching the deadly barrage blasting away the ridge, his ridge.

His carefully constructed signal beacon got a direct hit, sending a hundred fiery tree trunks spinning through the air like Catherine Wheels. He hoped desperately that the gunners stayed on their mark, or at least fell short rather than over.

As salvo after salvo pounded the ridge a dust cloud of spent explosives and pulverised granite drifted down the slope to envelope the shoreline. To escape the choking fog Patrick swam out to the reef from where he continued watching the onslaught, balancing with his toes on a submerged rock amid the coral. When the bombardment stopped he waited for a few minutes to see if it would start again.

He was halfway back to the shore when he heard once more the approaching chop of rotor blades. He trod water and watched the broken ridge where the last vestiges of airborne debris were drifting away.

And suddenly there it was, a beautiful angel in drab light grey, cutting a magical swathe of clear air through the thinning smoke, sunlight glinting brightly from the double windscreen.

Patrick kicked his feet with all the vigour he could muster so that his body raised in the water almost to his waist and waved both arms.

Then the helicopter was thundering overhead, kicking up salt spray from its downdraught.

~ Chapter Two ~

Patrick took a long wondering look at himself in the full-length mirror. 'Ben Gunn', he said aloud, and sniggered at the appropriateness of his observation. Then he sobered as he tried once more to get his head around the staggering events of the past few hours. He felt disorientated and somewhat confused by the abrupt change of environment; his first encounter with humanity had been strangely surreal, and not a little intimidating.

At first, he had forgotten that when someone spoke to him he was supposed to reply. Instead, he had internalised his responses to their endless questions, avoided eye contact with the concerned faces of his rescuers, trying to make sense of the new and scary experience of being once more amongst people.

His over-weathered frame was a shocking sight: ribs and hips sticking out, legs flamingo-skinny with unnaturally large and flappy feet. 'You look like a famine refugee,' he told his reflection, 'you could set up a slimming club for anorexics.' He giggled at his own joke, and then he remembered where he was and looked round guiltily and began once again to question his sanity.

No, don't go there.

Instead he started thinking about food, fantasising about what his first meal would be like. On Folly he had grown accustomed to eating like a bird, a subsistence diet of sea grapes and conch, having rendered the tiny island's iguana population extinct and swept the narrow reef clear of lobsters. The taste and smell of conch had become so hateful to him he never wanted to see another one in his lifetime.

He tugged at one of the thickets of hair that sprouted maniacally from his head and covered most of his face. It was the colour and texture of washed-out coconut rope.

He spent a luxurious half hour under the shower; he had to start it cold because the hot water was unbearable on his skin, and then gradually turned up the hot in stages.

Afterwards he allowed the ship's barber to go to work on his head and face. He spent some time convincing the slightly camp hairdresser that he normally wore his hair long and didn't require the close-cropped style mandatory for his sailors.

'My God, actually in a ponytail? How very sixties.'

However, as hard as the barber had tried, he hadn't been able to deal with the wild tangle. Finally Patrick agreed to a complete head-shave.

~.~

The young surgeon lieutenant wrapped the BP cuff around Patrick's upper arm, and then shook his head as he pumped up the pressure.

'It's unbelievable how you survived for over a year on that rock. And to think we nearly blew you to pieces.'

Patrick stayed silent. He didn't think it was unbelievable. The only thing he was having difficulty coming to terms with was the fact of his rescue, and those thoughts were coloured by a disturbing wistfulness.

Christ, he actually missed that fucking island already.

Life there had been simple. All the anger had gradually worn away, and his grief became just a constant ache that he came hardly to notice. Now all the implications of his liberation began to crowd in on him. For the first time in many months, he started once more to think about Stella. After more than a year of isolation, was he still in the same frame of mind?

He didn't know.

The medical officer nodded satisfaction at the BP result and unbound the cuff. Patrick felt again at his chin and cheek, marvelling at the novel feel of hairlessness. He explored the bizarre baldness of his head. Stella would be in hysterics…

His fantasies about food had been dashed. They hadn't allowed him any solids, explaining that until his fluid and nutrition levels were back to normal his body would simply reject the rich food. Therefore, they fed him thin soup and milkshakes and promised him a light meal in the morning. Right now, he could have walloped down a New York Strip with all the trimmings.

He had had several visitors to his bedside, including the aircrew who had rescued him, and a couple of curious officers that came to gawp. Knowing what warships were like, he realised that by now he would be the main topic of gossip in the wardroom and on every messdeck.

He still had no clue about his immediate future. Though he had told a little of his story to the Exec - the USN equivalent of the First Lieutenant - the information flow had been largely one way. He gathered the ship was on an operational mission of some kind and there would be a delay before he could be set ashore, and that was all he knew. But he felt no urgency on that score; he had some serious thinking to do.

That evening the Captain popped his head into the sick room door. 'Is this a good time, Mr Redman, or do you need more rest?'

Patrick spluttered his willingness for the officer to come in; his conversational skills seemed to have deserted him.

'Sorry I couldn't drop by earlier,' the Captain said, lifting a chair to the bedside, 'but we've got a lot of stuff going on right now.'

Patrick just nodded and kept a diffident silence.

'I also should apologise for not being able to drop you ashore right now – you've caught us at an awkward moment.'

Patrick thought of the irony of that explanation and almost laughed, but remembered in time the seniority of his visitor, 'I understand, Sir, operational reasons and all that,' he managed to stop himself tapping the side of his nose.

'Quite, but I think I can share with you the main points of our mission,' he looked pointedly at Patrick, 'because by tomorrow morning it will be common knowledge.'

Patrick found himself oddly detached from this revelation, but nevertheless was mildly intrigued and felt the need to make some sort of response, 'Don't say Cuba's waving nuclear missiles around again, Sir?' he said, and immediately regretted his choice.

However, the Captain only laughed good-humouredly, 'No, nothing quite on such an international scale – I assure you we're not taking you into World War Three.'

Patrick felt hauled back into the world. After all, a lot could have happened in thirteen months.

'Tomorrow morning,' the Captain said, 'October 25, at 0545 Eastern Standard Time, we commence Operation Urgent Fury: a combined force of US and OECS troops will land on the island territories of Grenada to oppose Cuban forces and local Marxist militia.'

Yes, the real world was finally forcing itself back into Patrick's life. He recalled a conversation with a brash Bostonian who had hinted at this very possibility. Patrick had argued that Grenada was in the British Commonwealth, so an invasion by the US would be somewhat tricky without upsetting the Special Relationship.

But that recollection brought back another, more poignant one. Without warning, he saw Stella – her wretched look of despair when their eyes met for the last time, the pistol-shot deafening in the enclosed room, the crimson bloom sprouting from her head and dotting the wall behind her, her body floating to the ground like an autumn leaf. A wave of grief swept through him.

'Are you okay, Patrick?'

He pulled his thoughts through the blackness back to the present and realised the Captain must have misinterpreted his expression as a response to the impending action. He cleared his throat and looked up brightly.

'Ah, so that's what the gunnery practise was all about.'

After the Captain left the duty medic dimmed the lights in the sickbay. At first, Patrick couldn't get off to sleep, despite the unaccustomed luxury of a soft mattress and cool clean sheets, or perhaps because of them. His mind was a whirlpool of thoughts and memories. Eventually the medic gave him something in a small beaker, and within minutes he was overcome with drowsiness.

~ Chapter Three ~

The following morning, two hours before *H-Hour*, Patrick was moved into a spare cabin in "Officer Country" to make ready the sickbay for combat casualties.

Dressed in crisp new khaki shorts and shirt, he accepted an invitation to breakfast in the Wardroom. The two lieutenants at his table were keen to get first-hand the story of his life as a castaway, so between mouthfuls of fried egg, pancakes, and sauerkraut, he responded politely, keeping his replies short and vague; he remained especially circumspect about how he came to be there.

After a time he became irritated by the questioning and tried to steer the table conversation to the forthcoming operation.

'I thought Maurice Bishop was one of the good guys.' he said, mopping up the last streaks of grease and egg yolk from his plate with a chunk of bread.

'Bishop?' said a boyish looking lieutenant whose shirt badge said Clements, 'he was the guy they killed, right?'

'Yeah,' said another, a big man in camouflage fatigues, who hadn't spoken until now; like Patrick, he had been studiously stuffing his face with calories. He wiped a napkin across his mouth and continued, 'the fuckin' commie bastard that started all the shit here. Austin's drivin' the show now and he's even fuckin' worse,' he smiled and reached a big beefy hand across the table to Patrick, 'Name's Rick, by the way, Rick Paul, Captain, US Marine Corps.'

'Patrick Redman. Pleased to meet you, Rick.'

'Hey man,' a voice down the table called, 'every sailor on this ship, and probably the whole freekin' Task Group, knows your name – you're famous! A limey version of Robinson Crusoe.'

'He was a Brit too, numb-brain!' chipped in another, to an uncertain chitter of laughter.

Patrick ignored the banter and addressed Rick, 'So what happened to Bishop? I've been out of touch for a while.'

His understatement got another laugh.

'Executed a couple months back,' Rick said, 'along with his whole goddam cabinet. You're right about Bishop though; Raegan thought he was okay - the devil you know? But this motherfucker Austin's beyond the pale. So here we are, to kick his ass, and his Cuban mercenaries, outa here.'

'And to repatriate the med students,' chirped Clements.

Rick let out a contemptuous snort, leaned across to him and said in lowered tones: 'You know jack shit, Clements. Those students are just pawns to cover up the real deal.' He turned back to Patrick, 'Regime change, that's what this mission's all about, trust me.' He pushed back his chair and picked up his plate and cup, 'Now if you will excuse me gentlemen, I have to rustle up some marines.'

~.~

Patrick met up with Rick again later that morning.

The Executive Officer, who seemed also to be responsible for Patrick's welfare and security, had given him freedom of the ship, except … 'Do not enter any compartment marked Restricted Access without permission from someone who works there. And wear this badge at all times outside of Officer Country.'

The badge said: 'Authorised Visitor'.

One of the crew had given him a baseball cap to protect his newly bald scalp from the sun. The donor was a young sailor with a homely southern drawl who seemed in awe of Patrick. The cap was emblazoned with the ship's name, *USS Charles Walther*.

Drawing curious but benign glances from the crewmembers briskly going about their business, he found his way to the main weatherdeck and stood at the guardrail watching a humongous aircraft carrier close abeam. She was launching aircraft at the rate of about one a minute; it brought back memories.

'That's *USS Independence*', said a voice behind him.

Rick joined him at the guardrail, 'she's the reason we're here: Carrier Escort. Those A6's are supporting our Rangers out there on Point Salines.'

Patrick looked to where he pointed, astern of the carrier, and recognised, about four miles away, the spit of land where he and Stella had made their first landfall in *Spirit of Carriacou* after crossing the Atlantic over a year ago. Only now, there was a pall of thick grey smoke over the promontory where the new airport was. He couldn't hear any gunfire over the noise of the two ships and the roar of jet engines from the carrier's deck, but as he watched, he saw the flashes and plumes of new explosions.

'So what are the Marines doing on a Carrier Group Destroyer?' Patrick shouted.

'Small Boat Interdiction. When the Rangers have done their work, we'll be patrolling the coasts around these islands for commie insurgents and PRA militias.'

'So how long do you think it'll be before I can get ashore?'

'Who knows?' shouted the marine, 'a week? A month? Depends how long these fuckin' Cubans hold out."

The noise level suddenly dropped as the last aircraft off the catapult banked to starboard and headed inshore.

"What's your hurry Patrick? You've been stranded alone for a year, and now you've got a ringside seat to history in action – relax and enjoy the show.'

'I have something to do' Patrick said.

Rick leaned heavily on the guardrail, 'You wanna tell me about it?'

They gazed down at the fast rushing water for a few moments, Patrick agonising over whether to tell the big marine officer his story, the latter clearly giving him space. He had to tell someone, and he had taken a liking to Rick; he seemed like someone who would listen.

It was Rick who broke the silence.

'I take it this is something connected with why you were stuck on that island all alone?'

Patrick nodded, and coming to a decision, began telling it. They walked slowly aft while he talked, down the waist towards the flight deck, the big man stooping and listening attentively. The helicopter that had picked Patrick up stood lashed and blade-cuffed, with a couple of grubbers wiping down its fuselage with cloths.

Patrick and the marine officer continued past the aircraft and stood at the very stern, where the wake of the destroyer stretched away to the horizon; a straight white highway on a windy blue sea.

~ Part Two ~

September 1982

~ Chapter Four ~

The naked Rhododendron bends
her bloom-bare branches to the stream.

I scrambled out of the companionway into a night blasted by howling wind and a madness of driven spray. Our yacht had broached in the heavy seas and now wallowed with her leeward rail under water, as nearly on her beam-ends as I ever wanted to see. Stella had the starboard lazarette open, heaving out fenders and mooring lines.

'Steering gone.' she called, as ever, calm and in control.

I snapped on my harness and held open the lid for her while she dug down for the emergency tiller. I used the moment to assess our situation. 'What about the autohelm?'

She put her head close to mine to be heard, 'Perhaps, but there is a risk of more damage. We must get her pointing upwind, and then I will take a look.'

I left her to ship the tiller while I furled up the headsail before it flogged itself to shreds. Then I released the preventer that was holding out the half-submerged boom.

It took both of us on the tiller bar to heave her up to windward. At last, the boom swung clear of the water and as she came head up, I took up the slack on the mainsheet.

'Quickly, the washboards!' Stella said.

I slipped the two panels into place just in time as a big wave slopped into the cockpit. Then we were head to wind and pitching into giant seas, still shipping water over the bow, but safe. Stella throttled back the revs until there was just enough power to make headway.

'Take over,' she said, 'I will go below to investigate.'

She slid back the hatch, put her hands on the coach roof, chose her moment then vaulted lightly over the washboards onto the ladder inside.

Keeping the boat into wind with the emergency tiller was brutal work and I hadn't yet made the mental transition of it working opposite to the wheel. I had just about got to grips with it when the companionway hatch slid back, and Stella's head popped up.

'Try the autohelm,' she called.

I aligned the course to ship's head, hit the Auto button, and held my breath. A complaining groan of the servo from below, then the tiller kicked against my hand as the electric steering took charge. I slumped down gratefully on the bench. Stella vaulted out, secured the hatch and came aft to sit by me.

'Well, Skipper, what's the verdict?'

'As I suspected, the steering chain is broken,' she said, without the slightest hint of anxiety, 'it is lying in the bilge.'

She could have been talking about how nice a night it was. As if I needed proof of the calamity, she reached up and gave the useless wheel a spin. Then she looked up brightly. 'But the good news is, only a link has snapped, it can be repaired.'

Which was just as well, I thought. Then I thought about it again. Repairing it at sea with the autohelm running would be like fixing a bicycle chain with someone jiggling the back wheel. It was a job for the boatyard. On the other hand, the autohelm could only be a temporary solution. Continuous use would soon drain the batteries once we stopped the engine, especially running downwind with those walls of sea chasing us. Steering with that sod of a tiller for twelve days didn't bear thinking about.

Stella had been watching me work it all out, as if she could see the synapses firing in my brain, and now turned a palm up expectantly for my verdict. She never stopped teaching me, even in a crisis.

'We haven't got fuel to keep the engine running all the way to Grenada,' I said, 'so we have to fix it ourselves.'

'Exactly,' she confirmed, 'But not in this, and not in darkness.' She sounded tired; the last four hours must have been exhausting.

'Want me to take the watch early?'

She gave me that imperious look of hers, and ignoring my ridiculous offer, pulled herself up to the pilot console. 'We will turn back downwind. If you will see to the genoa I will manage the helm and mainsheet.'

When we were running free again I went below and made a hot drink: tea for me, coffee for Stella. I passed up the two steaming mugs from the companionway ladder, then came up and sat opposite her in the cockpit. Stella sipped her coffee appreciatively then looked across at me.

'Thank you darling, and well done just now.'

Sitting there with her pretty face poking out of her foulie hood with her lifejacket collar cradling her damp cheeks, she looked curiously vulnerable. I wedged my mug in the cup-holder, leaned across and planted a kiss on wet, salty lips.

'That was good practice for your exam.' she said.

'I didn't know I had to snog the examiner to get my ticket – I won't do tongues, mind.'

I enjoyed seeing her laugh, eyes sparkling in the dim light from the console.

She sobered and tried again, 'you know what I mean. You handled your part very well.'

We stared at each other as I waited for the penny to drop, then we both collapsed giggling again. Juvenile, I know: I suppose it was relief after our recent scare.

'Seriously though,' she persisted, straightening her face, 'what to do when the steering fails is a common question. You can now reply with confidence.'

'As my Granny always said, it's an ill wind that blows nobody any good.'

She thought about that, and then beamed, 'Very apt. Nikkie would have enjoyed that.'

We let the sentiment ferment a moment as we slurped our drinks. Niklas was Stella's previous partner, a Swiss guy who had been a friend of mine, had always latched on to my English aphorisms, and before long I would hear them repeated to others, often hilariously misspoken. I had noticed recently that Stella had picked up the practice.

Eventually she said, 'How would you like to build on the experience and do the repair?' She must have read my flicker of doubt, for she quickly added, 'I will do it myself if you do not think you are up to it.'

I bridled at the implication, 'Can't be rocket science, where do I start?'

'I will brief you in the morning, *schatz*. You should go and turn in. You have the watch in two hours.'

When I came up to relieve her at eight the wind had dropped to a pleasant fifteen knots. With her customary flamboyance *Spirit of Carriacou* was again riding the trade wind and prevailing ocean rollers, though her charm was somewhat marred by the rumble and stink of the idling engine.

~.~

Access to the steering gear compartment was through Stella's cabin on the starboard side: a small hatch in the bulkhead at the end of the bunk. I found the broken chain in a pool of oily gunge in the bilge.

In order to get both hands to the job I needed to stick my head and arms right in amongst the moving pulley wheels and cables. Stella lowered a length of line through the gap where we had removed the compass binnacle, and I tied it to the end of the chain, so she could pull it up and locate it over the top chain sprocket. Trouble was, the lower chain sprocket was still engaged to the steering quadrant, so it kept jiggling back and forth at the whim of the autohelm while I was trying to join it with the new split link. I quickly grew to hate that dark sweaty hole, dodging the moving components with the boat bucking and tossing. It was a real pig of a job: it took me an arm-aching eternity to get that chain joined up again.

Do you think I came out of there flushed with success? Forget it. Right then I was knackered, bruised and scratched all over, filthy and sweaty, and as pissed off as a three-badge rock ape.

However, Stella always knew which buttons to press to snap me out of a mood. Thanks to that long spell with the engine running, we had hot water from the calorifier, of which she reminded me and suggested a hot shower. We hadn't used the shower since Santa Cruz, La Palma - twelve days ago.

Bliss!

~ Chapter Five ~

Without the engine noise and drifting diesel-exhaust, the tranquillity of ocean cruising returned. Her batteries now fully charged, we left *Carriacou* on continuous autohelm for a couple of hours while we took a shared break. We talked little as we cleaned up the saloon and then set to work on dinner, she, preparing the food, me, washing up the things as she finished with them. We opened a bottle of wine and ate together under the bimini.

Carriacou was making eight knots, genoa poled out to port and our huge red and white spinnaker nicely ballooned to starboard. We had dowsed the main to ease the load on the steering and give her an easier ride.

Partly shaded by the genoa, the autumn sun drifted toward the horizon on the port bow, where wisps of alto cirrus promised a spectacular sunset.

Stella sat opposite me in shorts and bikini top, fresh and crisp from her shower. I recalled how she had looked after her release from that god-awful prison in Kenya: grey-faced and painfully thin, scarred all over from untreated sores and insect bites, hair butchered ragged, hands broken-nailed and discoloured with ingrained filth.

Now she was a picture of health, her golden-brown hair had grown back to shoulder length and the scars from her holiday in hell all but disappeared.

'Do you still get flashbacks of Shino?' I said.

'They do not seem so real anymore. These longer passages are helping; I always feel more at ease once we get into the cruising cycle.'

I knew what she meant. Back in the Med, anticipating our first ocean crossing I had expected to be bored shitless, but there is an ethereal quality to long sea passages. It's just the boat, the endless ocean, and us; nothing else seems real. Passing time is measured by the regular highpoints; snatched conversations at watch changeover, solo night watches gazing up at the blaze of stars, and watching the sun come up astern at the end of a six-hour watch. Then there are the many unbidden events that stay in the memory: a pod of dolphins cavorting and showing off under the bow, the sudden zipping of the reel as a yellow-fin takes the trawl line; and this: sitting together under the bimini eating a meal at sunset.

I helped myself to another piece of fish. Few would consider Dorado the most appetizing gift of the ocean, but she had turned my catch of yesterday into something special.

'This is awesome sweetheart; I don't know how you manage it.' I was referring to the ever-present ocean rollers that gathered up behind then lifted *Carriacou's* stern skywards before dropping her back into the next trough, simultaneously slewing her side to side. The resulting corkscrew motion was erratic and unpredictable, and made working below with hot food a precarious affair.

'I was well trained, remember? I had a good teacher on Kos, and then I had my own restaurant on Kalimnos.'

I realised she was so adapted to sea conditions she had completely missed my point.

'The secret is to enjoy good food,' she continued, 'I am convinced Nikkie first only took me on for my cooking - he liked to eat well, even on long voyages.'

'Well, he was a big guy,' I said, 'needed his calories.' I gave her my best smile, 'but sitting across from me now is all the evidence I need that it wasn't just the cooking.'

Given how long we had been together and what we had shared I was surprised she could still blush, but then I noticed the glassiness in her eyes.

'Sorry sweetheart, I didn't mean to upset you; I know you still miss him.'

She smiled through unshed tears and waved a hand in front of her face.

'No, *schatz*, please ignore my silliness.'

~.~

When she was feeling fruity, Stella got this feline look in her eyes. Did I mention they were a startling pale blue? They pierced me with a directness that turned my legs to jelly and sent shockwaves to my groin.

Now I might forgive you for thinking that given the mutual attraction between us a bit of rumpy-pumpy might have been a regular feature of our crossing. However, a word to the wise: sailing two-handed in a regular Atlantic shipping route imposes certain limitations. It was likely there were half a dozen ships within twenty miles radius at any one time – we just couldn't see them. The horizon from the deck of a small yacht on a calm sea is just four miles. True, the superstructure of a large vessel poking above the horizon might be visible further away. But with closing speeds of up to thirty knots, the time from first sighting to collision can be as little as twelve minutes.

Therefore, while a little romantic canoodling wasn't out of the question we couldn't risk taking our eye off the ball for long. We hadn't seen a ship for five days, but I'm sure you have heard about sod's law? The one that says, if something bad *can* happen then it probably will.

Having said all that, there was still that idyllic setting and overriding mutual attraction. She had that playful kitten look now, and I knew one of those rare unbidden events was imminent. She came around the table and sat by me. Our lips touched, and I breathed her sweet warm breath.

I felt her hand arrive at the inside of my thigh, moving up towards my crotch. She scraped her nails softly up and down beneath the leg of my shorts. Our lips pressed closer, her tongue forced its way into my mouth, found mine.

I reached behind her and flicked open her strap. She lifted her arms and let the bikini top slip to the deck. I cupped one of her breasts in my hand and bent my head to it, flicked the soft nipple with my tongue, licked around it until it swelled and hardened. She laced her fingers through my tied-back hair.

The table was getting in the way, so we shuffled along the banquette for more space. I took both her hands in mine and eased her up so she stood in front of me, bracing against me because of the motion of the boat. Steadying her with one hand in the small of her back, I placed tiny kisses in a line down her belly until I got to her shorts.

She pulled the band from my ponytail, scrunching up the folds of my hair in both hands. I thumbed open the button of her shorts and pulled down the zipper, letting them slip down and flop to the deck.

With my free hand, I explored the silky inside of her thigh, her fingers tightened into my hair in anticipation. I touched a delicate wisp of hair and felt the cool beads of her readiness. She parted her legs a little and then gasped as my fingers slipped into her smooth wetness.

'Patrick!' she breathed, 'I must have you now - you are driving me crazy.'

I stood and released my shorts, took her shoulders and eased her onto her back along the banquette cushions. She reached her arms over her head for the grab-bar on the bulkhead, keeping one foot on the cockpit sole to brace against the roll.

I climbed a little awkwardly over her, taking the weight on my arms, and she took one hand from the grab bar to help steady me. I gazed into her eyes, letting out a gasp to match hers as I entered her velvet softness. Despite the urgency of my desire, I kept my thrusts long and slow - only breaking rhythm when the boat gave a particularly violent lurch - enjoying the feel of her pelvic muscles rippling with each stroke.

'I love you Patrick,' she whispered, and I felt the first hot squirt of her orgasm and could hold back no longer.

We lay there in each other's arms for a time in semi-wakefulness, until a sudden change in the ocean's profile shook us out of our reverie; and *Carriacou* started rocking from side to side like crazy, as if she was applauding our performance.

Our eyes met, and we both jumped up, casting around for the cause, and there, about a mile on our port quarter on reciprocal course, was a ship, a great big bulk carrier. She had passed easily within half a mile of us and her expanding bow wave had disturbed the ocean's natural rhythm.

We looked at one another for a moment, and then fell about laughing. The first ship in five days and we had just shagged our way through its transit. Good old Sod's Law.

~ Chapter Six ~

Filipe's shabby old Cape Islander chugged its way across the bay towards a narrow isthmus of low-lying sand, while the man next to him in the pilothouse searched back and forth across the water with binoculars.

Suddenly he pointed out to starboard and spoke in rapid-fire Spanish, 'There it is, over there, Felipe, see the plastic container? Steer to your right.'

The captain nodded, throttled back and spun the wheel over. It was almost dark, but he could discern the improvised buoy bobbing on the calm water. Felipe cupped his hands and shouted through the open window.

'Manuel, get ready with the boathook.'

The big man standing on the foredeck looked back slack-jawed, the boathook, like a child's toy in his enormous hand, still pointing skyward.

'Elías, please go and tell that big slob to point the boathook at the mark so I know which way to steer, and as we get close please call out the distance to go.'

When he had hooked the buoy and pulled it inboard, Manuel took the rope and hauled up the heavy load. As it reached deck level Elías leaned over and removed two of the plastic bags from the cargo net. Manuel then carefully lowered the remainder back to the seabed.

'Why did you take two packets?' Felipe said.

'One we take ashore for him to test. The other is for our trouble, it will not be missed.'

'You hope. Gonzalez's men in Guanica will count them you can be sure. If they find there is one short they will make you pay, maybe with your life.'

'Felipe, you worry too much, I fix everything with Gonzalez, you will see.'

'Anyway,' Felipe insisted, 'why steal it now, when the nigger has still to check the shipment before we leave? You could have taken it when we are on our way.'

'Manuel here needs a fix; he's been nagging at me all day that he's run out.'

'Yeah,' the big man agreed, 'Manuel want to get coked up tonight. If the nigger make trouble I pull his balls off.'

Felipe steered the boat back to the island. He slowed her as she approached the beach and let her drift in until her foot nudged the sand, allowing his two passengers to jump off the bow.

'See you here in the morning,' he called, then backed off the beach and went to find an offshore mooring. It had been a long day and he was looking forward to a light supper and an early night.

He had made up his mind that this would be his last job for the contrabandistas. It was getting too dangerous. Besides, he suspected that the mentally subnormal giant, Manuel, was a complete psycho: Felipe was secretly terrified of him.

~.~

He woke up with a start. He had heard a bump and the boat still rocked slightly from the impact. A vessel coming alongside. He had no sooner swung his legs off the bunk than the clatter of boots on the deck above confirmed his worst fears.

Cops!

Ah! Jesus, he had just remembered that idiot Manuel had left a kilo bag of coke in the wheelhouse.

Before he even had his trousers on, the cabin door flew open and a bright light dazzled him.

'Armed Officers! Sit back down on your bunk and do not move.'

~ Chapter Seven ~

The RYA Yachtmaster exam was something I had never imagined doing. Stella had all but bullied me into taking it. 'If we are to sail together we must *both* be properly qualified,' she insisted, 'and there is a great deal for you to learn before you are ready.'

So she taught me, and despite my years at sea and recreational sailing with the navy, I found out she was right; I learned something new nearly every day since leaving Mombasa. That was one hell of an introduction to sail cruising by the way: up the Indian Ocean, transiting the Gulf of Aden and Arabian Sea to Oman, then back up through the Red Sea and Suez, and across the Med. I lost count of how many places we stopped off along the route. Of course, we had to explore them all. 'Expanding our geographical and cultural experience,' Stella had called it. I told you she was imperious.

Under Stella's severe instruction I learned to handle the sextant with something like confidence, got on first-name terms with the most useful astronomical bodies, and almost understood Sight Reduction Tables. When we reached the Atlantic she had me navigate the whole way across, and I have to say I got good at it, with my fixes hardly ever more than ten miles out from hers.

However, as we motored into the clear waters of Port Louis Marina, even all that hard-earned knowledge couldn't appease the anxiousness I felt for the coming test. Ignoring my protests that I wasn't ready, Stella booked me in for the exam by radio almost as soon as we tied up.

"There is no point in delay,' she said, 'you are as ready now as you will ever be.'

We spent the whole first day shopping in St Georges to re-stock supplies. Afterwards we fell into the forepeak's double bunk together for the first time since the Canaries, and for a couple of pleasurably distracting hours my queasy apprehension went on hold.

After the exam (a doddle really, don't know what I was so worked up about), we had sailed on north to Carriacou, the island Niklas had named his boat after. Following a relaxing day swimming and snorkelling, we had made the half-day passage here to Pipah: a tiny island paradise, population six hundred.

~.~

'One, two... one, two!' the Rastafarian singer tested his microphone again while the one with the electric guitar leant down to tweak the amplifier controls before repeating the same chord he'd been strumming for the past half hour. The other two band members, keyboard and drums, sat disconsolately at their instruments having abandoned all hope of getting started tonight.

'One two, one two'

Sitting at the bar, a man in lurid knee-length shorts and a hairy beer gut scowled at the band.

'Okay, that works now play some music.'

'One two, one two!' the singer boomed again, unperturbed by the interruption.

'So you can count to two,' the American said darkly, 'now play some music!'

'One two, one two!'

'The fuckin' mic works goddammit! Play somethin' or pack up and go home.'

Some of the young women clustered on the dance area turned worried glances towards the bar. A swim-suited woman perched on the next barstool put a hand on his shoulder. 'Cool it, honey, you're scaring the French girls – they think you're serious.'

'I am fuckin' serious dammit!' he said, glaring at the singer.

A stocky black man in an apron came out from the kitchen and spoke quietly off-mic with the singer, then went behind the bar to help serve the growing crowd of thirsty customers.

'What'd the guy say Kenny, they gonna start tonight or next week?'

'Dey ready just-now, done worry.'

At the mention of his name, I realised I knew Kenny from my last visit, but he hadn't noticed me yet, or just didn't remember me.

'One two, one two!'

'Put a tape on Kenny, and make sure you turn it up loud. I don't know why you use these guys.'

He leaned over to me and said, 'Same story every fuckin' Wednesday.'

Kenny reached across the bar and dug him on the shoulder with a black pudgy finger. 'Dem need da money Frank, dey try hard yanoo, equip-mant git damp in back o truck all week.'

'Then tell 'em to get here early and set up so they're ready to go on time. That's what you pay 'em for, goddammit.'

'Happy-*shance*, Frank. Dees boys out fishin' all day, yanoo.'

'Have patience? Jesus. I just hope they're better at fishing than setting up their fuckin' music.' He turned back to the band. 'Play something guys. Who cares if it's not perfect?'

'One two, one two,' The singer grinned big white teeth at Frank, and then ducked the empty calabash ashtray the American threw at his head.

Amused by the little sketch, I picked up our beers and made my way back to Stella, dodging around a table where two men sat alone talking quietly to each other, and from what I could make out, in Spanish. I wouldn't normally have noticed them except they fell silent as I passed.

One of them, the smaller of the two, compact, tidy and sporting a neat chinstrap beard, held up his drink to me, 'Great party eh?'

'Yeah, nice atmosphere,' I said, trying to keep my voice natural, 'better when they get some music started. Looks like everyone's itching to dance.'

His companion, dark, scruffy, and as big as a Small Bus, grinned on inanely as if waiting for a cue to speak.

When I had last visited here, Hispanics had been a rarity. As I threaded my way back to Stella I vaguely recalled rumours of Cuba's involvement in the Grenadian revolution. I didn't really care why they were here, not my business. But when the Chinstrap guy had raised his glass to me I had spotted a dull glint of metal inside his jacket, something that definitely looked like a gun.

Stella was laughing; she had been listening to the antics between the band and the loud American, 'It is like a comedy review,' she said, 'It is wonderful here, so relaxed and simple.'

All around the beach groups of babbling visitors squeezed together at bench-tables under strings of lights, stretched between coconut trees and palm-thatched pagodas, and slender black waitresses weaved back and forth between tables balancing plates heaped with lobster and salad. A skeletal figure with a mountain of dreadlocks appeared, shovelled up bright-glowing embers out of an iron cauldron and carried them spitting and crackling back to the open-air kitchen.

At last, a tape came on: a pulsing reggae song with French lyrics that aroused a sudden flurry of movement in the bar. Frank grabbed his wife and whirled her around the patio, and they were soon joined by the young French girls and some of the local boys.

Out over the bay the full moon cast a silvery path along the water. Half a mile off, a floodlit superyacht sat graciously at anchor, her two boats that had brought her all-female crew ashore lay bobbing at the water's edge, too big to haul up the beach.

Several smaller inflatable tenders were there too: visiting crews from the line of yachts moored a mile away across the bay, their dim masthead lights swaying in the gentle swell. *Spirit of Carriacou* lay in sight, moored to a buoy a little way offshore.

I watched Stella watching the lights twinkling faintly along a silvery horizon made sharp by moonlight. The air was soft and warm, carrying the smell of wood-smoke and spices, with the occasional whiff of marijuana.

I said, 'I told you I'd show you something special.'

'It is magical!' she said, reaching for my hand across the table. 'Nikkie and I sailed the Caribbean for almost a year, but I don't remember any island like this, it is so primitive. How on earth did you find it?'

'Don't let the locals hear you call it primitive,' I grinned, stroking her hand with my thumb, 'they might get offended, even though it is. I was here three years ago on the old Rusty P. Remember me telling you about the '79 hurricane that flattened a couple of the islands up near Martinique?'

She nodded. 'Yes, when you had that awful job of pulling bodies out of the mangroves, ugh.'

I was quiet a moment, remembering. Hurricane David, it was: that island got a direct hit. After we had done what we could we came down here for a bit of light relief.

'We anchored just out there where that gin palace is,' I told her, 'had a fantastic couple of days: snorkelling, windsurfing, water-skiing, getting pissed-up right here, the whole works. Always knew I'd be back one day.' I squeezed her hand and went for the big finish: 'I couldn't have wished for better than to come back like this, with you.'

'Oh you...' she laughed, 'stop it at once.'

'Got to keep my hand in you know, otherwise you'll think I'm taking you for granted.'

Her eyes turned sober, 'Do you miss the navy?'

I paused before answering, thrown by her sudden change of tack. 'No, not really. I was already quite disillusioned with the Mob, even before the brown stuff hit the fan, and look at it this way, we wouldn't be here now if I hadn't screwed up. One door closes another one opens.'

'Very philosophical, *Schatz*, but sometimes I wonder if you are truly happy away from your old comrades.'

"All in the past, Stella, this is my life now,' I waved an expansive arm out across the bay; 'I mean look at this, what's not to be grateful for?'

Kenny came out to our table with two loaded plates and set them down on the place mats in front of us.

'Hi Kenny,' I said, 'remember me?'

He bent down to get a better look at me in the dim light, then his face lit up with a broad grin of recognition, 'Yeah man, meh 'member. You was here on dat war-ship four yeego.' He held a loose fist towards me and I bumped it with mine.

'Good memory! I'm guessing you won't remember my name though, it's Patrick.'

'Kenny, this is my skipper, Stella. Stella, meet Kenny, runs the best beach bar on the finest island in the Caribbean.'

After he left I turned to see Stella laughing quietly into her hand. 'I hardly understood a word that man said,' she explained, 'it is a strange form of English for me.'

'No, well they're a bit posh up in the north where you were,' I told her, 'the Grenadine patois takes a bit of getting used to.'

After dinner, we danced. The band had sorted out their technical problems and were now covering a recent Bob Marley number, a happy song, presumably calculated to summon forgiveness for the long delay in the live music.

...Singin': done worry 'bout a ting,
'Cos every liddle ting, gonna be all right...

Despite claiming never to have danced to reggae before Stella turned out to be a natural and outclassed many of the more experienced hip-grinders on the dance floor. The band followed with covers of Jamaican acts like Steel Pulse and

Black Slate. Stella's body rippled with movement and the local boys stood by clapping and cheering her on.

They seemed fascinated by her tattoos: I haven't mentioned those have I? Something like leopard spots on her left shoulder that cascaded down her bicep, and weird black Gothic markings that started in the small of her shapely back and disappeared into her shorts. Clearly, I wasn't the only one turned on by them. I remember her telling me that when she first met Niklas she was a rebellious punk rocker with metal piercings and a bright red Mohican haircut. Hard to picture her like that then, but those tattoos helped conjure up an image I found strangely erotic.

After a couple of dances I stood aside and watched her dance with some of the local boys, intervening only once when one got a bit too fresh with her. I couldn't really blame him: she was ravishingly sexy on the dance floor.

The guy bore my ticking off in the way typical of the islands: no apology just eyeballed me with a hurt expression, but he behaved himself thereafter. Stella flashed me a smile of gratitude, but with a look that reminded me she was no blushing maiden.

The only discordant moment was when a Police Landrover coasted down the track and parked on the hard sand next to the bar. Its approach drew my attention when the music stopped, and half a dozen local boys scuttled out of the bar and merged into the darkness of the surrounding trees.

A uniformed police officer with sergeant's stripes stepped out of the vehicle and pulled on a peaked cap; I watched Kenny come out to meet him, and the two of them disappeared behind the shack together.

I turned my attention back to the party. Stella who had danced herself to a standstill ran over to me: she looked ready for a drink. 'Was that a policeman I just saw?' she said, still breathless.

'Yeah, scared some of your buddies away,' I laughed, 'they were probably carrying weed.'

Before driving off again, the sergeant took a tour around, stopping to chat occasionally with people he clearly knew. Though he nodded and said Good Evening to the white people he passed, including us, I didn't see much smiling back. I noticed he completely avoided the black locals, as well as the two Hispanics still sitting at their table.

When he left the collective sigh of relief was palpable. The people in the band trickled back and the music started up again.

~.~

After midnight, everything quietened down. The French all-girl crew climbed into their boats and sped off towards the glittering superyacht, the local boys looking wistfully after them before walking off down the shore, while the resident whites that hadn't drifted home sat around on the quirky beach-furniture chatting.

Stella and I took a rum punch nightcap to our earlier dinner table and were joined there by the owner, Kenny, and the loud American, Frank, and his wife, who introduced herself as Martha.

As they took their seats I overheard Frank say to Kenny, 'That depraved bastard sting ya?'

'Yeahman, he sting, but no problem. If I done pay, I got no business. Dat jus life man.'

'Ah, it stinks Kenny, you know that.'

Kenny shrugged indifferently and turned to Stella. 'How you likin' Pipah?'

'It is a beautiful island,' Stella said, 'I was wondering about the name, what it means?'

'Used be pipah factory here, no more now, but de name remains.'

'Pipah factory?' Stella said quizzically.

'Pipah, like de newspipah, yanoo?'

Stella looked stunned for a moment, then put a hand in front of her mouth and tried not to laugh, but her eyes and shaking shoulders gave her away.

Kenny grinned good-naturedly and turned to me. 'So, Patrick, you a yachtie now, no more in da navy?'

'No man, all that's finished. We had a little trouble in Africa…' I caught Stella's warning glance and broke off, changed the subject. 'I got chucked out of the navy for smoking weed.'

'Aww man, me sorry to hear dat. What doin' liv-now?'

'We might do a little chartering here eventually,' I said, 'but for now we're just chillin' out, man.'

'We also plan to help a friend with his dive business in St Vincent,' Stella said, mainly I suspect, to forestall any questions about Africa, about which we had agreed to divulge as little as was polite.

Kenny looked interested. 'So you goin' into dive school business?' he said, 'Frank he own dive shack hee on Pipah.'

'That's good to know,' I said, 'we plan to do a little diving ourselves while we're here.'

Frank, who had been looking a bit the worse for wear, now perked up. 'How long you planning to stay? We could show you some awesome sites.'

'That would be nice,' Stella said glancing at me.

'Yeah, that would be good,' I agreed, 'we'll probably hang around here a week or so before heading north.'

'Who da guy in Vincy?' Kenny said.

'He's called Thomas Dennie,' I told him, 'local guy we worked with at one time.'

'Ah knows him man!' Kenny said. He paused and thought for a minute. 'Yeah man, he bin Africa a few years but come back wid new woman. She mudder passed,' he added sadly, 'yeah man, me knows Thomas Dennie, good guy. You need anyting up dere you let Kenny know. Keep in touch yeah? On de radio, yanoo, channel six-eight.'

Stella reached down absently and slapped her leg and Martha dived into her beach-bag. 'Here honey, rub some of this on your legs. *Nosee-ems*, pesky things.'

'Thank you,' Stella said, climbing from the bench to treat her legs with the tube of ointment. 'It is so wonderful here I think I can tolerate even the sand flies.'

'You guys gotta come to our house for dinner,' Martha said, 'Frank never appreciates what a great cook he's married.'

'Naw, c'mon honey,' Frank said, 'you know I die for your cooking.' He turned to me. 'Wait till you try her lambi stew, best lambi stew anywhere.'

'I too love to cook, Martha,' Stella said, 'perhaps you can show me some local recipes?'

Martha grinned delightedly. 'Sure honey, we'll have a ball in my kitchen – a real girly ding dong. You guys free tomorrow night?'

~.~

The following afternoon we loaded the diving gear and a cold-box lunch into the tender and motored over to a tiny strip of sand at the edge of the bay where a ring of green sea encircled a stretch of dazzling ice blue.

We descended into impossibly clear water into a world of wonder; clouds of brightly coloured fish and forests of delicate purple sea fans that rose up amongst blue and red razor corals. We thrilled at close encounters with giant groupers, reef sharks, turtles and huge shoals of glittering little fish. The highlight was when a gigantic sting ray came up, winged lazily around us then soared away, fading into the deep blue at the reef's edge.

After the dive we ate lunch on the sandy strip, snoozed and canoodled a while under the shade of a clump of sea-grape trees, then took the dingy back to the boat.

I didn't know it then, but that was to be our last dive together.

~ Chapter Eight ~

The house was a big single storey affair secluded on the wooded hillside overlooking the bay. We mounted a short flight of steps and skirted a ceramic-tiled swimming pool to the front of the house. Here was a splendid marble patio where Frank and Martha stood, waiting to clink iced gin and tonics into our hands.

The view over the moonlit bay was stunning. The place where we had been diving that afternoon was a delicate silver strip set in dark velvet. Beyond, the lights of more densely inhabited islands shimmered and threw glitter paths across the sea towards us.

What we could see of Pipah was mostly in darkness with the treelines silhouetted against the starry sky, a few sporadic lights of dwellings dotted here and there amongst the trees.

A faint warm breeze cooled our faces and wafted in the distinctive Caribbean scents. It was soothingly quiet, the only sounds, the soft swish of a ceiling fan inside the house and the occasional chirrup of an amorous tree frog in the foliage outside.

Immediately below we could see *Spirit of Carriacou* sitting under her anchor light, now the only boat in the bay. To the left, separated by a tall headland was another smaller bay, more enclosed and surrounded by mangroves. There were several other sailboats moored there but without lights.

'That's the hurricane hole,' Martha told me, 'owners moor up in there when they go home for the summer. Most of them will come back and sail away when the season kicks in.'

'Fantastic view.' I said.

'Yeah, we love it,' Frank said, 'been here fifteen years and we never get tired of it,' he slapped the back of his neck and inspected the bloody smudge on his hand, 'but right now the mosquitoes are biting so we better go inside.'

The interior of the house was a big open plan living space with the kitchen area at the back. Three settees and two recliner armchairs positioned around a long coffee table marked the lounge area, and a dining table set for dinner stood off to one side. There was a wall on one side with four doors off to other rooms; the other three sides were floor to ceiling windows, no glass; just fine insect mesh with vertical louvre shutters on the outside. The floor was shiny black marble tiles. The overall effect was of elegance and tasteful practicality.

'C'mon honey,' Martha said to Stella, 'let's you and me get some food cookin' and leave these guys to talk.'

Frank took one of the recliners and I chose a settee.

He nodded at my glass, 'You ok with the gin or would you prefer a beer?'

I looked and saw I was empty, 'Must have been thirsty,' I said, grinning ruefully, 'I'll have a beer please.'

'Get us a couple of beers, honey,' he called, 'Patrick and I got us some serious drinkin' to do.' He turned back to me, 'Now, did I hear you say you sailed here from Africa?'

'Yeah, not in one go, of course, it's taken nearly ten months. We left Mombasa just before Christmas.'

'You guys must a come up through the Gulf of Aden. Christ that's some serious shit going on there, with the piracy an' all. You get any trouble?'

'Not really, we pretty much hugged the coast around Yemen going up to the Red Sea. Most of the pirates are operating over on the Somali side. We had a bit of a scare when a Yemeni speed boat buzzed us but they just waved us on when they saw the Swiss flag.'

'Yeah, I noticed that. How come your boat's Zurich registered?'

'She used to belong to a Swiss guy, Stella's partner. He died, and Stella inherited the yacht.'

'No kidding? Hey that's sad,' he twisted round and called to the kitchen, 'Hey Stella, I'm sorry for your loss.'

She smiled acknowledgement.

He turned back and said in hushed tones, 'Wanna tell me?' He suddenly looked abashed, 'If not, just tell me to shut my fool mouth.'

I looked towards where Stella was mixing something in a jug. She glanced across at me and gave a minute shrug, lifted her eyebrows: *It is okay, tell it if you want.*

'Shark attack during a dive.' I said.

'Jesus H Christ, that's fucking awful.'

'Yeah, it was tragic all round, but especially for Stella. They'd been together a long time.'

I was starting to feel uncomfortable with the topic, so I switched the subject onto his diving school. He told me he had been doing great business for the first twelve years, but it had fallen off since the '79 coup.

'Those idiots really fucked up the tourism around here, leisure diving took a big hit, and now they're only just starting to realise it.'

Stella chipped in from the kitchen area, 'What is *leesha* diving?'

I drank my beer as I thought back to try to decipher what she was talking about, then guffawed and nearly choked. Even funnier was the puzzled expression that appeared on Frank's face.

'He means *leisure* sweetheart,' I said, when I had recovered, 'it's the way Americans say it.'

'Oh, I get it,' Frank said, 'it's the two cultures divided by a common language thing, right?'

'Right,' I agreed, still laughing.

'So is it coming back now?' I said, getting back to the subject, 'the tourism I mean.'

'Bishop's working on it, the new airport and all, but this guy Coard, his deputy's a wannabe democrat and doesn't like his boss. Bishop better watch his back. If he goes, the hard liners will take over and then Reagan will probably step in.'

'Step in? A US invasion you mean?'

'Yeah, like you guys did in the Falklands.'

I prickled at that, 'Oh, come on Frank, it's not the same thing at all. The Argies invaded those islands, our forces just kicked their arses out,' I paused, as a thought struck me. 'Anyway, Grenada's a member of the British Commonwealth. You can't just march in.'

Martha came over and replaced our empty beers, 'C'mon you guys, no politics. Lighten up.'

'Okay, honey, sorry,' Frank said, 'but it was just getting interesting. Say, Patrick, let me show you round the house.'

There were two enormous bedrooms with proportionally enormous beds, a palatial bathroom, and finally a food storeroom. Here he stopped me at the door and gave me a conspiratorial grin, 'Come look at this,' he whispered, 'it'll blow your mind,' he lifted a piece of sacking.

'Sugar?' I said, looking at the stack of bulging plastic bags, 'On a Caribbean island, who knew?'

He didn't get my irony, 'Not sugar,' he whispered, 'coke. A million bucks worth.'

My chin hit the deck. I couldn't speak.

'Found it out there, in the bay near where you guys were diving today. Cool eh?'

At last, I found my voice, 'Frank, you've got to hand it in to the cops, or get rid of it at least. They'll hang you if you get caught with this stuff.'

He looked at me horrified, 'Go to fucking McCredy? He's crooked as the criminals that brought the stuff here, hell he's probably one of 'em.'

He pulled the cover back over the cocaine haul, 'Listen Patrick, I'll be straight with you, my business is just about down the shithole. I'm broke man. There's a guy in Vincy'll take this stuff off me for half its market price. Half a million bucks, man. More than I need to get straight.'

'I think "straight's" the wrong word Frank,' I said, hardly believing what I was hearing, 'our friend in St Vincent tells me there's a big purge going on with cocaine smuggling. Apparently, they've set up this special unit, the Black Squad.' I glared pointedly at him. 'Frank, they do summary executions! Shoot on sight,' I made a gun with my hand, 'you know? Bang-bang, dead.'

'Patrick,' he put his hand on my shoulder and stared me in the face, 'you know, you worry too much?'

I didn't speak. My guts were starting to churn up and I felt sick.

'Listen up buddy,' he said, 'you got a Swiss flag, they'll never suspect you if you cruise it across for me. Fuck, I'll even split with you, fifty-fifty. Wadya say buddy?'

'I say you're a fucking loony, that's what.' I turned to go, and almost bumped into Martha.

She stood staring at her husband, face screwed up in rage, 'Frank, you didn't ask him?' she hissed, 'I told you he wouldn't go for it, you fucking moron!'

'Come on Stella,' I said, 'we're leaving.'

'Sorry.' she mouthed at Martha as I stalked past.

I didn't look back, heard Stella's footsteps following me, and walked quickly out. As we rattled down the steps outside Frank called after me: 'You're making a big mistake, Patrick, great opportunity!'

'Fuck off!' I shouted back.

'Ah, limey chicken-shit!' I heard as I turned onto the dirt track leading down the hill.

'Are you going to tell me what that was all about?' Stella said, struggling to keep up with my angry strides.

'Not here. Let's get back onboard.'

~.~

'Cocaine? Are you sure?'

'Sure I'm sure, you think I made it up just to fuck up the party?'

'Patrick, please? Calm down and tell me what happened.'

I took a deep breath. 'Sorry, darling, but the guy's a cunt.'

'Patrick!' she said, shocked, and then she laughed, 'I've never heard you use that word before, it sounded... strange.'

I had to smile, 'Look, he found a million dollars' worth of the stuff on the reef, out where we were today, of all places. He's stashed it in his storeroom and wants us to ferry it over to St Vincent for him. Offered me half the proceeds.'

'So, you did the right thing, well done. Now let us forget it and leave here in the morning. We can go to Bequia; I have always wanted to go there.'

I went to the fridge and pulled out a beer, 'Want one?'

She nodded. I flipped open two bottles and handed her one. 'You do realise if he gets caught with that stuff he faces the death penalty?'

'That is not our problem, Patrick. He is responsible for his own actions.'

'Yeah I know you're right. But just because he's a c... an arsehole it doesn't mean I don't feel sorry for him. I think he's just misguided. He's not thinking straight because his business is down the pan.'

'So what are you thinking?'

I didn't answer, afraid of what I was thinking.

'Patrick...?'

'Okay, he needs to get rid of the stuff. He doesn't trust the local police and it sounds like he's probably right not to. What say we go back up there in the morning, give him an ultimatum? Either he dumps the stuff, or we tell the cops he's got it.'

'How will he "dump" it? Put it back where he found it, you think?'

'That's where we can help. We'll take it out to sea and rip the bags open, disperse it into the water as we're underway. Minimum damage to the environment if we spread it wide enough.'

'This is assuming we do not get stopped before we have dumped it. You want us to risk this for someone we have only just met?'

'Like I said, I feel sorry for the guy. He's just a loser who thinks he can see a way out. What do you say? Let's do the guy a good turn.'

She flopped down on the banquette and sipped her beer thoughtfully. 'Very well, I agree. But *he* might not. If he bluffs your call about the ultimatum, then we leave and forget the whole thing.'

'No problem with that darling,' I laughed, 'by the way, I love you.'

~ Chapter Nine ~

Next morning we ate an early breakfast in the cockpit and watched the sunrise. Another boat had entered the bay overnight and was anchored a couple of hundred yards further out; a scruffy gaff-rigged wooden ketch with a tatty brown sail hanging from the mizzen. There was no sign of movement aboard her, just a wisp of smoke issuing from a flue on her cabin roof.

After breakfast, we took the tender ashore and trudged back up the hill to confront Frank again, hoping we could get Martha to support our plan and help persuade him.

It was eerily quiet as we mounted the steps and walked around to the front of the house. I stopped on the corner, looking at the open patio doors and motioned to Stella to wait. If they were up already, they were not making much noise. I could hear the fan humming softly inside but sensed something was wrong. I almost baulked at the whole idea then, prepared to turn around, forget it, and leave this island for good.

I wish to God I had, now.

We walked quietly to the door, Stella grasping my arm as if she too had that same sense of uneasiness I was feeling. Frank was sitting in the chair - the same one he had occupied last night while we discussed Grenadian politics. His chin rested on his chest, for all the world asleep.

Except for the dark round hole in the centre of his forehead. Stella took a sharp intake of breath and squeezed my arm so tight it hurt. Absently I patted her hand, as much for my own comfort as hers. We didn't speak, not much to say really. We had both seen violent death before, it was more the circumstances of this one that disturbed us.

The door to one of the bedrooms was ajar. Together, dreading what we would find, we stepped towards the doorway. I had forgotten how to walk and stumbled a bit. My throat was suddenly dry, my tongue felt like a roll of number one canvas.

Martha lay propped on her pillows on the giant bed, eyes open but vacant, nobody home. She had on a flimsy pink nightgown. Pink. Except for the front that is; that was dark burgundy, glistening wet blood. It had poured from the wide gash that had been her throat. Flies buzzed and hovered around the blood, some settling to feed.

Stella pulled urgently at my arm, 'Come, we must leave.'

I had to agree, but couldn't move, just stood transfixed. She tugged at me again, and this time managed to unstick my feet from the floor. I put my arm round her shoulders and we huddled out of that hellish room. As we emerged from the bedroom we both froze, palpable fear bouncing back and forth between us.

I recognized the two men in the patio doorway immediately; dark-skinned, Hispanic, one, a small bus with a mass of curly black unkempt hair, the other shorter and skinny, chinstrap beard. They held their handguns almost lazily at belt height, but most definitely pointing at us.

Another figure emerged from behind them. I registered dark blue trousers, light blue shirt, crisply pressed, with police epaulettes, sergeant stripes and a smart peaked cap. It was the cop, McCredy, who the night before last had bid us a cordial good evening.

My momentary relief was somewhat automatic; it ignored the dreadful logic of the situation. However, it quickly dawned on me the true meaning of his presence here. Now it was all terrifyingly surreal. I felt Stella shivering and I pulled her closer, realising I was shaking too.

McCredy stepped into the room and stood off to one side of the two men.

'What's going on?' I said.

'It is really quite simple,' the cop said evenly, 'these gentlemen have come to retrieve their property. I am merely here to make sure they get it.' He looked every inch the provincial black police officer and spoke with an urbane West Indian accent.

'Quite simple?' I gasped, 'there are two dead people here, and it looks clear to me who murdered them - and I can probably guess why,' I could feel my face reddening in frustration, briefly blunting my dread with outrage. 'Aren't you going to do something?'

The cop didn't reply, just stared blandly back as if everything was perfectly normal.

Chinstrap gestured to me with his gun, 'You, *hombre*, come over here. *Mujer*, you stay.'

I didn't move but grasped tightly onto the woman who was the most important thing in my life.

'If you're going to kill us get on with it,' I grated through a constricted throat, 'if we're going to die we'll die together.' It wasn't bravado. I was shitting bricks. The defiant cliché just blurted out of me and I immediately wished it hadn't.

'Oh come now,' the police sergeant said reasonably, 'this is no time to be melodramatic. You must do as the gentleman says; you will not be harmed if you just obey orders.'

'Melo-fucking-dramatic?' I said, 'they've killed these people. You're supposed to uphold the law, what's the fucking matter with you?'

The cop was unruffled, 'You can choose; it is all the same to me. I will put it more plainly: obey orders or you will both be killed.'

Stella, now looking remarkably calm, loosened her grip and eased my arm off her shoulder, 'It will be all right, *Schatz*, I am sure. Go to them.'

Indecision. Would my compliance save us both? God knows I had no reason to trust these animals. In the end, Stella decided for me, she just stepped away from me and shooed me away.

So that's what I did, I walked over to them – just like that. Chinstrap now beckoned me to one side and held the gun pointing at my midriff, 'Stay there and do not move,' he said.

'What do you want with us?' Stella said flatly.

'With you, nothing,' the Small Bus said in a sinister growl that sent cold fingers creeping down my spine.

I saw her face suddenly change from calm control to dread realisation. The colour drained out of her and she looked at me, finally an expression appeared on that face, especially in those lovely eyes that would stay with me always, a look of deep regret, as she understood before I did. Because my mind was unable, or unwilling, to accept the hard evidence of my eyes; the gun lifting and firing in a dreadful single action that defied comprehension.

Stunned and deafened by the dreadful noise of the shot I watched vacantly as blood from her head splattered the wall behind her and she floated to the floor. I don't know how long I stood there trying to unscramble the message that had just passed from eye to brain, but then the truth of what I'd seen struck me like a shock wave.

In that dreadful moment I died there with her. I buckled and sank to the ground, but my hands and knees of their own volition began to crawl towards her.

'Keep still or you will suffer the same.'

I've no idea which one said it, and didn't care.

'Do your fucking worst you murdering bastard,' I said, and continued crawling towards the motionless form on the floor; crawling because my grief had turned my knees to jelly.

I didn't feel the blow, just the marble floor slamming cold against my cheek. I welcomed the blackness that bloomed into my brain, hoped I would never wake up again.

~ Chapter Ten ~

I woke up to the thrumming of an engine matching that in my head. I recognised the fuzzy edge of the saloon table above me, and realized I was flaked out belly down on the port side banquette. Through the table's underside, a pair of legs in jeans and white trainers came slowly into focus.

'So, he wakes at last. Get up *gringo*, we have work for you.'

It was Chinstrap.

I didn't move. I had just remembered Stella, lying there, not moving, a dark island growing by her head. At first, I wasn't registering any feeling, like a tooth extraction under anaesthetic; you can feel the pressure of the forceps, hear the cracking of nerve fibres breaking, the tooth sucking from its bloody socket, but no pain, not then. However, the numbness quickly fell away, exposing me to a wall of raw agony.

'You evil murdering bastards' I said. I sat up and blinked through a fuzz of tears, ignoring the gun pointed at me.

'You're dead, you fucking animal,' I snarled, 'you don't know it yet but you're dead!'

He just grinned calmly, my rage just so much pissing into wind.

'No *Gringo*, we are not animals, we are worse. When we have no more use for you we will just snuff you out,' he clicked his fingers above his head, 'like we did your woman. So you better make yourself useful, eh?'

His words, softly spoken, sobered my immediate urge to lunge at him. From that moment, I wanted desperately to stay alive, determined to do anything to save my life until I got the chance to flush away these two worthless pieces of shit.

'What do you want me to do?' My voice was hoarse with grief, but I kept it dull and resigned, the way I wanted it to sound.

'We have many skills between us, Manuel and I, but we know not sailing or navigation. You will do this for us.'

For a moment, I forgot to keep up the act of a broken man. 'You stupid bastard,' I said, cradling my aching head in my hands, 'you killed the wrong one. She could have done a better job for you.' I felt the lump on the back of my skull, the hair matted and stiff around it. 'Fuck, what did you hit me with?'

'If you are telling me you cannot sail this vessel then you are a dead man,' he said, 'as you see, we manage release buoy and start engine, Manuel drives us – we could maybe work it out without you.'

'Oh, I can sail her alright, you just killed the better sailor, that's all.'

'Well that is unfortunate, but not important. You are here now, you will do it.'

'Where are we headed?' I said. I was getting into my part now, my anger unassuaged, just deferred for now.

Just then a stream of Spanish came down the hatch from the cockpit, '*Hey, Elías, es el gringo despierto todavía? Necesito un curso.*'

Chinstrap looked at me and grinned amiably, then called back: '*Sí, está despierto, espere un momento.*'

'My friend needs a course to steer,' he told me, 'we are going to Guanica, in Puerto Rico. By the quickest route.'

I stood up, swaying slightly, not with the motion of the boat, the sea was calm, but because I still felt woozy and had a pounding head.

That's when I noticed the bags of cocaine stacked up on the bench seat next to him. I opened the medicine locker overhead, ignoring his sudden start of suspicion, found the packet of paracetamol and held it up for him to see. The gun tracked me as I crossed to the sink. I pulled a cup of water and downed two tablets, then crossed back to the chart table.

Before I got the lid open Elías jumped up. 'Wait!' He came over, lifted the lid and checked inside, scattered through the instruments lying there, lifted the pile of charts to check underneath. 'Okay,' he said, 'continue, but do not take me for a fool, *Gringo*. I want the quickest and most direct route and no tricks, you understand?'

I found the chart I wanted, small scale because it had both our departure point and destination on it. I didn't want to mess about with multiple charts. I checked the compass repeat above the chart table; 270, due west. The log showed five and a half knots. I glanced at the two radios but didn't dare risk switching them on. Even these jerks would know what they were, and I didn't want to draw attention to them. I checked the ship's clock on the bulkhead. Ten past nine.

'How long since we left Pipah?' I said.

He looked at his watch, 'About forty-five minutes.'

I plotted a rough dead-reckoned position.

'Steer three-zero-zero for now,' I said, 'I'll refine it shortly.'

Elías called up the ladder: *'Oye, Manuel, dirigir trescientos'*

Time to test my boundaries. I said, 'At sea we spell each figure out phonetically. It's three-zero-zero, not three hundred.'

'So, you speak Spanish, *Gringo?*'

'Not speak it, but understand a little.' I said. I thought to push my luck a little further. It couldn't hurt, could it?

'Look, if I'm going to do this then we speak English for sailing and navigation, and please stop calling me *Gringo*, my name is Patrick.'

His smile was evil, but I felt I had won a point when he said, 'Okay, Patrick, but you make sure you behave, otherwise I make some rules for you, eh?'

I heard muttering from up in the cockpit, '*Jesús, lo que está mal con esta cosa?*' I looked up at the compass repeater, it was passing 240 and we were still turning to port.

'Starboard,' I shouted up, 'you need to turn to starboard, to the *right* for fucks sake.'

'Once you have completed navigation you will drive.' Elías said.

'We'll need to get the sails up first.'

'Sails? Why such?'

'It's just over four hundred and fifty miles, we don't have the fuel. This is a sailboat, or didn't you notice? Besides, it will take four and a half days to get there at this speed. We can go faster under sail and make it in three.'

Actually, we did have the fuel, more than enough. The engine burned two litres per hour. Four fifty miles at five knots takes ninety hours, and that's 180 litres. We had two hundred litres capacity in each of two tanks, and they were just about full.

However, these twerps didn't know that, and I reasoned that if anyone was trying to find us then the sails would make us that much more visible. Anyway, I figured the speed argument would win them over. I didn't think they had considered the passage would take so long.

Fucking lubbers, I've shit 'em!

I looked at the compass again. It was way off course; Manuel couldn't hold a course to save his life. Not that I wanted him to; save his life I mean.

I grabbed the hand bearing-compass from under the table lid and slung the lanyard round my neck, took out my notepad and a pencil and noted down five possible fix points from the chart then stuffed the pencil and pad into my shorts pocket.

'I need to go up to the cockpit.'

'Okay, you go up, I follow, no tricks. *Manuel, que están subiendo.*'

First, I engaged the autohelm and set us on course. I noted Manuel had his gun tucked into the back of his belt. 'Now you don't touch the wheel,' I told him, 'you just sit and look out for ships, can you manage that?'

That upset him, 'Watch your mouth, *Gringo.*'

'His name is Patrick.' said Elías, smirking.

Another point. I tried not to look smug.

I looked around. Pipah stood on our starboard quarter, its sandy shoreline now receded below the horizon. The two peaks of Union rose on our port bow, with Mayreau coming up on the starboard: we would pass between them. My DR position wasn't too far out. I took three fixes with the compass and noted down the bearings and time. I scanned around, taking in as much information as I could; not much shipping about, a few smudges of white sails on the southern horizon and that was about it.

I was glad to see the tender had been tied onto the stern, but they had left the engine mounted, trailing in the water. It was causing a lot of drag, but I didn't mention it. I might get chance to make a quick getaway in it sometime and that would save precious seconds. I checked the painter was properly secured and not chaffing.

Finally, I took a look at the anemometer. The apparent wind was a little north of east at eleven knots, and from that I mentally calculated true wind due east at fourteen. Good for nine knots on a starboard broad reach.

'I'll plot this fix and then get us a more accurate steer.' I said, heading for the companionway.

'Wait,' said Elías, 'I go first, you come down when I say.'

Manuel pulled his gun out of his belt and trained it on me. He looked like he wanted to shoot me. I felt I had made progress with Elías, but Manuel was going to be a problem. Not that I had a plan. Not then. However, Manuel had killed Stella, and seeing him sitting there in the cockpit of her boat with his malignant glare was the most difficult thing to bear.

'Okay, come.' said Elías from the saloon.

He certainly knew his business, standing well back in the saloon out of reach of my descending feet, gun trained steadily on my midriff. Back at the chart table I plotted the fix and dead-reckoned it on for one hour at our current speed. No point in rushing things, it wasn't yet noon, but in the next hour I planned to hoist sails and kill the engine. From there I drew the line of our intended true track to our destination in Puerto Rico. Then, assuming eight knots, I marked it off at four-hour intervals. Next, I took down the East Caribbean Pilot from the bookshelf and turned to the Tide Tables.

Tides in the Caribbean are generally negligible but certain areas have prevailing currents that you need to account for on long deep-sea passages. I marked tidal vectors for each four-hour section along the route. When I got roughly to the halfway section, I noticed something on the chart that I'd missed before: a symbol marking an uncovered pinnacle, about ten miles to the right of our track. That's when I got the first glimmering of an idea for my escape.

~ Chapter Eleven ~

Elías came and stood beside me looking down at the chart and the open book lying on top of it. 'What doing now, why taking so long to make course?'

I felt his suspicion and my hackles twitched.

'Currents,' I said, without looking up, 'tides and currents. I need to adjust our headings to keep to our track; otherwise the currents will take us off course.'

I pointed to a random column of figures in the Pilot, 'These tables tell me the tides and currents in the area at the times we transit the sections I've marked on the chart.'

I lifted the book off the chart to indicate the points marking the first four-hour track. 'I've nearly finished, and then we can go up top and hoist the sails.'

He grunted and returned to his seat. With my heart in my mouth, I lifted the table lid and flicked through the pile of charts. A peek at the larger scale commercial chart of the area showed the charted 'obstruction' in a bit more detail: a small islet with vegetation and a surrounding reef, no navigation marks, no conspicuous landmarks – good! So long as some enterprising developer hasn't come along since the last survey and built a holiday resort on it.

I could feel suspicion glaring across the saloon and so covered myself by dragging out the big book of tidal charts from underneath the pile. Its pages were entirely irrelevant to where we were, but I made pretence of consulting them.

I then went back to the Admiralty chart and worked out we would be ten miles abreast of the islet about one am tomorrow night. The almanac told me the moon would be waning gibbous and just past meridian, so I would have good visibility if it didn't cloud over.

What gave my plan credence was the east-west shipping route thirty-two miles to the north of the islet, and the fact that I would have a radio. Without those two factors, I would find myself marooned, with little hope of a passing friendly vessel in these empty waters.

Now I just needed to get us a bit closer in without the two goons noticing. I took up the pencil and dividers and got to work. When I had finished I entered the important details of the nav-plan into my notebook, all the time thinking furiously through the details of my other plan, hoping my misapplied tidal corrections would take us directly to the islet.

Under any other circumstances, I would have tried to teach my two passengers the rudiments of sailing a boat. Now it served my purpose to keep them as ignorant as possible. Therefore, I worked single handed, the two morons looking on uncertainly from beneath the bimini as I unzipped the mainsail cover and undid the ties. Manuel's grizzly face glowered at me as I disengaged the autopilot and took the wheel.

'What for you need for turning the boat, *Gringo*?'

'I need to get her into wind to hoist the sail,' I said, 'can't hoist the mainsail otherwise. And it is still Patrick, if you can't manage that, try Mr Redman. It's a name you'll come to remember one day.'

His face grew dark and he made to get up, but a restraining hand from Elías settled him back down. '*Cálmate Manuel, su tiempo vendrá.*'

The look on Manuel's face made my blood run cold. Here was a man who killed people with as little sentiment as squashing a mosquito.

'Let us see if you are so brave when I tear out your guts, eh, *Gabacho*?' he growled.

As she nosed into wind, I re-engaged the autohelm, then grabbed the main halyard and hoisted the sail, sweating down the last few inches on the winch. I could still feel the small bus's eyes boring into my back, and for a moment, I hefted the heavy winch handle thoughtfully before slipping it back in its stowage.

I would need to disable at least one of the goons in order to make good my escape. I still didn't have a plan for that.

I unfurled the genoa and snapped in the starboard sheet. She took the wind like a racehorse coming out of the paddock and suddenly given its rein. Despite my situation, I thrilled at her weatherliness. As she laid to the wind, the two morons swore in Spanish and grabbed onto the bimini frame. I cut the engine, waited for the ignition alarm then switched it off.

Silence. Always a high point for me, *Spirit of Carriacou*'s smooth transition to sail.

I watched them struggling to keep their seats on the windward bench, Manuel gawking petrified at the rushing water lapping at the rail. My quick elation and his fearful stare made me reckless. 'This is sailing,' I said, laughing at Manuel as I reached to grab the nav console, 'get used to it, arsehole.'

Too late, I realised I had crossed a line. Despite the sloping deck Manuel stood, bracing himself against the console, a dark tower, black as thunder, and backhanded me so hard I went down like a skittle. No sooner was I down on the cockpit sole than I saw his boot approaching with frightening speed, the toe connecting perfectly with that vulnerable spot just below the ribcage.

The wind whooshed out of me and stayed out, as if the entire atmosphere had escaped the earth, leaving me gasping in the vacuum. It seemed like an age before I could once more draw breath, and even then, the agony in my diaphragm kept me doubled up on my side. Through watering eyes, I saw the small bus was steadying himself against the boat's motion, rallying for another kick.

'No, Please, No!' I croaked from tortured lungs.

However, the killer kick never landed. Instead, the quiet voice of Elías drifted down through my desperate haze. '*Manuel suficiente, que necesitamos de él consciente*'

I heaved myself onto the banquette and sat doubled over, trying to get my lungs working.

'You get back on course, you fucking *Gabacho*,' Manuel hissed, clearly still in the grip of his rage, 'and watch your fucking mouth. Next time I kill you.'

I stood and grasped the console, forcing a reluctant abdomen into an upright position and flexing my aching jaw.

When I could move again I flipped off the autopilot and called 'Coming about'. I turned the wheel to port and reached down to release the starboard foresheet, for a moment forgetting about Manuel standing there.

I looked up just in time. 'Head down!' I shouted at him.

For a big man he moved surprisingly quickly, ducking just as the boom swung across to port, missing his head by a millimetre. Shame, I thought, regretting the automatic reflex that had triggered the warning call. He looked as if he might come at me again, as if I had arranged it on purpose.

'Best stay sitting behind the wheel,' I said quietly, to try to calm the pressure in his boiler, 'it'll be safer there.'

I could almost hear the steam escaping his ears as he shuffled his way unsteadily past me at the wheel. I glanced behind at Elías; he was sitting relaxed and comfortable staring out to sea, and smirking. Interesting, I thought, there didn't seem to be too much love lost between these two.

I busied myself with the boat: engaged Auto and set the heading to 332. I then bent my back to hauling in the leeward genoa sheet, kept headsail and main sheets in hand to check away together as she swung away downwind. When she had settled onto a broad reach, I eased off the vang, bringing her lee rail clear and a look of relief to Manuel's face.

I was thinking hard as I made up the sheets. My head was still thumping like a pile driver but for the first time I was feeling a hint of optimism about the future. Grief, anger, fear; they were still all on hold. The boom incident had given me an idea.

Systematically, my plan was coming together.

~ . ~

By mid-afternoon my two hijackers had broken into an argument. Their Spanish was quick-fire and heated, but I understood enough to know it was about food.

'I'll cook us something if you like,' I said, interrupting, 'it'll be safer that way.'

They stopped arguing and looked at me suspiciously. Elías said, 'maybe you think to poison us, eh? Patrick, eh?'

'No, of course not,' I said. The thought had crossed my mind, but I hadn't worked out a way of achieving it. 'I just don't want you blowing us up with the gas, and besides, I know where all the food's stowed. Just makes sense that's all.'

Moreover, I didn't want those two morons rooting around the boat either.

'What you got eat, *Gringo*?' said Manuel, a little calmer now.

'Hungarian Goulash, Coq au Vin, Chicken Supreme, Fish Curry, take your pick. All with rice, of course. Whatever you choose, we all have to have the same.'

After another brief spat they settled for the Coq au Vin. We went through the ritual once more of Elías preceding me down to the saloon; he watched me like a hawk as I rummaged in the fridge through the plastic boxes of Stella's pre-cooked meals. I put the one she had marked C/V on the shelf above the cooker and set to work preparing the rice.

The saucepans were stowed in a locker under the seat opposite where he sat, and when I lifted the seat cushion, he got jumpy.

'Wait! What you doing?'

'Relax, I'm getting the saucepans… you know, to cook the food?'

He came over and watched me as I opened the lid. There were a few things piled on top and I dragged these out first and put them to one side before selecting the two big pans I wanted. Thankfully, he didn't watch me re-stowing the surplus items, deciding instead to start mooching in the side lockers above and behind the seats.

What I didn't put back in the locker was my folded up dry bag. This I left underneath the banquette cushion. I watched him out of the corner of my eye as I poured rice then water into the saucepan. He was pulling stuff out and examining each article.

'Have you thought about when I'm going to sleep?' I said, talking to distract him, 'I obviously can't stay awake for the whole three-day trip.'

He glanced round and the look on his face told me he hadn't.

'We will see, you just do what I tell you.'

He went back to searching the lockers, getting closer to the one with the flares and portable VHF in it.

'What are you looking for?' I said, 'maybe I can help.'

His mouth turned up in his usual sneer.

'You have a weapon maybe, something you use for self-defence maybe, eh?'

'We don't carry firearms,' I said, 'we like our boat, and value our freedom too much.' I looked pointedly at the pistol in his hand then at the bags of coke stacked on the seat.

I quickly turned back to light the hob with the gas sparker. I didn't want him to see my sudden rush of anguish. I had just remembered there wasn't a "we" anymore.

'Try the wardrobe by the heads,' I said, hoping to sound casual, and jabbed a thumb into the forepeak lobby, 'there by the toilet door… there's a couple of spear guns.'

I didn't mind him finding the spear guns; they were not part of my plan, half-baked as it was. He stepped into the lobby, threw open the door and dragged out the two guns and the bunch of spears. He called Manuel to the hatch and passed the bundle up to him. '*Tirar por la borda.*'

I didn't try to protest: losing a couple of fifty-dollar spear guns was the least of my worries. At least I had distracted him from finding the portable radio, for now.

~.~

After the meal I gathered up the dishes into a bucket and went to go below. Once again, Elías jumped up to get down ahead of me.

'Look pal,' I said to him, 'this is stupid. If I'm running this boat, I need to move around *mucho*. You've had a good look round down there, there's nowhere to go and no weapons.'

He studied me for a moment, and then said, 'You wait here, I go down alone then we see.'

My heart sank, and I cursed my stupidity. Now he would find the portable. From the cockpit, I watched him scanning around the saloon. He walked forward, and I heard him open the forepeak cabin door. He spent a few minutes in there and I listened to him pulling the spare sails out from under the double bunk and overhead stowages, going through all the lockers.

He went into the heads and rattled around in the cabinet, opened the under-sink lockers where the seacocks were. Finally, he came back into view and approached the chart table. He pulled out the toolbox from its stowage under the pilot seat and clattered through the tools inside, checked behind the bookshelves and examined the sextant box. Then his eyes fell on the instrument panel.

Fuck! He was looking at the radios.

He stared at them for a few seconds, then reached down to the SSB, our long-range communication for ocean passages, and turned the volume knob. As it powered up a soft hiss of static noise faded in. He took the mic from its clip and examined it, then looked up at me with that by now irritating smirk.

'Ah! Patrick, you take me for a fool, eh?'

I wasn't too surprised when he bent down to the toolbox and grabbed the two-pound hammer, hefted it once then laid into both radios, the VHF and the SSB. I was surprised how long it took to make any visible impression on them; several blows to even crack the plastic readout screens. He kept on until they were just a useless mess of mashed circuitry.

'Happy now?' I said as he came up the ladder, 'We've got five hundred miles of empty sea to cross with no emergency comms, you better hope we don't run into trouble.'

'You make sure we have no trouble, Patrick,' he said, smirk now combined with a warning glance as he brushed past me, 'Now you can go downstairs, but no clever ideas.'

I was pissed off about the radios but if that was the price of being allowed below unsupervised then it was worth it. When I had washed up and stowed the cooking stuff I set to tidying up the mess Elías had left in the forepeak cabin. That was where we kept the emergency grab bag. I fished out a plastic bottle of water and a small knife in a sheath.

When I came out into the saloon with them, my blood froze to see the shadow of the small bus filling the companionway hatch. I let the two incriminating items slip out of my hand onto the seat cushion, but I was sure he must have noticed. However, if he had, it didn't register. He was nowhere near as sharp as his oppo.

'Hey, *Gringo*,' he called down, 'my friend he say you have beer in icebox.'

I had been holding my breath and now let it slowly out. Relieved, I went to the fridge and passed two bottles up to him with an opener. He took them and flicked his fingers at me 'Más, más.' I passed up four more bottles.

I listened to the two off them settle down to drink in the cockpit, still bickering away in Spanish.

I packed the knife and water bottle into my dry bag and a couple of cereal bars from the breakfast locker. That should be enough food, I thought, space in the bag was limited and I didn't intend to stay on that islet very long. Finally, I took down the portable VHF and two flares and shoved them in. Sealing the bag was difficult because it was full to bulging – I hoped it would still float. The most important item in the bag was that portable radio. Without it, my plan would ultimately backfire, and I would be fucked.

I went back to the forepeak cabin, flipped open the clips on the deck hatch and eased it open just enough to slide the bag out to wedge between the hatch coaming and the front of the coach roof. Not ideal: a bit of roughers could wash it away, but what the hell? I was taking huge risks every step of the way – Christ; they were endemic in my madcap plan. I secured the hatch and returned aft, closing the cabin door quietly behind me.

'What you do in there, Patrick?'

Elías was standing at the foot of the ladder, a dark scowl of suspicion.

'Just tidying up the mess you made in there,' I said, 'it doesn't do to have gear sculling about.'

He eyeballed me, and I held his look, a spasm of fear as he lifted his gun. However, he merely jerked it towards the seat, motioning me to sit down. I complied, and he walked past me to the forepeak, opened the cabin door and looked inside, then closed it again.

'If you have finished down here you come back upstairs where I can see you.'

~.~

Elias had the cheek to offer me one of my own beers. Obviously, I refused it. Socialise with those bastards? That was just too much to ask and buoyed up with alcohol my contempt would have got the better of me. Instead I busied myself with a cloth and cleaning fluid, getting rid of the black marks on the teak and paintwork from Manuel's boots. Just because I was probably not going to have the boat much longer, one way or another, that was no excuse for dropping Stella's high standards. Every so often, I stopped to check the sail trim and made minor adjustments. The wind held a steady easterly as evening and sunset approached.

'I need to go below to put a fix on the chart and check the nav lights before sunset.'

'No lights,' Elías growled, 'we sail in darkness.'

I didn't bother arguing. Maritime Law and navigational safety seemed now irrelevant. Besides, collision with another vessel was probably the best outcome for which I could hope.

We were now beyond range for accurate fixing from Union, but knew we were due for a satellite pass, so I switched on the *Transit* receiver.

Elías must have heard the click. He scrambled down the ladder and stuck the gun into my ear, using his free hand to force my head down onto the chart table.

'Tell me, what is this machine?' he grated.

'Relax,' I managed through a mouth crushed down on the table, 'it's for navigation. It can't transmit, only receive.'

He grunted and let me up, stepped back and looked suspiciously at the small box in the console, flashing red light and a line of zeroes on the readout.

'Explain how work,' he said.

'There are satellites up there, orbiting the Earth roughly every two hours. One is about to rise, and when it does, we get our position on this readout. That's all there is to say about it really. I needed to switch it on to get the signal.'

He jabbed the chart with his finger, 'And this satellite, she give you position for map?'

I hesitated; a part of my stomach fell away. Whatever I thought about Elías I knew he wasn't stupid. If he followed me through the process of plotting our true position on the chart it would be blindingly obvious we were drifting well right of track.

'Yes,' I said, trying to sound matter of fact, 'once I've applied a correction from the tables.'

'Where tables? Show.'

Oh, he was a sharp all right. I took down the Pass Tables and slowly opened it, trying to think how I would bluff this out. There were not many pages – it was a simple book, just a listing of satellites and times of passes during particular months, with a drift extrapolation table at the back. I opened it to the current month.

Then I had it. The satellite passes were for the first of each month. I wouldn't use the extrapolator but bluff it out instead. Our Latitude and Longitude had just appeared on the screen. I checked the chart and did a quick mental calculation.

'There,' I pointed to the readout on the screen, 'that's our uncorrected position, now I just need to add seven days drift, twenty seconds latitude and twelve seconds longitude for each day after the first of the month.'

He grunted, and I knew I was losing his interest. He watched as I opened my notebook and wrote down the time and the current position from the satellite, then manipulated the figures to what I hoped was close to the track I'd marked on the chart. When I plotted the position, I found I had overcorrected by almost a mile, but that showed us to port of track, so no problem.

'So, we are incorrect course,' he said, studying the chart where I had just marked our position and time, 'you will change this now?'

'A bit more leeway that I expected,' I lied, 'but I expect the current to take us back towards our track, so we shouldn't need to alter.' The more bullshit I could feed him the happier I was. The last thing I wanted was to teach him navigation.

'I warn you, Patrick,' he said, 'I am watching you. If you trick me I let Manuel tear you open, he no like you since you insult him.'

'Did he ever?'

Just then, Manuel gave a shout from the cockpit and Elías motioned me to go up ahead of him. The small bus was crouched in the cockpit, pointing astern. I looked where he pointed and suddenly there was a glimmer of hope. About a mile astern stood a sleek grey vessel, bow-wave reflecting pink from the setting sun. She was following, overhauling, and would be up with us in a few minutes.

~ Chapter Twelve ~

'Patrick, you tell all is well, understand? We will be downstairs, but my gun will be pointing straight at your heart.'

I nodded, wondering if it was a naval vessel or the police, perhaps chasing Stella's murderers. Then I remembered the bent copper and had to admit that was unlikely.

'And think of this, Patrick, we have nothing to lose – if they take us we are dead, so if you say anything to make them suspicious you will be the first.'

With that, he backed down the ladder, reinforcing the threat with a malevolent stare. Down in the saloon behind him Manuel's face glared up at me and I saw his fear, as if sure I would give them away despite the dire warning. I might have done so if it had been a warship, after all, I had nothing left to lose either and I would have died knowing I had avenged Stella's murder.

However, it wasn't a warship. As it drew up on our starboard quarter, I saw the blue, gold and green flag of SVG fluttering at its stern, and "Coastguard", in big black letters on its superstructure. I thought of the bags of coke down in the saloon, remembered Thomas's letter telling us about the Black Squad – they shoot cocaine smugglers on sight, no questions, he had said.

If I were very honest, I would say I was scared that Elías would carry out his promise first.

A loudhailer crackled into life. 'WHAT IS THE NAME OF YOUR CAPTAIN?' The big man calling from the bridge wing was black, and I mean completely black, from his black beret to his black battledress tunic and the black submachine gun hanging from its black strap over his shoulder. He had obviously clocked our name and port of registration (Zurich) painted on the stern.

I cupped my hands and called back, 'Patrick Redman.' If I had told the truth, they might have asked to speak to her.

A short pause, then 'GOOD AFTERNOON, MR REDMAN, WHAT IS WRONG WITH YOUR RADIO? WE HAVE BEEN CALLING YOU ON CHANNEL SIXTEEN.'

'It's switched on, but I haven't heard any traffic since we sailed, so it may be faulty'

'PLEASE SAY YOUR LAST PORT OF CALL AND DESTINATION.'

As I raised my hands to answer Elías called urgently from the saloon, 'Dominican Republic, tell them we are going to Dominican Republic.'

I felt a tickle in my chest where I imagined the bullet entering. 'We left Pipah Island this morning and we are heading for Dominican Republic.'

The man disappeared into the enclosed bridge, but the patrol vessel kept station alongside. After what seemed an inordinately long time he came out again onto the bridge wing and lifted his hailer.

'THANK YOU, MR REDMAN, HAVE A SAFE JOURNEY, AND PLEASE GET YOUR VHF CHECKED WHEN YOU REACH DR.'

With that, the cutter's engines gave a roar and she sheared off to starboard. I watched her head back the way she had come, suddenly feeling very alone and scared, and regretting my fainteartedness.

Why the hell hadn't I just jumped overboard?

'Well done, Patrick,' Elías said, coming back up the ladder. He cocked a mocking eyebrow, 'maybe we invite you to join our little enterprise,' he turned back to Manuel, 'what you think amigo, would not Patrick make a fine compadre?'

'*Creo que hacer banquete muy bien para los tiburones.*'

Elías laughed. 'He say you make good shark food. I think he loves you eh?'

The small bus just scowled, resumed his seat and drank deeply from his beer bottle, unmindful of the dribble down his bristled chin onto his stained t-shirt. He wiped his mouth with the back of his hand and belched loudly.

~.~

I spent virtually the whole night in the cockpit, the two crooks taking turns to watch me while the other slept in the saloon.

Manuel, I discovered, was a coke junkie: three times I saw him sniffing up a couple of lines down on the saloon table. That explained the erratic behaviour and maybe the contempt in which Elías held him.

I went below a few times to make a cup of tea and get a satellite fix, updated our false position somewhere near the fake track and marked the true one with a faint pencil dot that I hoped would be taken for a bit of dirt if Elías decided to inspect it closely. After each fix, I made a slight adjustment to the autohelm heading. If the goons noticed at all, they didn't comment.

I did manage to snatch a little sleep, dozing fitfully by the wheel as the boat plodded her way northwest through a moderate following sea. It was more difficult when Manuel was on watch because he made me nervous.

He couldn't seem to sit still for long and kept moving around the limited confines of the cockpit, one moment standing staring out into the darkness, the next sitting shuffling his feet – more black scuffs from his boots on the teak sole.

He drank beer continuously – when the fridge supply ran out I pulled the last case out of the forward bilge space and he drank it warm. He didn't speak, just grunted and belched the watch away, casting baleful stares my way.

It was always with relief I watched him stumbling down the ladder after Elías relieved him, never quite mastering the art of getting his big frame elegantly down the companionway.

Somewhere in my basic military training I had been told that conversation with one's captors was an important rule for survival; invoking empathy made it harder for them to hate you. Much as I despised him, Elías was at least someone with whom I could have some kind of dialogue.

'Why did you want the Coastguard to think we were going to DR?'

'It is less suspicious – if they know our true destination they might come onboard to look for drugs.'

'They wouldn't have been disappointed.' I observed drily.

He sniggered.

'So why Puerto Rico and why Guanica in particular?' I tried.

In the gloom, the habitual smirk made his hair chinstrap look like a lopsided question mark and I almost laughed aloud.

'None of your fucking business,' he growled, 'you ask too many questions, just keep your mind on getting us there.'

'Just making conversation,' I said, 'helps pass the time, you know.'

He was quiet for a long time, brooding. Eventually he said, 'We get best price for cocaine in Puerto Rico because it gateway to United States.'

I tried a question that really had been puzzling me, 'How come you brought the stuff to Pipah in the first place? You must have had a boat; you could have gone there directly from wherever you picked it up.'

Another long silence. I waited.

Finally, he spoke, 'I think it does not matter Patrick, you know Manuel will kill you when we get to Puerto Rico, so I tell you – to pass the time, as you say.'

The chill I had felt when that fact had first become clear no longer wilted me. I had a plan to make it turn out otherwise –-delusional I know, but that was all I had. I gave a shudder nonetheless.

'We work for Sherwin,' he said, '*El Negro*, cop on Pipah – he bring the stuff in from Venezuela, always hide on reef for safe pickup.

'This time our boat driver, Felipe, he get himself arrested by Grenada Coastguard while we visit on shore with *el Negro* - lucky thing it was before picking up. We try to get another boat, but the goods are down there four days – too long. It get more complicated when the Americano diver find it. *El Negro*, he blame us, say we have to kill him and his woman, otherwise business is blown, you understand?'

I nodded, quietly appalled at the matter of fact logic of his explanation. 'And shooting Stella, was that the cop's idea too?' I squeaked the last two syllables.

'He would have ordered it, but Manuel, he decide it first.' His face grew stark and serious, the smirk almost disappearing. 'He likes to kill - he get excited, you know what I mean?'

I knew all right. I struggled with my emotions. 'Why do you think McCredy would have ordered it anyway?' I said eventually, back in control, 'couldn't you just have brought us both back to the boat?'

'It is simple logic Patrick - that is how this man thinks. Why take two boat captains when one is enough and two are harder to manage – and a woman makes life complicated. We could not leave a witness. Next to this, with you and the girl turning up *El Negro* has a good case to explain the deaths.'

'What do you mean?' A cold finger had touched my spine.

'You, Patrick, do you not see? You are the killer. *El Negro* will investigate the murders and he conclude that you and your girlfriend went up to the house to rob the Americanos, but the man, he have a gun and shoot in self-defence, kill your girlfriend, you kill them both in revenge and then get away on your boat, simple, eh?'

I was shocked but had to admit it made sense. Any concocted scenario would, when the only investigating officer had carte blanche to invent what truth he liked. 'And what about the boat driver,' I asked, trying not to think about the implications, 'won't he talk?'

'Not now,' he said ominously, '*El Negro* see to it.' He drew a finger sideways across his throat.

~ Chapter Thirteen ~

My last day on *Spirit of Carriacou*. I got more and more nervous as the day wore on and the time to execute my escape plan drew nearer. There were just too many variables; so much that could go wrong – remember Sod's Law? By mid-afternoon my plan was starting to feel like a hopeless fantasy.

My biggest worry was the Small Bus; the wild look in his eyes was starting to scare me, and he was getting increasingly aggressive, eyeballing me and shoving me around whenever he came near, as if he wanted an excuse to lay into me again. He had drunk all my beer, but he was going hell for leather on the cocaine. When Elías told him once to lay off it, his reaction was to go below and snort another two lines.

Manuel's deteriorating condition could work to my advantage later, but it cut both ways: I worried that Elías wouldn't leave him alone with me when the time came. It was already a bit of a gamble that he would be on watch then anyway. I wasn't at all sure I could get away with it if Elías was on deck. I guessed on a window of three hours when we'd be within swimming distance of the islet; if my navigation was any good, between one and three miles.

At four o'clock it was time to execute phase one. I plotted the satellite fix and checked our distance to run to the island. Then I flipped open the fuse-box cover and pulled out the fuse for the autohelm.

I went up on deck where my two guests were chatting, sat down and waited. With the sails so well trimmed it took a while before we started to veer off course. However, she gradually poked her head to windward and the sails started to flog. I stood up and checked the compass.

'Autohelm's gone,' I said, taking the wheel and turning her back downwind.

'Okay,' said Elias, looking up casually from his conversation with Manuel, 'so now you steer with the wheel, no problem?'

'Actually it is a problem, I can't steer the boat for another two days without sleep - I need to fix the autohelm.'

'We can take a turn on the wheel while you sleep here,' Elias said, 'we both know how to drive boat.'

'Yes,' I agreed, 'but you don't know how to sail. Unsupervised you could get us into all kinds of trouble.' I nodded towards Manuel. 'And there's no way I'll be able to sleep with him on the wheel under sail.'

Manuel fixed me with a look of pure animosity.

'Okay, you fix,' Elias said, 'I drive.'

I stood aside, and he stepped up to the wheel. I pointed out what to watch out for about shifting wind. It wasn't rocket science; in these conditions and he would manage quite well, but it suited my purpose to have him nervous.

Down below I grabbed the toolbox and a skein of nylon line and put them on the bunk in my cabin. I shuffled my way aft to the steering gear hatch and pulled the toolbox and line with me, opened the hatch and got to work, not on the autohelm, but on the steering chain. It occurred to me that when Stella had said this would be good practice, neither of us had reckoned on how handy my knowledge of the steering gear would become.

I levered the retaining clip from the joining link from my previous repair. Given time, it would gradually work its way loose, but right now I needed to control exactly when that would happen. I cut off a long length of line and led it forward through a structural cross member then back to the chain, tying it through the sabotaged link.

Next, I cut another longish length and tied it around the two electric cables on the autohelm servo, led the line up through a hole in the side of the lower chain sprocket and tied it tight around the spindle. I watched this arrangement for a while to make sure nothing would happen for minor rudder corrections. It would take full rudder to pull out the wires and that would simultaneously cause the chain to part.

Taking care to leave enough slack to allow minor course alterations, I led the first line back out through the hole and closed the hatch, effectively trapping that line in place. Just to make sure, I tied a knot in the end to stop it slipping through when it pulled taught. I snipped off the loose end and shuffled back out, stowed the stuff back under the chart table seat, then replaced the fuse for the autohelm.

Phase one complete, the whole operation had taken just six minutes.

~.~

At sunset, I cooked us a farewell meal, another one of Stella's ready meals. I heaped by far the biggest portion on Manuel's plate, and true to form, he scoffed the lot. By the time it was fully dark he was snoring loudly in the saloon, leaving me alone with Elías once more.

He sat opposite and treated me to the grimmest version of his smirk, glaring at me pointedly.

'What you up to, eh?'

I felt a cold sweat break out down my back.

'Up to?' I said, 'What the fuck are you talking about?'

'Do not fool with me, Patrick, I know you planning something. You think maybe you escape eh?'

I gave him my best look of incredulity.

'How the fuck could I escape out here? Where would I go? Get real for fuck's sake!'

'Last evening you talk like you got no problems, like you relaxed, even because we going to kill you. Why so?'

'Well, there's not really a lot…' I began.

'And then today you act different, you tense, no more relax. I watch you, Patrick, I know. Don't try fooling around with me, I warn you.'

'What do you expect?' I said, letting my voice slide up an octave, 'With that fucking nutter of yours on a coke bender, pushing and shoving me around all day, I'm pissed off and, if you want the truth, I'm shitting bricks about what he might do next.'

I was surprised to see him grin, white teeth intense through the evening gloom.

'*Sí,* that is a good name for him, "fucking nutter" – I like this.' He leaned across and lowered his voice: 'I tell you a little secret, Patrick, after this trip I finished working with him. He is becoming, how you say...*un peligro*?'

'A danger? Oh, a liability you mean?'

'Yes, a liability... to me.' He leaned back and sighed.

I was getting uncomfortable with the way he was confiding in me, not sure what game he was playing – it felt like a psychological one.

'I need to plot a satellite fix,' I said, 'and I'm going to make a cup of tea, can I get you one?'

'Such good manners, Inglés, even in the face of death you offer me tea.'

Without warning, he leaned across again, and this time stuck the gun under my chin. 'I still think you up to something, remember, I watch you, no tricks.'

Before sitting down at the chart table, I filled the kettle and lit the gas. My offer of a cup of tea was to give me a moment longer alone to think, because something was nagging at me. Elías had inexplicably taken me into his confidence about his plan to ditch his partner. Why would he do that? He would surely realise I might try to exploit that weakness between them to engineer their downfall, and my survival?

On the other hand, perhaps he did. Suppose it was just a subtle lie, to allow me a secret hope, to mislead me into the idea of a safer alternative to jumping ship. Otherwise, how could he expect me to keep meekly submitting to his threats until the inevitable end?

What knocked my confidence was that was it was so clever, his grasp of human nature so complete, that it left me wondering how I could ever hope to deceive this man long enough for my plan to work. However, it was too late to back out now; I would just need to be ultra-careful not to arouse his suspicions further.

After plotting the pseudo fix, I measured the distance from our true position to the island. Twenty-two miles, and we were nicely on track. The clock read eighteen forty-three, the log showed seven point three knots. We were going too fast: at this rate, we would be on it in three hours. I needed to delay our approach to the island by at least another hour, to give Manuel time to recover sufficiently to stand his watch.

I passed the two mugs of tea up to Elías and then joined him on deck.

'On track,' I said, looking around the horizon. As my eyes swept astern, I caught sight of something in the water, in the middle distance about a mile away, indistinct in the twilight gloom. Then I looked down at the stern and realised what the object was.

'Fuck, we've lost the tender,' I said, 'need to turn round and recover it.'

'No we do not,' Elías said, 'I released it, just in case you plan your escape, eh?'

'Ah, I see, well that's not going to help you much when you want to get ashore. I hope you can both swim.'

I couldn't have manoeuvred the boat to recover the dingy anyway – it would have triggered my booby trap. Now I came to think about it, using the dingy to make my getaway would make me an easy target. No, I would need to swim for it.

I continued sweeping round the horizon. There was a thickening bank of cloud to the west.

'Looks like the wind will get up tonight,' I said, 'I need to reef in the sails.'

'You try to slow us down?' suspicion etched in his voice.

'It won't slow us that much, but if we get caught in a force eight with no reefs in we'll be in real trouble, trust me on this. Sailing is about planning for the worst.'

He still looked doubtful, looked around the horizon for himself.

'There,' I said, pointing to the cloud bank just visible in the last dying glow from the sun, 'that's heading our way and it will bring a stronger wind.'

For the first time I decided to elicit his help, mainly to distract him from asking any more questions.

'Can you ease out the main halyard for me as I pull the reefs down?'

'So you get me put the gun down? You think me stupid? You stupid!'

'Look,' I said, snapping off the halyard brake lever and picking up the rope, 'with power on the sail there's very little weight on the halyard, you can ease it with one hand, just let it slide through your palm as I pull down the reefs.'

I passed him the halyard and he took it, still looking suspicious.

'Watch what you're doing with that gun,' I said, 'please?'

I unsnapped the reef lines and pulled them in, one, two, then three, nodding at him to ease away as I did so. Finally, I closed the halyard brake and took the line from him.

'Well done,' I said lightly, 'we'll make a sailor of you yet.' Just for good measure, I furled in the genoa to the third mark as well. Better to be late than early.

When I sat down again and reached for my tea Elías stopped me with a waggled finger. He grunted and shook his head picking up my mug and passed me his. I looked at the horizon ahead.

There was no way that weather was coming our way, not with an easterly wind. For all his wily intelligence, Elías was no sailor.

~.~

The moon rose on our starboard quarter at around half past eight, a great big silver egg, and clear of cloud. By ten thirty, it was half way to its zenith on the beam. That's when Elías finally went below to wake Manuel for his watch. He summoned me to stand in the hatchway, keeping the gun firmly trained on me as he shook the snoring animal by the shoulder. At the third attempt, Manuel finally stirred and sat up, looking about in a stupor like he had been on a twenty-four-hour bender. Well I suppose he had.

When the Small Bus sat down opposite me, more-or-less awake, Elias sent me below to make the dozy bastard a strong coffee, remembering to make me drink some before passing it to him. Only when he was certain Manuel was fully awake did he finally go below and stretch out on the saloon seating. By then it was just after eleven.

For the past fifteen minutes, I had been covertly watching the horizon ahead. In particular, fine on the starboard bow, a barely discernible swelling on the moonlit sharpness. When I had first spotted it, the island was directly in line with the foresheet winch and the running backstay. Now it was a little to the right: we were drifting too far to port, I needed our track to pass closer. I made a point of looking at my watch.'

'Satellite pass,' I said, 'I'm going below to plot a fix.'

Manuel just grunted and gave me a baleful stare.

There was no pass, the acquisition light burned red, the readouts frozen on the last recorded position. There would be no more satellite fixes that night, because I opened the fuse box and pulled the aerial lead out of the back of Transit Box. I spent two more minutes looking busy then returned to the cockpit.

'A little to port of track,' I said, turning the autopilot dial five degrees starboard, 'that should do it.'

I was convinced the moron was quite mad. He just stared at me with a creepy malevolence. I was going to have my work cut out manipulating him.

The course alteration required a sail trim, so I heaved in the mainsheet a couple of inches and did the same for the genoa. The hump of the island was now clearly visible to the right of the forestay. If Manuel looked there, he would be bound to see it.

'How will you do it?' I said.

'Do what?' he said slack jawed and dull.

'How will you kill me, when the time comes?'

He looked suddenly interested. I had his attention. 'You want to die, *Gringo*? You welcome death?'

'Of course, I've nothing to live for now.'

'You lie,' he growled, 'No peoples wish to die, all want survive. I know this, I kill many peoples.' He sounded aggrieved at the notion I had proposed, disappointed. I realised then that it wasn't the killing, but the power that excited him. He wanted his victim begging for mercy. My death, if he got his way, would be a long drawn out affair. If I had any doubts about what I was about to attempt, that moment dispelled them.

I faked a yawn and lay down on the bench, closed my eyes. The next half hour would be make-or-break.

'You will be tied up against a wall…' he said, 'you listening, *Gringo*?'

'I'm listening.' I said, stifling another fake yawn.

'I will slowly open your belly with my knife. You will feel nothing at start, my knife is very sharp. Then it will begin ache as I let your guts spill out onto floor. Then you will feel pain, pain like you cannot imagine. You will scream like a woman, beg me to kill you. But I will not kill you. I will make you look down at your intestines; spread them out so you can see them more clearly. It will take one hour for you to die, and while you are dying, I will cut off your dick and balls and stuff them in your mouth. You like this, *Gringo*, is this what you want to hear?'

I felt sick, certain that he meant every word.

'A bit graphic for my taste, got anything else?'

Then I felt his hot breath on my face, smelled its foul cloying odour. I opened my eyes to see his bloodshot ones just inches away. I wanted to get away, to puke. Fear and revulsion were vying for position. And an almost irresistible loathing: I imagined smashing that foul visage to pulp with a winch handle, but forced myself to stay calm, cleared my face of any expression and let my tortured thoughts dissipate.

'You act very brave now, Patrick,' he snarled, drops of spittle flying into my face, 'but I think you lie, you really just chicken shit.'

It was the first time he had ever used my name, and I found it creepy. He returned to his seat, oozing malevolence, but under control. I closed my eyes again and listened to the soothing sound of water rushing past the hull, the creak of rigging, the soughing of the following breeze, letting the calm wash over me, savouring my last minutes on the yacht that had been home for so long. I knew he was still watching me, could feel his resentment, his innate hatred. Unbelievably I think I dozed off for a few moments.

Then it was time. I stood up, stretched and yawned. Manuel was still watching me; I ignored him, moved up to the console and checked our heading, looked up at the sails, looked out ahead, and feigned surprise, then horror.

He responded, stood and looked where I looked. 'What is this, you say no land, but there is land!'

He lifted his gun towards me.

'Uncharted rock,' I said quickly, 'not marked on the chart, that's why it's uncharted.'

I disengaged the autopilot and gently turned the wheel to port, watching Manuel out of the corner of my eye, standing there stupidly.

Indecision. Exactly what I wanted. I heard a clunk from below as the chain parted and I held the wheel steady.

'What that noise?' Manuel said.

'Just the rudder, the seating's a bit loose, nothing to worry about.'

I imagined the chain now only connected to the bottom sprocket by a few links under tension. I watched with grim nervousness as the bow came round, putting her stern through the wind. If this had been my Yachtmaster exam I would have failed it instantly with this manoeuvre, and now I made sure of the worst possible outcome:

I pointed toward the island. 'Watch out over there for submerged rocks,' I said, quietly so as not to wake Elías.

He looked where I pointed, and I grabbed the nearest winch handle from its pocket just as the wind got behind the mainsail.

The heavy boom whipped across with terrifying acceleration: an unstoppable juggernaut with power in the sail to speed a ten-tonne boat through the water. It caught Manuel squarely on the back of his ugly head with a satisfyingly loud clang and sent him sprawling onto the guardrails. The mainsail thwacked into place on the new tack.

With the genoa backed, held there by the windward sheet, the loose rudder clunked home, and *Spirit of Carriacou* hove to.

Then a shout from below and Elías was coming up the ladder. I hurled the heavy winch handle at his emerging head, missed my mark but hit him squarely in the chest, and unbalanced as he was, he tumbled backwards into the saloon. I knew I had failed to put him out of action, but it would still give me a few vital extra seconds.

Manuel's huge prostrate form lay sprawled face down with his toes hooked over the cockpit edge, head and arms hanging over the guardrail. Summoning all my strength, I grabbed the heavy body by the belt of his trousers and bounced him forward on the top wire until he overbalanced, but not before I heard Elías come stomping back up the ladder.

I should have just left Manuel there and run forward, but my hatred suddenly had the better of me, and now I had left it too late. Aware of Elías's head already emerging from the companionway, and galvanised by sheer terror, I ran forward, ducked under the boom, grabbed the dry bag and jumped over the starboard rail, oddly thrilled by the crash of gunshots behind me. The whole exercise couldn't have taken more than ten seconds.

Silence as I descended into cool dark water, above me I saw the wobbly outline of the moon. Struggling to stay down until the yacht drifted clear I slipped the dry bag's lanyard over my left foot and pulled it tight around my ankle. The stuffed bag was more buoyant that I had anticipated and was dragging me upwards. I let it go and it bobbed up to the surface. Then I heard the ominous popping sounds, and saw luminescent streaks slicing down into the water all around where the bag now floated above me. The angle of the bullets entering the water resolved my disorientation, telling me which way to swim. I needed to breathe soon, swam with deep long strokes until I could hold it no longer, pumped spent air from my lungs as I surfaced, then took a hurried breath, diving again as bullets smashed into the water around me.

The next time I surfaced, I trod water and turned to watch the boat. Her moonlit hull was clearly visible, starboard quarter aspect, about a hundred yards away, and as far as I could make out, still hove to. As I floated there watching, a bulky figure climbed out of the water onto the stern platform. I felt stab of disappointment.

The Small Bus had survived a blow that should have felled an elephant.

~.~

I made it ashore to find my dry bag was no longer a dry bag. Two of Elías' bullets had punctured it. The two flares (actually, one red flare and one orange smoke) were intact; they were waterproof anyway, but heaven knows what would have happened if a bullet had struck one of them. The water bottle was ok, and that had been a godsend.

One cereal bar was still in its cellophane wrapper, the other had turned to soggy crumbs at the bottom of the bag, among broken pieces of orange plastic and loose shards of electronic circuitry.

~.~

I slept fitfully up near the tree line that first night, became intimate with the sand flies and crabs, and woke up itching and shivering in the cool light of dawn.

Carriacou was still in sight; maybe four miles away, both sails still up, though I couldn't make out from that distance if they were drawing. If my hijackers had been seamen, they would have known a sea anchor would help them get some sort of directional control under sail. It occurred to me they might try the engine, in which case they would just cruise in huge circles for days until she ran out of fuel.

However, I didn't put it past Elías to work out how to fix the steering chain, eventually. The tools to do it were all there and he had Manuel to help him. Hell, even I had managed it - in the mid-Atlantic swell at that!

What I wasn't sure about was whether they would return here for me. I had gambled they wouldn't. Besides, I could now see that without the dingy they wouldn't get through the reef. I took a dip in the sea and stood there neck-deep watching the sun come up.

Back on the beach, I took out the pieces of the ruined radio and laid them on the grassy margin of the beach to dry. But I knew it was pointless: I'd found a squashed bullet lodged in amongst the printed circuits and a hole punched through what were almost certainly the radio's vital innards.

From the top of the hill, that VHF radio would have given me contact with any vessel within maybe forty miles.

~ Chapter Fourteen ~

Stella once told me she had seen a river in Kenya running red with petals.

'I thought they must be all the rhododendrons in Africa,' she'd said, 'I imagined all those bushes leaning over and letting their delicate flowers drift down into the water, watching to see what happened to them as they journey on their Big Adventure, who would survive, and who would succumb to the swirling river, or get swept into the waiting-pools.'

My fellow traveller has withered and died on the river's muddy bank, ripped from me in the first flowering of our Big Adventure. My petal floats stranded temporarily in the eddy - Stella had called it the waiting-pool, one of her endearing mistranslations - but hopes soon to be nudged by some unseen hand and sent on its way once more with a new mission: sweet retribution.

Now I'm just trying to survive, and not think too much about what happened to Stella. Today was my first full day on the island I've dubbed Redman's Folly. Not that I've had chance to air that name in conversation with anyone, except maybe the odd frigate bird that occasionally swoops inshore or the little sand crabs that scuttle in and out of holes on the margin of the shore, holding up their claws to me like arms in an invitation to dance.

By any measureable standard of Caribbean islands, this one is small, and uninhabited. In addition, as far as I can recall from memory, it's at least three hundred miles from anywhere else. When I say small, I mean I can walk completely around it in twenty minutes. It has a pristine sandy beach all round its perimeter, except where a line of jagged rocks extends out to the south west for about fifty yards. The end of it marks where the shallow coral reef throws a complete circle around the island with no breaks as far as I can see.

There is a swathe of trees and shrubs just above the beach. The interior is a hill wreathed in sea grape bushes. The bad news is that most of the fruits have dried up and fallen. Still, I did manage to forage a few edible ones. Ripe sea grapes are the colour of burgundy and about the same size as a true grape. They have a big seed in the middle with a thin but juicy covering of sour/sweet fruit. Not bad to eat but acidic, and you must work hard and gather hundreds to get any nutrition out of them. They will not keep me alive, that's for sure.

I found two tall coconut trees with big green fruits on them, but the trunks are vertical, so I cannot climb them. I've tried throwing rocks at them, but they will not budge, so I reckon they are not ripe yet. However, later as I explored the beach, I found three coconuts washed up. I have a small knife in my meagre survival kit, so I'm making progress getting into one of them.

Water is the big problem, and that's why I don't simply smash the coconuts with rocks: I want to preserve the shells intact, because this afternoon I'm going to try to make a solar-still. I haven't done the Robinson Crusoe course so it's going to be trial and error, but I've got an idea and think I've got some things to make it with, including those coconut shells, which I need to store water in as well. (There's never a Calabash tree when you want one, have you noticed?)

I could also do with making a fire, so I can cook a lobster I managed to snag off the reef this morning. Otherwise, I might eat it raw and hope it does not poison me.

I have a Maasai friend in Kenya who once showed me how to make fire. Now I just have to find some suitable pieces of wood and some dead dry grass. No luck so far. The wood is either green or so rotten it falls apart. There are plenty of dead leaves but I'm not sure if that will work.

~ . ~

Well, I built that solar-still. I eventually managed to cut the top off one of the coconuts; sawing for what seemed forever with my pathetic little knife. However, I got there, and praise the God of castaways; it was almost half-full. After I scoffed the nut-flesh, washed down with the sweet milk, I lay flaked out in the shade wallowing in the wonderful feeling of rehydration and a full belly.

Refreshed and with revived optimism I dug a hole in the sand and filled it with sea-soaked grass and leaves. I nestled my precious shell in the middle and covered the hole with the torn-out cellophane panel of my dry bag. Fortunately, there was only one bullet hole in it and that was near the seam. I wedged the corners in place with four big rocks, and then put a smaller stone in the middle to make it sag down over the coconut.

All that remains is to see if it works, and for that, I need sunshine. That should start happening in the next hour.

Meanwhile I'm thinking about food. Hunger is gnawing in my gut right now, but I'm not starving yet, nowhere near. It is just that I'm used to eating well and regularly, thanks to... no, let us not go there.

I've not dared risk the lobster yet, and it's starting to smell a bit now. Yesterday I fished out a couple of conches and managed to crack one open with a rock. However, it looks like a giant slug and I couldn't bring myself to eat that raw either.

I remembered something this morning from my sea survival training in the Mob, making me quite relieved I didn't eat the lobster or conch. Fish is protein, and protein makes the body consume more water to process it. So avoid eating fish if water is a problem.

In theory, I can go a couple of weeks without food, but in this climate, only a day or so without water.

Therefore, until I have the solar-still working, I'll stick with coconut and sea grapes.

I found some Aloe Vera plants growing among the sea grape bushes, so I've split one open and daubed myself all over with the sticky gunge inside. It may not be ideal for sun block but at least it will keep my skin from shrivelling up. Helps with insect bites too.

At first light, I'm going to circumnavigate the island to look for passing ships. Or boats, windsurfers, canoes, man on a log, anything.

Today I'll try to make fire.

~.~

Hey, guess what? The solar-still works! Well, it makes water, anyway, not a lot, but a life-saving mouthful every two hours or so. Not working now of course. I've just emptied the last mouthful for today, and now it's nearly dark. If it's cloudy tomorrow, I'm fucked. Unless it rains of course.

However, it gives me a sense of achievement. I did a little victory dance when I saw the first water condensing inside the plastic and dripping into the coconut; whooping and cavorting around like a nutter, actually.

Making fire? Sadly no. My efforts so far have been frustratingly pathetic. On the plus side, I did find some suitable wood, a piece of dried log and a strong stick. I also picked handfuls of the hairy filaments I found growing on some of the drier shrubs.

The way Ayo had shown me in Kenya involved a hole in the split log and a sharpened point on the stick, then a kind of bow with a turn round the stick to get it drilling fast into the hole in the log. The bow would need some strong cord and the pointy stick, a sharp knife; well, need I say more?

So I went to plan B, something I've seen somewhere but cannot remember where. I carved a channel along the flat length of the split log, and then I wedged it into the sand and started pushing the stick vigorously back and forth in the groove to make friction. It was getting warm, then hot to the touch and I got quite excited.

Then the fucking stick broke.

I tried again with what was left of the stick, and then went to find a whole bunch more. What I wanted to see was a wisp of smoke. Then I could offer it the tinder. Now my shoulders are aching like hell with the effort and I'm giving them a rest before trying again. I've gathered a load of firewood just in case of success.

The broken conch shells are quite useful as rough blades. However, they are brittle and soon crumble so I need a constant supply. Tomorrow I'll make a spear and try to catch a proper fish, one I know I can eat raw.

~ . ~

Last night I dreamt that Stella had come to me, snuggled up against my back; I could feel her naked breasts against my skin. She felt real, the fantasy vividly erotic. She whispered something in my ear, and I turned to her, kissed her. She murmured softly as I ran my hand down her smooth body, I felt her thighs part to welcome my probing fingers; and felt her hand close softly around my ready erection. I moved over her and saw again those gorgeous eyes gazing into mine.

However, on the very threshold of consummating the fantasy I awoke with a groan of disappointment. The hand I had felt on me was my own, so while the recollection was still hot …

It was a welcome release, but frustratingly transient, and all too soon the dark reality imposed itself once more.

~.~

Another little success this morning. Yes, I made fire.

I've learned a lot here, and the one big piece of advice I can now offer to manage survival is to take your time. Think ideas through and let your natural creativity drive the project.

My first two days were filled with febrile but mostly useless activity, trying one idea after another but not sticking to any of them long enough for success, rushing everything and making a good enough job of nothing. The results so far have fallen far short of fit for purpose.

So I've redesigned the solar-still, dug it deeper to accommodate more wet vegetation and a greater volume of moist air to condense. So now, it makes water at a higher rate. Each time I open it I take out a good half shell-full, so now I don't need to disturb the process so often.

When I sat down and started thinking properly about fire I realised I might after all be able to make the bow to drive the spindle that in turn drills the hole that heats the wood and makes the spark that starts the fire.

You remember the dry bag I cut up to make the still? Well of course, it also has a lanyard. It was a bit thick for a bowstring, but it's made of plaited nylon, so I just picked it into smaller strands.

I've no idea how I missed this before. It is so fucking obvious. So anyway, I sharpened my knife on a stone (another obvious idea that occurred when I started thinking straight) and cut a nice springy length of stick from the sea grape up on the hill.

I saw an iguana while I was up there, but it scuttled away into the bushes before I realised what I was looking at.

I took my time cutting and shaping the ends of my bow with broken conch shell, filing it smooth with pumice cinders. When it was finished, I carefully whipped the nylon strand into the grooves I had prepared at either end.

The bow and stick worked like a finely tuned machine, and soon I had a stream of white smoke pouring from the hole. I wasn't quick enough first time, but on the second attempt, I got a spark onto the hairy filaments, and with quick light puffs of breath, coaxed the smouldering ball into a flame.

Thanks Ayo, my friend, I'm glad I paid attention.

I'm finding it impossible to sleep for more than about two hours at a time – sleeping as often during the hot days as the nights - so keeping the fire going isn't a problem.

Last night I made a spear and after I've had my hopeful but probably futile morning walk to look for shipping, I'm going to try it out.

With luck, I'll eat today.

~.~

Today I found the highest point on the island and started building a beacon, dragging dried brush and dead trees up there and arranging them into a big bonfire. I must tell you it looks impressive. Now all I need is someone to sail past, so I can light it.

No luck with the spear fishing, only managed to spear myself. Now I've a wound in the top of my left foot that does not look as if it will heal up anytime soon, and it hurts like hell. I've daubed aloe jelly on it and at least that has stopped the bleeding.

The good news is I snagged another lobster off the reef, and so I've eaten at last. Now my stomach keeps quivering, probably a bit too rich after three days of near starvation. I know I'll get the shits later.

I need to find somewhere to sleep away from the ravaging sand flies. That means away from the beach. I've found a possible, a clearing about fifty yards in. Now I'm trying to work out how to move my fire without killing it, don't want to go through all that stuff with the bow and stick again.

~ Chapter Fifteen ~

I did try topping myself once, on the Dorset cliffs when a black depression was on me and all hope had gone, but realised it wasn't for me then, and it isn't now. My depression here feels many times worse than those dark days in England, because nothing can bring Stella back. But while there is a chance I can escape from here to go and find those bastards that killed her then at least I have a reason to keep on living, to survive this god-awful situation.

Last night I managed to move my camp away from the beach, a little way into the shrubs but still in sight of the shoreline. So I slept reasonably free from those persistent sand flies. It would have been a good night's sleep if I hadn't had to keep getting up to squat. Yeah, you guessed it, that bloody lobster.

I've made a device for catching iguanas from the trees where I've seen them. It is a long slender tree branch with a loop of line tied on the end – the rest of my dry bag lanyard – and a slipknot so it pulls tight around the animal's neck. It might not work but at least it keeps me busy.

Today I'm going to build a shelter. I'm not really getting enough water because it's cloudy right now. On the other hand, rain could solve that problem, at least for a while, and this is the wet season, after all.

~.~

Another day in paradise. The hole in my foot is not good. There is a red blotch spreading out from it and it feels hot to touch. Moreover, it hurts like hell, especially when I put weight on my foot. I keep dunking it in the sea but that does not seem to help. Not sure what to do for the best. Should I let it dry out, or put more aloe on it?

One thing keeps nagging in my head: even if some ship comes along and rescues me, I'm still going to face a raft of problems with the Grenadian police, thanks to that bent bastard McCredy. I'll be a wanted fugitive, my word against that of a police sergeant, one with enough influence to arrange the murder of someone in police custody.

Oh well, one-step at a time. Now I'm going to hobble up the hill to where my beacon awaits, watch the sunrise and look out for passing ships.

~.~

I caught an iguana today. Quite easy really: there he was, sitting on a branch about ten feet up, looking right down at me, head bobbing as if challenging me: *just try it, pal*.

Tell the truth I don't think he could have noticed my loop-on-a-stick swinging round towards him; I'm sure he thought he was safely out of reach. I got the loop over his head first time and flipped up the stick to tighten it.

Christ! He went wild when he realised he had been snagged, squirming and snorting as he fell to the ground then tried to scrabble away while I dragged him towards me. When I tried to hold him down, he fetched me a nasty scratch down my left forearm with his back leg; Jesus, those claws are lethal!

I ended up grabbing his tail and holding him up by it. In that position, he was strangely subdued, just swivelled his eyes at me and hung there.

'Sorry, mate,' I told him, just before I smashed his head in, 'it's either you or me, and today you lose.'

Now I'm looking at it roasting on a wooden spit I made – looks disgusting and smells a bit foul but I know people eat them.

~.~

It pissed down this afternoon for about an hour and now I have six half-coconut shells full of water and a full plastic bottle. I've covered the shells with leaves, but it will not stay good for long: I keep fishing out bugs and debris, and by tomorrow it will all have evaporated anyway, so I'll use those first and save the bottle for emergencies. My solar-still is good for about a half litre a day, but it needs sunshine. It has been cloudy all day today again.

Bad news on the medical front too! My foot has swollen up like a watermelon, and there's brown puss seeping out of the wound. It hurts like hell. I found some cobwebs in the bushes (I know, what an old chestnut, but hey, I have to try something) and I'm mashing it up with dry leaves and aloe jelly to make a paste to daub on. If it works, I'll call it *Redman's Spear-wound Balm* and patent it worldwide.

It's now more important than ever to try and get rescued. For that I hope for someone, anyone, passing within about four miles of this forlorn place, and then praying they'll be looking my way when I signal – I've got one flare for day, one for night, and of course, my beacon.

~.~

I found the only edible bits of iguana are the legs and shoulders: full of fine and tiny bones but worth the effort; the meat is quite tasty, rich and fatty.

I'm now seriously worried about my foot. The poultice I made has dried into a hard lump, but my foot continues to swell up and I now have a fever. It is a hot day, but I feel cold and I'm shivering: I mean, my teeth chattering like castanets. I get dizzy spells and there is a perpetual buzzing in my head.

~.~

Of all the possible worst outcomes this was one I hadn't thought of... I'm lying under a pile of dried out palm fronds, shivering like hell and too weak to get up. I've started on my emergency water bottle and there is about a quarter of a litre left. I've come to facing the real possibility of not surviving this.

~ Chapter Sixteen ~

Elías crawled back along the bunk, and stepped out into the saloon, wiping his grease-blackened hands on a piece of rag.

'The steering, he is fixed,' he called triumphantly up the companionway.

He had worked out days earlier how Patrick had tricked them and had located the steering mechanism. However, he had not discovered what the *gringo* had done with the chain. He and Manuel had searched the boat high and low, but nothing. They had found some spare links for it in the toolbox, but without the actual chain…'

Finally, he had concluded that the *gringo* had managed to throw it overboard.

They had tried driving the boat with the engine, but with the steering wheel not working, it had just sailed around in stupid great circles, so they had switched it off to conserve whatever fuel remained.

It was Manuel, this morning, after five wasted days, who had unwittingly given him the answer.

'Could not we just tie some string around the two cogs, to make one turn the other?' he had said.

'There is too much force, Manuel,' he had said kindly, 'it would just break.'

Then he had remembered the pieces of string he had found lying around down there and went back down to examine the compartment again. When he pulled at one of the pieces, it came up out of the pool of oily water in the bilge with the broken chain attached.

He called up to Manuel again. There was still no response. He looked down at the cargo of cocaine and swore at the ripped open bag lying on top of the stack.

He stepped up and looked out. Manuel lay recumbent on the cockpit bench gazing uncomprehendingly at the sky, and Elías knew he was no longer in this universe.

'Fucking imbecile, why did I ever team up with him?'

Shaking his head in despair, he looked around the saloon. He walked forward and opened the forepeak door, scanned around inside: recesses in the sides, all full of foul-weather clothing, lifejackets. He pulled off the mattresses and lifted one of the boards, but he already knew what was in there: full with sails, and the two scuba sets underneath them.

Then a board creaked beneath his feet.

'Ah!'

He stepped back over the doorsill and bent down, lifted one of the boards. There was some instrument or other poking up out of the hull, but apart from that, it was clear and dry, with plenty of room.

Room enough, he thought.

It took him ten minutes to pack all the cocaine into the space, and he had to compress it down for the boards to fit back properly. He repaired the torn bag with duct tape and tucked that into the only remaining space. When he was finished, he dragged out the biggest sail bag and laid it on top of the boards, then replaced everything else as he had found it.

He knew it would not bear a determined search, but at least it was out of sight, out of temptation's sight.

'He goes cold turkey, or I kill him,' he muttered.

He went to the chart table and scowled down at the chart. He had also worked out what the *gringo* had done here. He had spotted the tiny pencil marks that dotted their track towards the little island. The other course, plotted boldly with dates and times, had been a clever deception.

However, they had been drifting now for five days, and the island had long since disappeared. He had an idea they had been drifting west, but how far?

He had many times watched Patrick use the brass instrument and the plastic thing to plot their position and worked out the principles. He had also discovered that one measured distance from the scale on the side of the chart, and never from the top, which was slightly smaller.

He looked again at the satellite readout – nothing. The display was just a line of zeroes. Had Patrick sabotaged that as well? If so, how? The equipment seemed to be working, just no position. There was a panel next to it marked "FUSEBOX". Inside were two rows of blade fuses, like in a car. They all had labels. He had tried this before, but exasperation made him repeat the exercise. He pulled out the one marked SATNAV. The readout on the box went dead. He put it back, and the panel lit up again, still a line of infuriating zeroes.

He was just replacing the cover when he noticed the space in the fuse compartment that gave access to the back of the satellite device. He probed with his fingers and found a loose wire with a tiny plug on the end.

'Aha, maybe…'

He felt around the back of the box and found a hole. He plugged in the wire, then looked at the readout... and banged his fist on the desktop in frustration; still a line of fucking zeroes. Then he noticed something else: the word "searching…" was flashing above the figures. Had that been there before? He didn't think so.

Suddenly the box emitted a beep, the flashing stopped, and the word changed to "Acquired". The neon figures now read:

N15 43.4 W66 13.3

He let out a whoop of triumph.

'Elías the Navigator will get us to Guanica and deliver the cargo,' he declared aloud.

Then he froze. He was a week late with the delivery.

Gonzales does not tolerate mistakes. Gonzales accepts no excuses.

His previous partner had found that out the hard way, a bullet in the back of the brain. They had forced Elías to watch the execution: a warning not to fuck up.

He flipped over the folded chart and traced his finger along the Venezuelan coast. He stopped at Carupano. He was born in Carupano. His parents still lived there, and his brother, Enrico, a small-time dealer trading to touristas in Trinidad. Enrico did not work for the Cartels. In particular, and most importantly, Enrico had no contact with the Zamorano Cartel, Gonzalez's suppliers.

Patrick had also lied about the fuel, about how far the boat could go with the engine, though he was not sure what he had hoped to gain from that.

He had examined the engine. It was a small diesel, no more than 1000cc. The fuel gauge on the panel showed nearly two hundred litres. He reasoned a truck of a similar weight to this boat, with a much bigger engine, would go 500 miles on 200 litres of diesel.

He set about plotting a course to Carupano.

~ Chapter Seventeen ~

They say what doesn't kill you makes you stronger. Who the hell said that, anyway? I feel as weak as a baby.

I don't remember much, just weird dreams and short lucid moments when I managed to slurp a bit of water before falling back knackered from the effort. I've no idea how long I lay there under that stinking pile of palm fronds, it could have been two days; it could have been a week.

The fever broke sometime in the night and I just laid there exhausted, tongue stuck to the roof of my mouth, throat so dry I kept gagging, but of course, there was nothing down there to bring up. Eventually I crawled out of my hidey-hole to my solar-still. The cover had blown off but there were a couple of mouthfuls of bug-infested water left in the shell.

Then the rain came.

So now it's pissing down in sheets, my coconut shells are overflowing, sitting there neatly in a row, and I'm rehydrated but starving. The fire is long gone of course, so now I must start that all over again, when I can find the energy and the will to move.

When it stops fucking raining!

Finding something dry to burn is going to be impossible after this downpour. The good news is my foot's healing up. The swelling has gone down and it doesn't look so inflamed. The aloe and cobweb gunge I plastered on it is still in place, looks like a dried cowpat, but it's sitting on top of a healthy-looking scab. Redman's Balm, eh? I like the sound of that now, make my fortune maybe.

I don't know if I should share this with you, but I've just eaten a live cricket. It tasted foul and I nearly yacked it back up again, but hey, it's protein, don't knock it.

~.~

Well, that's my red night flare gone - used it to make a fire. Yes, I know, I'll probably regret it later when I see a passing ship. However, I still have my day smoke and the beacon on the hill. It was a hard decision, but everything is too damp. It does not rain on the Serengeti as it does here.

I almost came a cropper though. Gathering an armful of the driest leaves and twigs I could find I carefully arranged it in a nice stack, and then I held the flare into it and pulled the ring. Whoosh! I had stupidly overlooked that flares are supposed to fire two hundred feet into the sky. The fireball scattered my little pile of kindling then came after me, chasing me all round the beach. Luckily, it was still burning when it stopped moving and I was able to pile some of the scattered debris on it before it went out.

Anyway, I have a nice little fire spluttering away, albeit not in the place I had intended it to be. There's a pair of conches roasting away and smelling delicious. Life here is starting to feel normal, as if this is how I've lived my whole life.

That is worrying. Nothing outside my little universe has any substance anymore. I often wonder about my sanity. Will I know if I go slowly mad? Assuming I get off this island one day, will I spend my days believing myself to be the only sane being in a world full of raving nutters?

I think about Stella every day of course, mainly the fun moments we had spent, mostly funny incidents on the boat.

Like the night we were terrorised by a four-foot Wahoo, following the lure I had been reeling in for the night. It left the water going straight up like a Polaris missile, and two seconds later, it crashed through the bimini, ripping a big hole in the canvas. The two of us yipped and squealed trying to get out of its way as it thrashed about the cockpit.

In mawkish moments, I see her being shot, a deadening reminder that I'll never see her again. However, my pain now feels somehow dull and meaningless; a bright petal made soft and brown by prolonged swirling round in an endless eddy at the riverbank.

My emotions are shot. I'm like a headless cockroach, staying alive because I don't know how to die.

I'm having conversations with myself now, not just the odd word or two spoken aloud, but meaningful conversations and arguments, yes, even shouting matches that eventually fizzle out into a black sulk that lasts for hours. Only ten days but it feels like forever. Jesus Christ how much longer?

~.~

Livid with myself this morning. I cannot believe what just happened. I went off on my usual rounds of the island, feeling quite buoyant, picking up a useful-looking piece of driftwood on the way, and singing some idiot song or other, you know, to ward off the collywobbles.

I was on the other side, directly opposite from my camp, when I spotted it, a brown smudge on the horizon. At first, I thought it was something in my eye, but I closed first one, then the other, and the object remained. I think I screamed then, I remember screaming at some point, it still rings in my ears now.

I dropped the plank of wood and ran up the hill to my beacon, looked out again, and there it was, the top of a brown sail, maybe two brown sails, or maybe three, it was hard to tell at that distance. She was hull down, only the top half of her sail or sails visible, so no one on the vessel's deck would see the island.

However, they would if I lit the beacon!

I ran down to my camp and made a hasty torch from a burning stick, stuffed the smoke flare into my pocket, and ran back up the hill to the beacon. By the time I got there, the sail had moved a little way left of where I first saw it and seemed significantly further away.

She was going away from me.

It is perfectly understandable that people in boats look mostly ahead, and rarely glance astern, except perhaps when looking misty eyed at some receding shore. In theory of course, a good helmsman always keeps an all-round lookout, and it was this hopeful assumption that made me activate the smoke signal before thrusting the torch into the base of the beacon.

I held the smoke flare aloft long after its orange billows had dispersed on the breeze, long after the last sliver of brown sail had sunk below the horizon. Eventually I admitted the truth and threw the empty flare case onto the equally useless beacon that stood there, unlit and aloof, the torch having died without catching.

I need a better plan.

~ Part Three ~

November 1983

~ Chapter Eighteen ~

Adventure calls! "So onward, river steed,
and speed my courageous blossoms,
to bleed upon some foreign shore."

Patrick sat up suddenly in his bunk, wakened by the sound of gunfire. Realising where he was he lay back down and listened to the regular thump, one every three seconds, each accompanied by a clank that reverberated through the ship's ventilation network; he wondered what the target was. After a while he slipped down from the bunk and dressed.

The Wardroom was deserted, breakfast having finished some hours ago. A sympathetic steward pointed him toward the aircrew cafeteria, which was on the main deck just forward of the hangar.

Only two men were in the ACC, the helicopter pilot and his crewman, smoking and drinking coffee at the only table. Patrick asked if he could join them before grabbing a plate and heaping it with eggs, bacon, and beans in chili sauce.

'Not spotting for this one then?' he asked as he sat down.

'Marine ground-spotters,' the pilot told him, 'So, Patrick, how are you enjoying your cruise with the US Navy?'

Patrick paused from shovelling food into his mouth and realised how bad it must have looked. He put down the knife and fork and wiped his mouth.

'A bit more excitement than I would have expected on a cruise ship, but otherwise, very comfortable, thank you.'

'Go on, eat your food,' the pilot said, 'I guess it'll be a while before the novelty wears off and you realise how bad it tastes. Can I get you a coffee?'

'Thanks, and for the record, even after five days this is still the best food I've ever tasted.'

The crewman leaned over and said quietly, 'You know that rescue of yours probably ranks as one of the craziest missions of my career. What a story to tell back home.'

When the pilot returned with Patrick's coffee the two aircrew spoke among themselves while he finished the meal uninterrupted.

When he had done eating the pilot said, 'Captain Paul tells me you were in the British Navy.'

'The Royal Navy, yes,' Patrick said, with a disarming grin, and wondering how much Rick had told the pilot and whether his story was circulating the ship. He hoped not.

'Where is Rick today? I mean, does he have a place of work onboard?'

'Rick's at his place of work right now. He and his boys are out in a boat patrolling the coast around…' he turned to his crewman, 'what's that peninsular called, something French?'

'That'll be *Lance aux Epines*, boss,' he turned to Patrick and winked, 'he can't remember place-names, that's why he needs me.'

The pilot scowled and pointed a thumb at the crewman, 'And he can't remember his *place*, that's why he can't work with anyone else *except* me.'

'Hey, that's not fair, I saluted the Captain yesterday.'

'Careful, buddy, I could get jealous,' He turned back to Patrick, 'We were over there in UK waters a few years ago, with the NATO Standing Force.'

Patrick thought a moment, then said, 'We did a couple of months with STANAVFORLANT in '79 before we deployed here to the Caribbean. I was on *HMS Preston*.'

'Yeah, I remember Preston - DDG, right?'

'That's right,' Patrick said, 'and now I think about it, I do remember *Charles Walther* being one of the ships in the group. Funny thing is I might even have spoken to you on the radio. I was the Helicopter Controller on *Preston*.'

'Almost certain you did,' the pilot's grin widened, 'hey, that's *cool.* Hear that Dan?'

The crewman was at the coffee vendor refilling his coffee cup.

'Small world huh?' he called over his shoulder, 'hey, boss, you remember that Dutch ship with the giant radome? *Van*-something, but everybody called it *Kojak*?'

'Thanks a lot.' Patrick said with a self-conscious grin. He stroked the stubby bristles on his head then pulled on his cap. They all laughed good-naturedly, and Patrick savoured the old familiar glow of acceptance by fellow mariners the world over.

~.~

'Rangers lost four men dead and twenty injured today,' Rick announced to the table in general, 'all the survivors were stretcher cases, missing legs, arms...'

Everyone looked up, a mixture of shock and sorrowful head shaking.

'Poor bastards were in three Blackhawks that all crashed. Minimal enemy fire, just fuckin' pilot error. Darned fools panicked and brought each other down at the landing site.'

Patrick had wondered why the marine had been so quiet during dinner; he had tactfully waited until the meal was finished before breaking this news.

In the first days of the invasion there had been a kind of carnival atmosphere in the ship. Everyone he had met had been upbeat about the conflict, saying it would be over in a day, not much resistance expected.

'When they see the size of the forces against them they'll just give up without a fight,' had been the mantra on everyone's lips, and Patrick had bought into it too.

However, he had seen and heard the distant fighting along the coast between Point Salines and St Georges and heard about the difficulties the Rangers had had in locating and freeing the students at the True-Blue Medical School.

It also appeared that many of those youngsters were scattered everywhere at other campuses and private dwellings around the south of the island; and the Cubans, it was rumoured, were holding some of them hostage.

Suddenly it didn't seem such a picnic.

The officers had mostly drifted out of the dining area; Patrick too was about to retire to his cabin, when Rick came over with two cups of coffee. He placed one in front of Patrick and sat down opposite. He rubbed his eyes with thumb and forefinger then looked up at Patrick. He looked tired out, and Patrick noticed for the first time the silver streaks in his close-cropped hair. The captain was much older than he looked, probably in his forties and facing retirement.

'Bad day?' Patrick tried.

'One fuckin' hell of a day,' it was almost a groan, 'came across a bunch of five PRA men, a strip of pebble beach between some trees. Damn fools wouldn't drop their weapons. Fuckin' hell, me and six of my people had M16's trained on 'em from twelve yards away – they had no chance, but the crazy fuckers tried anyway.

"Drop your weapons," I tells em, "and we won't shoot."

Had a staring-down match for maybe ten seconds, nobody moving. I warns em again, but then one of em ups and shoots, and the rest follow like fuckin' sheep. We killed em all, goddammit, every single fuckin' one of em. Stupid bastards!'

Patrick stayed silent for a time, and then said, 'any of your men hurt?'

'Yeah, just a flesh wound to the shoulder. He'll be ok.'

~.~

As the days wore on Patrick became increasingly frustrated with his confinement onboard. Fair enough, he enjoyed the nostalgia of being back on a warship, especially one in action, but that was all it was, nostalgia. He longed to get ashore and start his search for *Carriacou*, and Stella's killers.

He had no illusions about the difficulties he faced, indeed, the impossibility of the undertaking, but he knew he had to try. He owed it to her memory.

He had started having dreams that relived his time on Folly. One night a tropical storm had torn away his makeshift shack and forced him to sit shivering on the hillside, exposed to the howling wind and lashing rain. The surreal moment in the dream came when the rain softened and turned pink, and when he held out his hand soft petals of rhododendrons floated into it.

Chatting with Rick after his daily patrols had become a regular feature of his evenings, and something which he increasingly looked forward to. Rick was a Vietnam veteran and, as Patrick gradually discovered, had a very cynical view of the current mission.

'This is Reagan's Falklands,' he'd said one evening, when they sat alone in the Wardroom lounge, 'he saw how good it was for your Margaret Thatcher, and he wants some of that post war popularity.'

'I can't believe your Military leaders would go to war on that basis?' Patrick said.

'Ordinarily I'd agree with you, but the generals in the Pentagon have their own agenda. They want to prove themselves after the debacle of 'Nam. A lot of the older guys here share that sentiment. So this little charade is very popular with Americans.'

Rick also supplied Patrick with daily updates of how the conflict was progressing. By the sixth day, Rangers and Marine forces had progressed to the north of the island where many PRA soldiers were still holding out.

'Today, the Rangers liberated a bunch of political prisoners from a gaol up there, but they realised too late that some real criminals were there as well. Another fuckup, but hey, that's war. Let me tell you, Patrick, when American soldiers fight, they fight like fuckin' tigers, but the knuckleheads that lead em get it wrong time and again.'

'I think the cockup syndrome applies to all armed forces,' Patrick said, 'not just Americans. I've had a few dunderheads for bosses in my time.'

He laughed at that, 'Yeah, you Brits have made fuckups throughout history, but you did it with such *Style*'

~ Chapter Nineteen ~

One evening Rick seemed preoccupied at dinner and didn't say very much but glanced at Patrick from time to time. The look was hard to read but he clearly had something on his mind.

When they had taken their coffee into the officer's lounge as usual, Patrick said, 'You look a little upset tonight, Rick. Did something bad happen?'

'Another bunch of idiots thought they could take us. We managed to take two of 'em alive though, so that's something, I guess.'

He took a sip of his coffee, and brightening, looked up, 'But that ain't it. I'm not pissed, I've just been strugglin' to work out if I should tell you what I'm about to tell you.'

Patrick said, 'You'll have to tell me now, Rick, so come on, out with it.'

'Okay, did you say your girlfriend's boat was called *Spirit of Carriacou*?'

Patrick's mouth went dry, 'Y-yes, why?' he managed.

'A white sloop with a red boot?'

'That's right,' he had painted that boot topping himself in Gibraltar, '*you found her?*'

'Now don't get too excited, if it's her, then she looks abandoned, and probably not seaworthy.'

Patrick lunged across and grabbed the big man's forearm, 'Where?' he was almost chocking with excitement, 'where is she?'

Rick shook him off and pulled a map out of his thigh pocket. He opened it out and pointed to a peninsula on the south coast of the island that bore an uncanny resemblance to the boot of Italy. A pencilled circle marked a small inlet, just where the boot's instep met the sole.

'That's where she lies,' Rick said, 'but she's aground in the mangrove, and she's got a good covering of green weed and algae. I nearly missed her; she's so merged with the vegetation. We banged on the hull, but no response, so I guess she's abandoned.'

'How is she grounded,' Patrick asked, still hardly able to believe what he was hearing, 'by the head or the stern?'

'By the head. I think the stern's afloat: she moved when I shoved her.'

'Can you take me to her, Rick, can you take me tomorrow?'

~.~

However, it was another two days before the Captain felt the situation ashore warranted allowing Patrick to leave the safety of the ship.

'I have to tell you, Mr Redman, I'm not entirely thrilled that you're deciding to leave us. But if that's what you want to do, then I've no jurisdiction to stop you. You're a British citizen, after all, and a free agent. But I strongly advise you stay away from population centres, especially around St Georges.

'Where Captain Paul is taking you, where apparently your boat lies, is in an area cleared by our forces, but it's pretty remote, so we can't discount an insurgent or two hiding out down there. Please be careful and avoid contact with anyone you aren't sure about.'

'Sir, I...', Patrick stopped, a sudden catch in his voice. He just stood, unable to speak, looking at the Captain through a fuzz.

The captain's hand clasped his shoulder, 'Mr Redman... Patrick, I can't begin to understand what it was like for you out on that rock, but I do understand delayed trauma shock. Stay with us a few more days, eat some food, relax, and give yourself a little more time.'

Patrick struggled a moment longer with his emotions. The offer was tempting, but the pull of *Carriacou* was stronger. 'Thank you, Sir, but I'm okay, really. I just wanted to say, thanks,' the word felt inadequate, 'to you and everyone on board, for saving my life, and... well, everything.' He took the Captain's extended hand and returned a firm handshake.

'You're very welcome, Patrick, it really was our pleasure. And good luck. Remember what I said. If you think you're in trouble, try to reach one of our units.'

~.~

The destroyer had resumed her plane guard duties - a dawn launch of F14's and A6's, - when the boat deck crew swung out and lowered the marine's forty-foot RHIB to within a few feet of the fast surging water.

Rick had insisted Patrick discard the loaned officer's khaki in favour of something less military-looking – a pair of nondescript blue shorts, a plain grey T-shirt, and a pair of leather sandals donated by one of his marines.

'Y'all ready down there?'

Patrick looked up to see a ruddy-faced Petty Officer leaning over the guardrail looking down at them.

'Ready when you are, sailor' Rick called back.

A staccato voice rang out over the intercom, 'BRIDGE, THIS IS BOATDECK, READY TO LAUNCH SEABOAT.'

'ROGER THAT, BOAT DECK, STAND BY.'

Patrick heard the great turbines winding down inside the ship and her speed gradually decayed.

'FIVE KNOTS, BOATDECK'

'AYE, SIR'

The petty officer appeared once more above and saluted, 'Slip at your discretion, Sir, and good luck.'

The marine sergeant sitting amidships pulled the pin out of the disengaging gear and took hold of the handle. He watched the flow of waves along the ship's side, nodding his head to pick up their rhythm, and then with one final emphatic nod, he pulled back the handle. His timing was perfect. The boat dropped onto the crest of a wave with barely a jolt, and surged forward as the big outboard dug in. The boat sheered away in a great arc, and then settled on course with the rising sun over the starboard quarter.

The destroyer, who had had to remain on station with the carrier during flying, was fifteen miles southeast of the small boat's destination at launch. From this distance and so close to the water, the low-lying coast was not yet visible. The long sea was almost dead astern, which made for a smooth but undulating ride, with the boat seeming to gain and lose speed as each roller passed beneath and overtook.

Forty-five minutes later the boat nosed gently through a narrow gap in the dense mangrove and glided into a small lagoon.

~ Chapter Twenty ~

Prepared as he had been by Rick's description of her, Patrick's heart sank when he saw *Spirit of Carriacou*. Her bow was stuck into the dense mangrove, her foot out of the water and resting on the thick roots of the stunted bushes, setting her low by the stern. He was relieved to see the rigging looked intact, and at least somebody had furled the genoa. But the mainsail lay un-stowed in green and grey crumpled heaps along the coach roof and in the cockpit.

As the RHIB drew closer, he saw her name on the transom. The fibreglass skin looked clean and pristine where Rick had wiped off some of the green filth. The Swiss flag hung forlornly from the backstay, faded and speckled with black mildew. The coxswain nudged the RIHB's soft bow against her stern and a marine took a turn round a guardrail stanchion with the painter.

'Want me to come aboard with you?' Rick said.

'You've done enough, thanks; I can take it from here. But please hang around while I check below. If there's fuel in the tank and she hasn't sprung a leak, then maybe you can tow me off into the middle of the lagoon where I can drop the pick.'

'Is that wise? What if the bow's damaged and you take water when she floats?'

Patrick swung himself up onto the stern gunwale, stepped over the wire, and into the cockpit. 'Don't worry; I'll check the bow for damage first.'

Rick stepped forward and handed up a canvass duffle bag. 'Here Patrick, a few things you might need. You didn't think about it, but I did.'

Patrick took the bag, 'Christ, what's in here, a gold bar?'

'Just a few things, check it out later. Let's speed it up; this unit has a rendezvous with some Navy Seals further round the coast.'

'Okay, quick as I can.' Patrick said, and turned to see what man and nature had done to Stella's beautiful boat. He pulled the algae-fouled mainsail away from the companionway and was surprised and delighted to find the hatch closed and the washboards in place. There was a good chance things were in better condition below.

Creepers had snaked their way along a deck grown green and slimy with algae. He grieved for the beautiful teak decking beneath the gunge. He slipped off his sandals and walked carefully along the starboard side to the bows, removing the offending foliage as he went.

At the bow, breaking off or bending back branches to give him clear access, he went down on his stomach and leaned over as far as he could reach to observe the hull around the solid steel foot of the boat, first one side, then the other. The skin was undamaged. A slimy rope fastened to a cleat led off into the trees beyond the bow. It was bar taut. He left it in place and returned via the port side. Here there was no creeping vegetation and the algae was less extensive, which he put down to the sunlight not getting to this side as much as the other.

The companionway hatch slid open easily, which surprised him; he had half expected it to be jammed through lack of use. Before he went below, he checked the gas bottles in their locker at the stern. The connected one was open. He shut it off. The spare still had its seal intact.

The saloon was in reasonable condition, but the banquette cushions had acquired a faint whiff of fungus and mildew. He lifted a couple of sole boards fore and aft. The bilge was dry. He stuck his nose in and took a deep sniff. No smell of gas.

He held his breath when he opened the locker above the chart table and let out a long sigh of relief when he found his and Stella's passports. He looked at her picture for a long moment.

It was from about five years ago, in Kenya, when her hair was long. Her beautiful penetrating eyes stared back at him, and although the picture was black and white, his mind filled in their startling blue. She had the beginnings of a smile and looked full of life and optimism. He snapped it closed and replaced both passports in the locker.

His wallet had only ten US dollars in it, but his Credit Cards were all there. Stella's purse was empty. He remembered they'd intended to go to the Western Union office on Pipah to get more cash that day…'

The electrical breakers were in the ON position, but the control panel was dead. The two smashed in radios were just as he had last seen them.

He would need to charge the batteries, and for that, he needed to start the engine. However, *Carriacou*'s engine didn't have a hand-cranking facility, so he needed a charged battery.

The toolbox was still under the chart table, so he took out the steel tape-measure and used it to dip the diesel tanks. The starboard one was empty but the port one was full. He checked the fuel changeover – it was pointing to the starboard tank. Whoever had used the boat last had thought they were out of fuel, but they had merely to change tanks. He did so now, and hoped the diesel was still usable after all this time.

He opened the engine cover and carried out the standard daily inspection. Everything checked out okay.

In the port cabin, he lifted the mattress and opened the battery compartment underneath. He disconnected the four dead batteries and connected the two unused ones they had always kept for emergencies.

He stepped onto the ladder and called to Rick, 'Stand clear, I'm going to try the engine.'

At the fourth attempt, the sixty-horsepower diesel shuddered into life and Patrick whooped with delight. Outside he heard a cheer from the marines in their boat. He returned to the deck and leaned over the port quarter, where the sight of engine cooling water pumping from the exhaust heartened him. He clicked the clutch into astern and eased up the revs until he felt the screw bite, then returned to neutral.

He held his breath as he reached for the wheel – it turned with reassuring resistance. Someone had managed to fix the steering. Elías? Or somebody else? Either way, he would need to check the repair, and if necessary, reconnect the autohelm leads.

He could still hardly believe his luck in finding her again and wondered at the unlikelihood of her being here in Grenada, hundreds of miles away from where he had sabotaged her before escaping.

He held up a thumb to the marines waiting patiently a few yards off.

'I'll be ok. She's dry and held into the shore by a rope. When I let that go she'll just slide off.'

Rick signalled the driver and the boat closed in once more to nestle on *Carriacou*'s stern. The Marine Captain extended his big hand and Patrick grasped it in both of his.

'Patrick, I want you to know, I think you're one plucky limey, a little crazy maybe, but I love ya man.'

'Thanks Rick, thanks for everything,' he let his eyes roam over the other marines in the boat, 'best of luck with your war, take care and get home safe.'

They all spoke at once to call their farewells and good lucks back to him. He watched the boat glide out of the little lagoon, and then went below to work out a recovery plan for *Spirit of Carriacou*.

He threw all the saloon mattresses into the forepeak out of the way. They would need some serious treatment in the open air once he had the topsides clean.

Then he remembered the canvass duffle bag that Rick had given him. Inside he found two US Marines Ration Packs, a portable VHF radio, and something heavy wrapped in a green oilcloth.

As soon as he picked it up, he guessed what the package contained. At the bottom of the bag were another smaller package, and a note from Rick.

Hey Buddy,
Some presents from Uncle Sam.
The gun's for self-protection. Hope you don't need it. And don't shoot your goddam foot off (I know you limeys ain't used to guns).

Radio's got a full charge. If the red light flashes it needs charging (but I guess you know that). US Forces monitor #16, but if you need to call our boys without telling the world, use #72. Range is line of sight (but I guess you know that too).

Best of luck, Patrick. Hope we meet again someday (maybe then we'll know what this fucking war was all about).
Rick

The gun was a Remington-Rand M1911. He was no weapons expert, but he knew it was the standard issue pistol favoured by the US Army. The smaller package contained two full clips.

He opened all the side windows in the saloon to let in some air, and then picked up the mattress from Stella's sea cabin. He was about to add it to the others in the forepeak, but then stopped.

He put his nose to it and sniffed; a faint smell of scent, and it wasn't damp like those from the saloon. He checked the cabin again and in the recess above the bunk found a bra, small size, a multi-coloured singlet, and four pairs of skimpy panties. They were certainly not Stella's; one, they were too small, and two, she *never* left her kit sculling.

'Who's been sleeping on my boat,' he muttered, 'and where are you Goldilocks?'

He checked his own sea cabin - and the mattress there was dry as well. At the bottom end, he found a small pile of clothes: a pair of orange shorts, a T-shirt bearing the logo of some ice hockey team, and several pairs of men's underpants in a plastic bag. All were dry, and recently worn.

'And her boyfriend?'

He opened the fridge and found two plastic bottles of UHT milk, one opened and still usable, a packet of ham, a chunk of cheese, a packet of butter, used, and a half loaf of sliced bread. All were in edible condition.

He looked around the saloon with fresh eyes and noticed how clean everything was. Anything they had used to prepare food they had diligently washed up and stowed. He tried the water hand-pump at the sink and it immediately issued a solid stream of water, indicating recent use.

When, after two hours running, the main batteries showed a full charge he killed the engine. With the control panel active once more, he saw that the port water tank was empty but the starboard one was nearly full: two hundred litres, that was good. He wanted to get her properly afloat, but he was also keen to welcome back his two squatters, whoever they might be.

If they returned.

~ Chapter Twenty-One ~

He heard them before he saw them, American accents, coming from behind the mangroves on the port bow. He went up top, padded down the port side and sat on the forward end of the coach roof. They were thrashing through the dense foliage, getting closer.

'Ow!' a female voice, 'you let that branch slap right into my fucking face.'

'Sorry, you shouldn't get so close behind me.'

'Shit man, just be more careful.'

They burst out of the bushes laughing and splashed into knee-deep water, a good-looking pair barely out of their teens, carrying lightweight backpacks. The girl noticed him first. She was smallish and pretty, short mousy hair; she gasped and put a hand to her mouth, staring up at Patrick. Her companion, taller, tousle red haired and massively freckled, gaped at him open mouthed.

'Don't panic,' Patrick said, smiling with hands raised submissively, 'look, I'm harmless.'

They continued staring for a moment, and then the girl broke the silence.

'I'm so sorry, we thought this boat was abandoned and we just had to get away from the campus because the Cubans were surrounding us and it said on the radio that they were taking students hostage and the Americans were having trouble getting through to rescue us and everyone was so scared so Tim and I escaped down the fire ladder and…'

Her companion put his hand on her shoulder. 'Tracey, please shut the fuck up,' he said gently.

'Oh, okay.' she smiled up sheepishly and turned an attractive pink, 'I always talk too much when I'm nervous.'

'Well, never mind,' Patrick said, 'you can tell me the full story later. You have my permission to come aboard.'

He held down a hand to the girl and she swung her sandaled feet easily up onto the rail, her taller companion waded aft a little then climbed aboard unaided.

'Now what a British sailor does in circumstances such as these,' Patrick said, 'is to make a cup of tea. However, my teabags being old and mouldy, and you being Americans…'

'Canadians actually,' Tim interjected, but without rancour.

'Okay, sorry - you being Canadians - probably prefer coffee, of which my supply of instant is welded solidly to the inside of the jar. So maybe you can help me out here?'

'Ah,' said Tracey, diving into her backpack, 'it so happens that we have been out shopping, and…Ta-rah!' triumphantly she held aloft a jar of Nescafe in one hand, and a box of Lipton's Teabags in the other.

'I like you already,' said Patrick, grabbing the coffee and ducking down into the saloon.

'No offence,' he called up the hatch, 'but you can keep the Lipton's, it's a poor substitute for the real thing.'

~.~

It transpired that Tracey and Tim were medical students at True Blue and had got caught up in the conflict when militias besieged their campus lodgings at the University Club. They had stumbled upon the boat by accident a week ago in their search for somewhere to hang out and had decided it was as safe a haven as any.

'You realise of course that most of the med students have been rounded up and flown out by the Americans?' he told them.

'Yeah, we just found out today,' Tim said, 'when we went to check out the campus. Just a bunch of army guys there now.'

'So why didn't you hand yourselves in?' Patrick said, 'your parents will be worried sick that you weren't among the survivors.'

The two looked at each other, Tracey chewing her lip in a slightly worrying way.

'We did tell them who we were,' Tim began, 'and they arranged for us to call our parents.'

'And? ...' Patrick prompted.

'They wanted us to go with them to the airport,' Tracey said, 'but... well it's kind of fun here, in the middle of a war, you know, kind of thrilling...,' she trailed off lamely.

'So we told 'em we'd be okay,' Tim supplied, 'they tried to force us, but we just ran. I guess they got the message cuz they didn't come after us.'

'They're probably too busy to worry about a couple of crazy med students, more like,' laughed Patrick.

Patrick couldn't hide his satisfaction at having the two youngsters for company. He had started to feel overwhelmed by his growing list of things to do and wasted no time in persuading them to help him prepare the boat for sea. They were thrilled by his promise of a sea voyage, and applied themselves enthusiastically, if not expertly, to the task.

'First job for you guys, sort out this crabby mains'l.'

While the two youngsters dragged the grungy sail away from the boat and scrubbed at it in waist-deep water, Patrick started work to get the boat properly moored. He got out the kedge anchor from the chain locker and prepared it on the stern. There was plenty of spare on the head rope, and despite its coating of slime, it seemed in reasonable condition. He took off the turns from the cleat and let the boat slide off the slippery tree roots, using her momentum to back off from the shore. Just before he ran out of rope, he turned up on the cleat to stop her.

Returning aft he slipped the kedge. When he was satisfied the anchor was bedded he returned forward and took up the slack, bringing the bow back to about three yards from the mangroves. He had her safely moored fore and aft, with a good four feet of water underfoot, and much more further aft where the keel was.

He would need to check the undersides for damage. He was particularly worried about the keel and rudder, but also wanted to make sure the log and transducer were clear of debris. He located his swim mask from his locker in the starboard cabin.

~.~

After three days of hard graft, the boat appeared in a reasonable state to go to sea. The hull and coach roof gleamed fresh and white, and apart from a few faint green stains, the mainsail had cleaned up nicely. Tracey squealed with delight when Patrick hoisted her aloft in the bosun's chair to clean the mast and wipe down the standing rigging with linseed oil.

However, no amount of scrubbing could remove the faint green sheen that remained stubbornly on the teak decks. At least they were no longer dangerously slimy, and Patrick decided to leave it at that until he could find a boatyard.

'We need to make a run ashore,' Patrick said, 'we need food and fresh drinking water; and I want to check with the US Rangers what the state of play is in Carriacou. If we can use the boatyard in Tyrell Bay, we won't need to haul all the way up to St Vincent.'

'Why not sail round to St Georges?' Tim said.

Patrick shook his head. 'Too risky. The US Navy has it blockaded – at least up until three days ago nothing was being allowed in or out. No, I believe Carriacou's our best bet – it's only a day's passage.'

~.~

Between them, Patrick and Tim moved the boat closer in, so they could wade ashore while keeping the rucksacks dry. Leaving Tracey to mind the boat, Tim led the way through the dense brush up to the main road. They headed north, towards the top of the peninsula where Tim said there were shops open.

The St Georges University Club, from where the two youngsters had made their spirited escape ten days ago, lay ransacked and deserted, broken glass on the pavements and mattresses in the windows.

'Anything you need from in there,' Patrick said, 'before we leave this island for good?'

'Na, we collected what little we could find the other day.'

They hurried on past. Thousands of empty cartridge cases and remnants of military uniform and equipment littered the road. Occasionally they saw dried up pools of blood among the debris: grim evidence of a hard-fought battle.

'I assume it was like this when you came back here?' Patrick said.

Tim nodded morosely, 'we heard this shit going down five, maybe six days ago from the boat. Man we were crapping ourselves.'

Somewhere far off to their right a dog barked for a few seconds then stopped. The air felt torpid from last night's heavy squalls. They had petered out by dawn and left a fresh zing in the air, but the mid-morning sun was rapidly consuming that.

The road ahead was devoid of people or traffic. Deep concrete-lined drainage ditches ran either side of the road, covered over where necessary to give access to a scattering of brightly painted shanty houses. Some of the gardens at the rear contained trees hung with ripe fruit: mangoes, papaya, and bright fingers of bananas.

'We'll pick up some fresh fruit on the way back,' Patrick said, 'the owners have obviously scarpered and it's a shame to let it go to waste.'

They found an abandoned US Army jeep at the roadside with its windscreen shot out. It looked serviceable, so Patrick looked inside.

'No keys,' he said, 'any good at hot-wiring?'

'Hey man, I'm a spoilt rich kid, not some street hoodlum.'

'Well, it can't be rocket science,' Patrick said, 'let's try it.'

He groped under the steering column and located a hole with some wires. He yanked them hard, but they wouldn't shift. He laid with his back on the floor pan for better advantage.

'Looks easy in the movies,' he grunted, as he tried once more to dislodge the connected wires.

'Try one at a time,' Tim advised, 'and just the two attached to the ignition switch, not the whole bunch.'

'Ah, that works,' he pulled the second wire out, 'amazing what they teach you at Med School, eh? Now what, just wind them together?'

'I would assume so.'

'Yeow!' shouted Patrick as sparks flashed from the touching wires, 'wasn't expecting that.'

Tim grinned, 'Dur, its electricity, man.'

He tried again, this time the engine turned once and coughed into life and he managed to get the wires properly joined together.

'Bingo, let's go.' Patrick had picked up the expression from the Marines, and he rather liked it.

'Now he's John Wayne,' Tim said sardonically, and climbed into the passenger seat.

~ . ~

Tracey used the time cleaning and tidying below. She switched on her portable shortwave radio that Patrick had left tuned to the BBC World Service; some old British comedy show she had never heard of called Round the Horn. She left it on because it made her laugh.

She had learned a great deal about the boat over the past three days and was looking forward to the Big Ocean Adventure. In fact the whole thing, with the invasion and all, had been an exciting interlude from her studies, scary, sure, but exhilarating as well.

Okay, so it would take a little longer than expected before she could tell Mom and Dad she was a qualified doctor, ready to start her internship, but that was fine. Shit happens.

Meanwhile she was going to have a little fun and learn to sail a yacht. Dad will be proud of that, at least.

She retrieved the dry, newly washed seat covers from the guardrails and took them below, measured them against the cushions to see which cover belonged to which, and then got to work redressing the seats.

The comedy show finished and the chimes of Big Ben came on, followed by the World News.

She couldn't remember whose idea it was to run – it had all happened so quickly. Although Tim had been her classmate, they hadn't really been friends until their joint dash for freedom. The rest of her class were Americans. They had seemed to have blind faith in their soldiers' ability to rescue them and insisted on staying put.

On the radio, some guy called Nielson in London had been found guilty on six counts of murder. A necrophiliac, apparently. Yuk! This was followed by something about a group of women in England camped outside some US Airbase. They were protesting about nuclear weapons.

'Go get 'em ladies.'

So she and Tim had made that crazy escape down a flimsy ladder from the top floor at the rear of the building, and since then, they'd become close.

They had had sex once, that first night on the boat, but by some unspoken agreement, had abstained from further intimacy, and Tracey had moved into the other cabin. Now Tim felt more like a brother than a lover. She found she preferred it that way and suspected he did too.

She wondered whether he was gay. That would explain the lack of passion that first night, and their mutual indifference to anything sexual subsequently.

There was a report about the war in Grenada and she turned up the volume to listen. Apparently, it was all over apart from some pockets of resistance in the north of the island. They played a clip from Reagan saying the operation (*Urgent Fury* for God's sakes!) had been a complete success and America should be proud of its military.

She zipped up the last of the seat covers and turned her attention to the bathroom... 'heads,' she corrected herself - remembering the origin of the term as Patrick had explained it - starting with that thick tidemark in the toilet bowl that had been so annoying her. She had found some bleach powder that she now applied liberally into the bowl and watched it bubble up in reaction to the seawater. The fumes made her eyes water; so she closed the lid and returned to the saloon.

She liked Patrick. Not that way, of course. He was little too skinny – emaciated almost - for her taste in men, and a little old maybe. And the shaved head didn't do it for her either. However, he was a really nice guy, and capable. Despite her fondness for Tim, she felt safer with him around.

She hadn't got around to asking him where he had been while his boat was rotting in this little backwater, and he had offered no explanation. Still, plenty of time for that while they were cruising.

She was polishing the big mirror on the outside of the heads door when she felt the boat lean abruptly to port. Someone climbing aboard. She went through to the saloon.

'You guys back already?' she called through the open side port, 'that was quick.'

Too quick, she thought, they must have come back for something. She switched off the shortwave and stepped up to poke her head out of the companionway, and then drew back in a sudden rush of panic. The footsteps thumping along the deck were too heavy for Patrick or Tim, both of whom always stepped lightly around the boat.

'Who's there?' her voice cracked with fear.

The footsteps stopped. She glanced back through the saloon ports and saw thick-soled boots and black trouser bottoms. Police, maybe? The boat tipped again. A second set of footsteps, lighter. A grubby pair of sneakers, turned up jeans, joined the boots out on deck. She stumbled up into the cockpit and turned around to face the intruders.

'Ah, look Elías, a pretty little *gringo* girl has serviced our boat for us.'

Tracey stood rooted to the spot. She wasn't sure whether to be more afraid of the ugly filthy-looking giant that leered down at her, or the automatic rifle aimed at her face.

~ Chapter Twenty-Two ~

'That's about everything, I believe,' Patrick said, stowing the last of the five-litre water bottles onto the back seat of the jeep.

For the first time in many months, he was sweating; a good sign he was recovering from his year of near starvation.

He surveyed the heap of stores they had amassed.

'That should keep us going for a week or so. Shame there isn't much fresh veg, but I guess we can stock up on fruit instead.'

They jumped into the jeep and Patrick re-twisted the ignition wires to start the engine.

'Thanks for paying for that lot; I'll sort you out when I can get to a Western Union.'

'No problem, Patrick, my treat. Spoilt rich kid, remember?'

Patrick smiled his thanks and made a tight turn back towards the boat. They hadn't seen any soldiers to ask about activity on Carriacou, and given he had sequestered one of their jeeps, he didn't really want to now. He had the VHF so he would be able to call ahead anyway. They stopped at one of the abandoned shanties and filled up all the remaining space in the two rucksacks with bananas and papayas.

'Choose only just-ripe bananas,' Patrick advised, 'otherwise they won't last.'

'What about some mangoes?' Tim asked.

'You know the best way to peel a ripe mango, Tim? Get naked and jump into the water. Cut some of that cactussy stuff over there.'

Tim looked at him uncertainly 'Are you serious?'

'Aloe Vera, trust me: it's a godsend when you need to wash in seawater. I thought you were a doctor?'

When they were on their way once more, Tim said, 'You know, Patrick, someday soon you're going to have to tell me where this world of wisdom comes from.'

~.~

They were still in thick foliage five yards in from the shore, when they heard it: a brief cry, then a yelp. Then silence. They froze in their tracks.

'That was Tracey.' Tim said.

Patrick put down his two water containers, raised a finger to his lips, and slipped the rucksack from his shoulders. Then they heard a man's voice, indistinct, but clearly not friendly.

'Oh fuck, the Cubans have got her.' Tim said, despairingly.

Patrick reached down and pulled the Remington from the rucksack side-pocket. 'Wait here,' he whispered, 'don't come till I call you.' He cocked a round into the chamber and checked the safety was on, then moved slowly forward.

There was no one up top but he saw movement in the saloon. He stepped carefully into the water and crouched under the bow, listening.

A loud slap, followed by another yelp from Tracey.

'Things will get worse for you *pronto* if you do not tell us where is key for engine.'

Patrick's throat constricted and the hairs on the back of his neck sprang erect. He recognised that voice.

Elías!

'I told you, you big oaf, I don't know where the fucking keys are.'

She screamed then, a frightened and frightful sound.

'How you charge batteries without start engine?'

Manuel! Cruel, sadistic, murdering bastard... Manuel.

'Speak bitch or I slice open more of your pretty face.'

Patrick fought to control the panic threatening to overwhelm him. He needed to think clearly.

What to do, what to do?

He took some deep breaths.

'Maybe, Patrick took it, I don't know. Just let me go mister, I can't help you.'

Manuel laughed. 'This not going to happen little girl, I been locked up in shithole for one year, you wanna see my big hard prick, eh?'

'Wait,' said Elías, 'who this Patrick? Speak!'

'The owner of this boat, you moron.'

'*Ese hijo de puta sigue vivo?*' Manuel's voice, the incredulity apparent even in Spanish.

'Describe him,' Elías said.

Silence, then another loud slap. She cried out again. 'Please don't hit me anymore, my head hurts.'

'That is whole point, Yankee whore, to make it hurt.'

Another dreadful slap and cry.

'Look you fucking moron, I'm at risk here of a serious cerebral edema. You could kill me, you know.'

'Cerebral…? What the fuck you talking about, girly,' Manuel said.

'Look,' said Elías, 'you just gotta describe this Patrick and we stop hurting you,'

'Okay, okay,' the girl said, 'skinny guy, bald, around five eight, five nine, English. Satisfied, arsehole?'

'Bald? Like you mean he got no hair?' said Manuel.

'*Es él, estoy seguro, se afeitó la cabeza, probablemente.*'

While Patrick had been listening, a plan had formed in his mind. It was risky, and sounded ridiculous when he replayed it, but it was all he had. He made his way back to Tim.

When he was satisfied the youngster knew what was expected of him, and with another assurance that all would go smoothly, and Tracey would be safe, he returned to the boat.

The two were talking together in Spanish as Patrick made his way along the port side towards the stern. When he was waist deep, he turned onto his back and swam to keep the gun clear of the water. At the transom, he placed the Remington on the dive platform then removed the pins from the dive ladder and slowly eased it out. When it was at full extent, he lowered it gently into the water.

Careful so as not to cause the boat to move, he stepped onto the bottom rung, and crouching, so only his head was above water, he waited, watching the shoreline over to starboard. He felt his heart thumping and he fought to control the bile of fear rising into his gullet.

Tim played his part magnificently. He came rushing out of the bushes twenty yards away to starboard, screaming and shouting like a lunatic, splashed into the water, clowning and cavorting, shouting nonsense at the top of his voice.

Someone came clattering up the companionway and stepped over to the guardrail. Only one – he needed both men on deck. His plan was falling at the first hurdle. He couldn't risk leaving one of them down there with Tracey while he took the other. That would be her death sentence, or at the very best, a hostage situation that could only end badly.

'What the fuck are you?' Elías' shouted.

Therefore, Small Bus was still below with Tracey.

'What the fuck are you, what the fuck are you…' mimicked Tim in a childish parody of the thug, still dancing and cavorting madly in the water.

He dared not risk looking over the edge of the deck in case Manuel was watching from the companionway, so he leaned back for an angle to get a look at Elías. He stood at the guardrail facing towards the redheaded crazy in the water. Patrick's heart froze when he saw the automatic rifle dangling from his right hand.

Chuckling, Elías turned back to the companionway '*Manuel, ven a ver este payaso. dejar a la chica por ahora, tendrá usted oportunidad posterior.*'

Patrick got close to the transom once more as Manuel grunted his way up the ladder. Now he had them both where he needed them. The plan was going to work – with some luck… with a lot of luck.

Then he noticed Tim had stopped performing. He was looking up to where the two men stood on deck, a look of dread expectation on his face. Suddenly his eyes swung towards Patrick.

Time to move.

He picked up the Remington and eased off the safety. In one swift movement, he hoisted himself up on the ladder, stepped onto the platform, and…

…froze as he stared into a rifle barrel.

'Patrick, what a surprise,' Elías said, smiling his sneering smile, 'but not the surprise you had hoped for, eh?' the smile stopped abruptly, 'drop the gun, now.'

The Remington thumped onto the deck – in his fear Patrick had hardly been aware of dropping it, and now wished he hadn't been so compliant – but too late.

Elías hadn't moved from his spot at the guardrail but was now facing aft, the automatic weapon trained unwaveringly at Patrick's torso.

Manuel, who had still been watching Tim when Patrick made his move, now spun round to catch up with a situation beyond his immediate grasp. Once again, it shook Patrick how fast the big man moved: dull, slow witted, but lightening reaction to danger.

'You?' was all he managed.

Elías smiled widely, genuinely amused.

'Once again, Patrick, you underestimate my intelligence,' he pointed a thumb back over his shoulder, 'how long you think it take me to work out why this *gringo* idiot here, eh? About two seconds, that is how long!'

Patrick said nothing. He felt numb. It would have worked if they had both come up at once. He could now see Tracey down in the saloon, or at least the back of her, hands bound behind the centre-post. He could hear her frightened whimpering as she struggled against her bonds.

Out of the corner of his eye, he saw Tim duck under the water. He hoped the youngster had the sense to swim as far away as he could.

Elías raised an eyebrow in query. 'This all very puzzling to me, Patrick, me and Manuel, we been in gaol for a year, this boat been here all this time, then the Yankees spring us, and here we are, all together once again. Very strange, do not you think?'

'I was always going to find you, arsehole, it was just a matter of time.' Patrick had noticed two sets of pale fingers clutching the toe rail by Elías' feet and forced himself not to look directly at them.

'Oh, look Manuel, he still grieving over his dead girlfriend. Never mind my friend; you are going to join her now. And for I like you, Patrick, I make it nice and quick – Manual, watch the *gringo* in the water.'

As Elías lifted his weapon to take proper aim, Manuel made to turn back towards the water where Tim had been, but kept his eyes fixed on Patrick, as if he didn't want to miss the show.

Patrick looked up and followed an imaginary swinging boom with his eyes. 'MANUEL, HEAD DOWN!'

The result was spectacular. Manuel snapped double like a sprung mousetrap, dropping his rifle and clasping his head with both hands, and in so doing butted into Elías, spoiling his aim. At the same time, Tim's hand came snaking over the toe rail and grabbed Elías' ankle, pulling him sideways with all the force of Tim's weight as he kicked himself from the hull. Elías crashed to the deck, knocking the crouching Manuel into the cockpit.

Dimly aware of Tracey's terrified screams from down below, Patrick quickly reached down for the Remington. Elías still had hold of his rifle, now pointing skywards but already chattering and moving in a fatal arc down towards him. By the time the pistol finally bucked in his hand, Patrick felt the hot wind of bullets on his naked scalp.

He barely had time to see Elías stagger backwards, spraying fire harmlessly skywards, before the scene was obscured by the Small Bus two yards in front of him, lurching forward with huge grasping hands.

He wasn't aware of pulling the trigger but was conscious of the pain in his right arm from the jolting weapon, as he put round after round into the advancing giant. He managed to step aside just as the maddened creature bounced against the wire taff rail.

Manuel reached up to grab the backstay to stop his forward momentum, and Patrick, now cold and calm, lifted the pistol to the monster's temple.

'This is for Stella,' he said, and pulled the trigger.

The Small Bus froze there a moment, and then slowly tipped forward and over the rail, its head leaving a bloody streak on the dive platform, and into the water.

Patrick felt nothing for the man he had just killed. Instead, he stared in disgust at the blood and brains splattered on the lifebelt and Dan buoy.

Then he was aware once more of Tracey's desperate screaming from the saloon.

'No, no, no, no, please don't kill them, oh my god, someone please help us…'

'It's all right, Tracey,' Patrick shouted to her as he scrambled over the taff rail, 'we're both safe, everything's okay.'

He opened the gas locker and reached behind the propane bottle, then went to Elías. Patrick had aimed for a torso shot, but it had gone high.

Elías lay sprawled on the cockpit edge clutching at his neck in a vain attempt to stem the flow from his carotid artery. His eyes were wide and sparkling with terror, a ghastly gurgle issued from his shattered throat. The unstoppable gush of blood pulsed over his clutching hands, covered his shirt and oozed across the deck into the scupper.

Patrick dangled the ignition keys in front of him. 'These what you were looking for?'

He left him and went below.

Keeping the shock from registering on his face, he quickly untied her, all the time cooing softly, 'It's all right, Tracey, you're safe now, we're all safe.'

He got her sitting on the bench just as Tim came charging down the ladder.

'Jesus, all that blood up there.' he said, looking down at Tracey.

'Just think of it as Rhododendron flowers,' Patrick said.

Tim gave him a quizzical look and turned to Tracey. 'You okay?'

'I guess,' she croaked. She was clearly in shock, shivering and sobbing and heaving uncontrollably. Her face was a mess: livid and swollen down the right side, right eye almost closed, a one inch cut on her left cheek (Patrick hoped she wasn't a vain girl, but he suspected not), and more bruising on her chin, and the beating had left her with swollen lips, the bottom one cut and bleeding. It was obvious what Manuel had planned for her from the torn open singlet, exposing her naked breasts. He found a blanket in one of the side lockers and wrapped it around her, then left Tim to comfort her while he busied himself selecting items from the first aid box.

'Do you have sutures in there?' Tim asked.

Patrick slapped his forehead.

'Of course, I was forgetting your profession. Yeah, we've got everything but the kitchen sink in there.'

He slid the box across the table to him.

'Fill your boots. You can thank my girlfriend for her diligence in stocking up. I'll go and tidy up top and then we can all have a cuppa.'

On the way up he turned back to look at Tim.

'Well done, by the way, you did a great job.'

'Thanks. So did you, *John*,' he paused then added, 'if a little brutal with the big guy at the end, there. Christ, it was like you executed him.'

Patrick looked back down the ladder, 'There's history, Tim. I'll tell you about it soon, then maybe you'll understand.'

~.~

Elías had bled out. Patrick looked down at the pathetic corpse without pity, just a vague sense of injustice; that mere death was somehow inadequate to pay for the loss of Stella.

He heaved the body over the side to join his pal floating face down a few yards astern and sluiced a couple of buckets of seawater over the blood on the deck and the lifesaving gear, to stop it congealing while he rigged the hose to wash it down properly.

Later he deliberated about the two rifles; Kalashnikovs, probably purloined from dead militias on the way here. In the end he sent them spinning as far as he could out into the lagoon.

~ Chapter Twenty-Three ~

'Now hold her there,' said Patrick, 'this is called a beam reach,' he pointed to the tell tail he had tied onto each shroud for teaching purposes, 'with the wind on the starboard beam, see?' He let out the main slightly, so the rail came clear of the water, and adjusted the vang.

'It's important to avoid overpowering, that's when more wind energy goes into keeping her heeled over than is pushing her forward. The twist I've just put in the main is now spilling wind from the top but increasing power at the bottom. It's given us an extra knot, do you see?'

'Yeah, I get it.' Tim said, gripping the wheel with white knuckles. His freckled face was a mixture of terror and excitement.

'Say, this is fun.'

'Perfect sailing weather,' Patrick said, 'you couldn't wish for a better introduction to it.'

In a stiff breeze, twelve to fourteen knots from slightly south of east, *Spirit of Carriacou* clipped along Grenada's east coast like the thoroughbred she was. Off to port the thickly forested mountains of the island's interior towered majestic above a coast lined with waving palms and silver sands.

Odd to think of it as a war zone, it looked so tranquil and idyllic from here. The only hint of a military presence out here stood a few miles off to starboard: the frigate *USS Clifton Sprague*, who had challenged them earlier on channel sixteen and then courteously wished them a safe passage.

Up ahead, marching off into the distance on a white-flecked azure sea, the Grenadines, a string of tiny, but lushly verdant volcanic islands that stretched all the way to

St Vincent, a hundred miles to the north. The most northerly of the chain belonging to Grenada was their destination, invisible yet, thirty miles away over the horizon.

Tracey came up the ladder to join them, the unbruised part of her face looking unnaturally pale, and sat on the windward bench next to Patrick, her bare feet braced against the pilot console. Patrick stroked her hair and put an arm round her thin shoulders.

'How now, sweetheart?'

'Okay I guess, just feeling a little seasick down there'

'Don't worry, it'll pass. Try looking out of the boat – there's plenty out there to feast your eyes on.'

As she gazed out towards Grenada, he looked closely at the wound on her cheek.

'Hey Tim, these stitches are brilliant, well done, buddy.'

'Thanks. Sutures are my speciality; it'll hardly show after a few months.'

Tim seemed more relaxed at the wheel now, clearly enjoying himself. After a time he said, 'I'm going into cosmetic surgery when I'm qualified, my Dad's business. He wants to take early retirement.'

'Well I'm sure you'll be very good at it. You certainly seem to take sailing in your stride.'

But now Tim had something else on his mind.

'You knew those guys, right?'

Patrick gave a mirthless smile and then blew out through puffed cheeks.

'Yeah, I did, and listen, I want to apologise to you both for getting you mixed up in that.'

Tracey turned and gave Patrick a thick-lipped smile, which quickly turned to a grimace when she found how much it hurt; she patted her swollen lips gingerly.

'It appears to me,' she said, 'those two hoodlums would have showed up anyway. It was our choice to live on your boat, and if you hadn't have come back to it when you did, Tim and I would probably be floating face down in that lagoon right now,' she put a hand on his and joggled it insistently, 'so Patrick, you certainly have nothing to apologise for.'

'All the same,' Patrick said, 'you deserve an explanation.'

~ Chapter Twenty-Four ~

When Patrick had finished telling his story Tracey stared at him looking shell-shocked while Tim at the helm wore a grim expression as he concentrated on his task. Finally Tracey broke the silence. She put a gentle hand on his.

'I'm so sorry about your girlfriend, Patrick.'

Patrick smiled his gratitude, thinking what a great doctor she was going to be, the touchy-feely kind with a caring bedside manner.

Sometime later Tim said, 'So if those two guys were on their way to Puerto Rico, how come they ended up down here? That must be eight hundred clicks away.'

'About five hundred miles, yeah,' Patrick said, 'that's the question I've been asking myself. Elías could have figured out the steering problem, might even have picked up enough from watching me to manage the boat. He was an evil bastard, but he wasn't stupid. But navigating it to Grenada? I'm not so sure.'

Tracey said, 'The big guy told me...' she shivered at the memory, 'told me he'd spent a year in some shithole. I guess he meant gaol.'

Tim looked thoughtful for a moment, and then said, 'Any chance they could have got caught smuggling drugs and gaoled in Grenada...?'

'...and the Americans freed them.' Patrick finished.

He remembered Rick telling him about the Prison breakout in the north of the island.

'Or maybe they were collared for the murders on Pipah.'

He got another image of Stella drifting to the floor and recoiled from the memory.

'Keep her on course and watch out for fishing floats,' he said, 'I'm going below for a few minutes.'

He remembered he had disabled the Satellite box before his escape, but now it was working again.

'Clever bugger, weren't you, Elías?'

He opened the chart table and found the small-scale chart he had used for the passage to Puerto Rico. Someone, probably Elías, had drawn a line from about a hundred miles west of Folly down to a place on the Venezuelan coast, Carupano. Scribbled next to the line was its bearing, one five seven. He checked it with the plotter, and it was correct.

'Aha!'

Now he knew why they had ended up in Grenada. Elías wouldn't have realised he needed to add fifteen degrees variation to get his magnetic heading. Steering one five seven would have resulted in a true track of one four two. That would have taken him straight to Grenada. Moreover, without switching to the full diesel tank they would have been running on fumes by the time they reached it.

He sat thinking through the possible scenarios once they had reached Grenada. The cocaine was no longer on the boat, so he could only assume they had taken it ashore to try to dispose of it and screwed up. If the cops had caught them with the stuff still on the boat, then they would have impounded her, not left her hidden in a remote lagoon.

~.~

Patrick's hopes of using Tyrell Bay's boatyard faded when they were still five miles from the island, when through his binoculars he saw several what looked like Blackhawk helicopters over the hills and surrounding coast. He tried calling on Channel 16, but the radio remained ominously silent. He switched to the local calling frequency, Channel Six Seven, and got a response on his second call, but not from the island.

'Sailing yacht *Spirit of Carriacou* this is sailing yacht *Venture*, moored in Tyrell Bay. Are you headed this way? Over.'

The voice sounded American.

'Good afternoon *Venture,* this is *Spirit of Carriacou*, affirmative, what are conditions like there? Over'.

'Not good. I guess from your boat's name that you're coming home, who's your Captain?'

'Captain is Ste... er Patrick Redman. You?'

'Sam Ledworth, at your service. Listen Patrick, we had a big invasion here three days ago, tanks, helicopters, troops, the whole nine yards. I spoke to one of the Marine guys and he told me they were looking for a battalion of Korean soldiers.'

'That's ridiculous!' Patrick replied.

'Exactly what I told 'em. I assume you know this island, Patrick: a few a thousand homely folk, religious as hell, and gentle as kittens. And they all know each other. Hell man, where would you hide a battalion here anyway? The Marines have gone now, but they left an airborne squadron behind, and those guys are making life here real difficult – and I sincerely hope they're listening.'

'Tell me, Sam, is the boatyard operating?'

'Sorry, Patrick, and besides, the Army has prohibited all movement. They won't let you in here. Hell, they won't even let me sail, and I'm an American Citizen.'

As if to emphasise the point a helicopter swooped down from the hills and came low over the sea towards them. By now, Tyrell Bay had come into view around the headland, and several bare masts were visible there.

Concerned about the effect of the approaching helicopter's downdraught Patrick started the engine and furled the headsail. He then put Tracey on the wheel and dropped the main, showing Tim how to flake and secure it to the boom.

'Turn to starboard,' he said to Tracey,' head for the bay – let's make our intentions plain.'

By the time the boat was steady on course, the big noisy aircraft was hovering at the stern. A crewman was holding up a chalkboard:

#16.

He picked up the portable, switched it over and stuck up a thumb.

The voice was a Texas drawl: 'This here's Bravo Niner One. Sir, this island is under United States Military jurisdiction and is out of bounds to civilian craft – please turn your vessel around and leave the area immediately.'

'I need to use the boatyard here,' Patrick replied, 'I have urgent repairs.'

'I say again, Sir, turn your vessel around and leave the area. This is for your own safety.'

Patrick knew further argument was pointless – he was talking to an automaton. He took the wheel from Tracey and turned north.

'Thank you, Sir, and have a nice day. Bravo Niner One, Out.'

The helicopter banked away and climbed, heading back to a peaceful paradise island to search for North Korean soldiers.

'Now what?' Tim said.

Patrick went below and retrieved the Remington and its spare clip, came back up and dropped them overboard.

'Now we head for Kingstown,' he said, 'another sixty miles, I'm afraid – an overnight passage. Let's get those sails back up.'

~ Chapter Twenty-Five ~

'We haul she out tomorrow for hull inspec-*shan* an' gelcoat, an' when de wood properly dried out we get to work sandin' down and treatin' de decks.' The bosun cast a bloodshot eye over the mast and shrouds. 'You wan inspect de rigging?' He held his notebook and pen ready and looked at Patrick expectantly.

The Kingstown Harbourmaster had recommended the boatyard when he had booked in. He had suspected a bit of nepotism, maybe family connections, but that was normal practice in the Islands. 'No, it's fine thanks, Beeno,' Patrick said, 'it's only eighteen months old.' They had changed all the standing rigging in Gibraltar and it was still in perfect condition, despite the months of festering in the mangrove.

'You sure now, Captain, dis climate rot wire rope real quick yanoo.'

Patrick laughed and clapped him on the shoulder. 'No, honestly, its fine.'

Sniffing a bit of extra cash, the wily bosun was trying to milk it for what it was worth. He didn't blame him.

'Don't worry, Beeno, there's plenty of work here: I want a new main made up, same pattern as this one, the log and sounder serviced, the diving sets hauled out from under the sails in the forepeak, serviced and charged up...' he paused to let him catch up with his scribbling.

'I need the VHF and SSB replaced, same make and spec as the broken ones already in there, and rub down and varnish the roof rails and the beading around the cockpit.'

Beeno finished writing then looked up woefully.

'Aw man, dat work for me colleagues, yanoo. You got nuttin' for a good bosun-rigger here?'

'I was just coming to that,' Patrick said, watching Beeno's eyes light up. 'I need the sheets and halyards, and all the berthing lines replaced. Oh, and new lanyards spliced onto the fenders. Best quality rope now, branded plait, eyes properly spliced and whipped, otherwise, no pay.'

'Oh yes, Captain, no problem.' Beano left grinning like a sneezing whippet.

Patrick had been up to the Western Union Office in town and confirmed he still had money in his bank account – he had wondered briefly if anyone at all had missed his yearlong absence and concluded that nobody would have.

Tim and Tracey had checked into a hotel in Kingstown. He had left them both on the phone to their parents – he imagined they would be long phone calls.

Now life was a little less precarious he was starting to feel the weight of the enormous problems ahead. He wanted to find out what happened on Pipah after his abduction: whether that crook McCredy was still operating there; and who, if anyone, the law had convicted of Stella's murder. He wondered whether anyone had told Stella's family in Germany of her death; there was the question of probate and the transfer of her assets to consider.

She had always said that *Spirit of Carriacou* would be his if anything happened to her - he would buy her from Stella's estate if necessary.

He decided to pay a visit to the Governor General's Office before calling on the Police. Later he would hire a car and drive round to the bay where Thomas and Adhra had made their home. If they hadn't heard already, then his news was going to devastate them.

~.~

'Take a seat Mr Redman.'

The Governor General, a dapper West Indian in his late fifties, sat behind an old-fashioned mahogany desk and peered at Patrick through an enormous pair of spectacles.

'Now, what can I do for you?'

'Thank you for seeing me so quickly, Your Excellency. I…'

Suddenly he didn't know how to begin, and just when he thought he was over the grief and trauma of the past year, felt the emotions rise in him once again.

'Alright, relax,' the Governor General said, 'I can see you are upset. Just wait a minute, just wait a minute.'

He pressed the intercom on his desk.

'Mrs Jameson, please bring in a pot of tea, and some biscuits.'

He looked up and smiled, 'You look as if you could do with feeding up a bit. Now, take your time and start at the beginning.'

'It all started just over a year ago,' Patrick began, 'when my girlfriend was shot and killed on Pipah.'

The Governor General, who had started taking notes on a foolscap pad, suddenly jerked his head up.

'Let me stop you there, Mr Redman. What is she called, your girlfriend?'

'Stella, Stella Friedmann. Anyway, these two Hispanic guys…'

The Governor General held up a hand, 'Stop, stop, stop, Mr Redman, I have some news for you, please be quiet a moment.'

He pressed the intercom again.

'Mrs Jamieson, please call the Attorney General, give him my compliments, and ask him to come to my office – tell him it is an urgent matter of extreme importance.'

A sense of deep foreboding swept over Patrick. Had McCredy succeeded in stitching him up for the murders?

'Yes, Sir Reginald, at once.'

He looked at Patrick again, a strange expression, almost of shock, on his face. Then he smiled.

'Mr Redman,' he began, then clapped a beefy hand to his forehead, 'Patrick Redman, of course, I should have recognised the name, but the connection failed me.'

He stood up, came to Patrick's side of the desk and sat on its edge.

'Patrick, brace yourself for a shock. Your girlfriend, Stella Friedmann, I am delighted to report that she is alive and well.'

~ Part Four.~

September 1982

~ Chapter Twenty-Six ~

> Crimson stained, the changing waters:
> now tranquil, slow, now rampant surge,
> then loiter in the waiting-pool, adrift,
> then swift emerge into the tumbling falls.

Stella became aware of a cool pulsating breeze on her face. And sounds: soft voices: clicking of heels on stone floors, strange beeps and hums, and a faint smell of chlorine. She had a memory of someone talking to her, a woman's voice, familiar, something from her past.

She opened her eyes, expecting to see her there. But there was nobody, just blank white walls and a windowed doorway in front, a fan turning slowly in the ceiling overhead. Disappointed, she concentrated on trying to make sense of her surroundings.

She was propped half-sitting, arms out on top of the sheet that covered her. Clean white linen, whiteness everywhere, stark. The sounds were coming from beyond the door, shadows passing the frosted glass window, footsteps clacking back and forth, subdued voices. It was all too confusing; anxiety came at her in waves.

There was a machine by the bed, a monitor, she realised, to measure vital signs, a cable from it down to a clip on her index finger. There was a drip stand on the other side, a tube hanging down from a bag of clear fluid. She lifted her right arm and saw the cannula taped to the back of her hand. She examined the hand, raised the other one and looked at that too. It was a very long time since they had looked like that. The nails had been trimmed, filed and shaped, coated with clear polish.

There was a red call button by the monitor. She reached her arm out and pressed it. It lit up and somewhere outside a buzzer sounded. Footsteps coming towards the door, a shadow in the frosted glass, door opening.

A black woman entered; dark blue uniform with a white pinafore and nursing cap.

'Hello Stella, welcome back.'

The nurse was middle aged, large and busty with a homely face. She glided to the bedside and picked up Stella's hand, held it in both hers.

'I 'spect you wondering where you is – an very confused moss like.'

Stella's reply came out as an incomprehensible croak. She found herself responding to the nurse's kindness with a rush of inexplicable emotion and began to weep uncontrollably.

The nurse pulled a chair up to the bed and sat holding her hand. She took a linen handkerchief from her pinafore pocket and gently dabbed the tears from her cheek.

'You every right to cry,' she cooed softly, 'it do you good, yanoo. We never knowed if you was ever gonna wake up, child. Praise de Good Lord you wid us at last. You friends will be sheer delighted.'

'Friends?' was all she could manage, feeling overwhelmed by the unanswered questions crowding her mind. Something bad had happened, but her memory remained stubbornly blank.

Just then someone else entered the room, white coat, spectacles, and stethoscope.

'Ah, Miss Friedmann, so glad you have woken up.'

The nurse made to get up but the doctor motioned her to stay seated, came to Stella's other side and remained standing.

'My name is Dr Hodge; I am the surgeon in charge of your care. I do not know how much Sister has told you, but you are in Kingstown General Hospital. How are you feeling?'

'Confused, and I have pain, here,' she lifted her hand, carefully because of the cannula, to pat the right side of her head.

'Oh,' she said, feeling the thick folds of crepe bandage that extended down over her ear on that side.

'You have a head injury,' the doctor said, 'I will explain everything when you are feeling better.'

'What happened to me?'

'You were in an accident, apparently on a boat. I'm afraid your injury was very severe; you have been in a coma for more than a week.'

She had no recollection of any accident. So many questions… one surfaced. 'Where is Patrick?'

He glanced across at the nurse, raised an eyebrow; she gave a sort of head-shaking shrug.

'I am sorry; we don't know anyone called Patrick. Perhaps your friends will know,' he checked his watch, 'they should be here soon.'

'Friends?' she said again, 'Where am I, exactly?'

'You are in Kingstown, on the Island of St Vincent,' the doctor said, 'Mr Hayward brought you here on his boat. He said you would not know him, but that you have friends here, Mr and Mrs Dennie?'

'Thomas?' she said, relieved at last to have something firm she could grasp, 'and Adhra? Yes, they live in St Vincent. They know I am here?'

'Dey been here many time,' the nurse said, 'dey spend long time speak – Mrs Dennie very convinced you hear her, even in de coma.'

The doctor added, 'A remarkable woman, albeit with somewhat arcane beliefs. But it gave her comfort to be with you.'

'I remember,' Stella murmured, 'and Thomas, I heard them talking to me, I thought this was a dream.'

Adhra, down to earth, well educated, self-assured; Adhra, child survivor of a village massacre in remote Northern Kenya. Yes, she could see Adhra chatting away just as if she were conscious, working on her neglected nails while talking of their African days, of Nikkie and Mombasa, the diving school (Stella's Dive Shack they had named it), and the charter business with *Carriacou*, her holiday chalets. They were good memories, high points in her life. And Patrick…

'You say they are coming here now?'

'Yes, they are on their way,' the doctor said, 'I spoke to Mr Dennie on the radio just now. They are delighted you have woken up.'

She wondered where the boat was now, still at that little island, or had Patrick sailed it here? Where was he now? She needed him here.

The nurse tapped the cannula on her hand and smiled, 'It is time you had some real food, no more dis intravenous stuff,' she detached the tube from the cannula and hung it over the drip stand, 'how 'bout some nice vegetable soup and a little soft bread?'

'That would be nice, thank you.' Stella said absently.

Her memory of events leading up to her accident was starting to return; she remembered an argument with the two Americans in their home. Then, later in the boat, she and Patrick had talked about some drugs. Trying to recall anything further felt like wading through treacle.

Where the hell was Patrick?

~.~

'Hey Boss, you looking good as new. Man we was worried.'

Thomas had not changed at all in the year since she had last seen him; weathered smile-creased face still alive with boyish mischief, belying his sixty-odd years.

Adhra looked stunning in her colourful kanga, black hair braids tied back with an ornate leather clasp, her extraordinary, pure-ebony face unblemished and beautiful.

For a long time Stella could not speak, just held the hands of her two friends, and wept. She had not known how she would react when they arrived; the sudden flood of emotion had been unexpected, something she could not quite explain. She realised it was a response to trauma, to having survived something awful, relief perhaps, brought on by the affection of dear friends from whom she had been so long separated.

'Aw, Boss.' Thomas said, his face crumpled in anguish, 'I feel, I really feel...' he squeezed the bridge of his nose and shook his head, got up and left the room.

'He gets very emotional these days, you know,' Adhra explained, stroking Stella's cheek. She smiled ruefully, 'I believe his hormones are imbalanced. He does not like to show it, he will return in moment.'

'Ach, he was always such a *weichling*,' Stella said, finding her voice and composure, 'can you tell me what happened, how I came here? The doctor mentioned a Mr Hayward?'

'Just Hayward, no "Mister" - he likes to be called Hayward. He is a strange old man, a sea gypsy with a shabby old schooner. He is always cursing, it is just his way, you know,' she gave a little laugh; 'I do not think he knows he does it. But he has a good heart, very generous – you will like him, everybody does.'

Thomas came back into the room and sat down, picking up Stella's hand once more. 'Sorry, Boss, me just upset to see you weep. You okay now?'

'I am fine Thomas, please do not worry. Adhra was just telling me about... Hayward?'

'Yeah man, me known him years, even from before me come to you in Kenya, you know. He famous sailor here in...'

'Thomas, I think Stella is more interested to know how she got here.'

'Yeah, sorry.' Thomas said, 'I guess you is. So, Hayward's kid find you in da woods on Pipah, you head all open an' bleedin evwhere, yanoo. She tell her dad and he go get Lazy Lobster Kenny and dey take you on Hayward's boat. To get you patched up cos der no doctor on Pipah, yanoo.' He looked a question at her. 'Boss, can you recall how you come to be in da woods wid a busted head? And where all dis time Patrick?'

The awful truth had rushed up on her a short while ago with sickening clarity. 'I... I think so; do you know the American man, Frank, and his wife that live in the house above Kenny's beach?'

'Yeamon, de dive guy – you know dem both killed? It all over de news and all.'

'*Ja*... Yes, Patrick and I found them, murdered...' She felt the anguish rise like a rip tide, paralysing her voice. Adhra gave her hand a squeeze and stroked her cheek. 'Take your time, Stella, just take your time.'

She let out a trembling sigh and forced herself to continue. 'It was *schauerlich* - horrible... we tried to get out of there, but then those two evil savages were in the doorway...'

'The killers of the Americans?' Adhra said, shocked, 'They were still there?'

'They had guns... and that dreadful policeman...'

'Policeman?' Adhra said.

She saw the blank incomprehension in both their faces. 'I am sorry, this must sound very confusing. I will start from the beginning.'

Therefore, in faltering steps she told them the whole story: from the night when Frank had revealed the haul of cocaine to Patrick, right up to the moment she realised what the gunmen had in mind for her, that final heart-stopping moment, when the big ugly one raised his gun. Then, nothing. She did not even remember the shot, nothing until waking up an hour ago.

'Hayward *thought* it was a bullet wound,' Adhra said, 'but he told us not to say anything. He told the doctor it was an accident on your yacht. He didn't think it was a good idea to involve the police.'

'But would not a doctor know it was a bullet wound?' Stella said.

'As Thomas said, Hayward patched you up,' Adhra said, 'in fact he did much more than that. He stitched your head up and nursed you on his boat at sea for two days. In the end, he became afraid you had brain damage and would not wake up. He also thought you had lost too much blood to recover without treatment, so he brought you here.'

Stella looked aghast. '*Zo*, under these bandages I have what, sail stitches? Made with sail twine, *vielleicht*?'

Adhra patted her hand reassuringly. 'Most probably he used something like that, but the doctor carried out a proper surgery later – I am sure Dr Hodge will explain what he has done.'

'*Alzo*,' Stella said after a moment's reflection, 'they have taken Patrick. We must assume so, *nicht war*? Otherwise, they would just have shot us both together. I take it my boat is still moored at Pipah?'

Adhra said, 'Stella, Hayward saw your boat motor out of the bay just before his daughter came and told him she had found you. A man was driving it, but his description did not sound like Patrick. He was big, Hispanic looking, black hair.'

~.~

'You suffered a severe trauma to the right side of your head,' the doctor said, 'behind the temple and the hairline, resulting in a near-avulsion, that is, a large gash where a triangular section of hair and tissue was torn off the scalp but remained attached – a flap if you will...'

Stella's sharp intake of breath stopped him. 'Are you okay with hearing this?' he said gently.

She nodded, biting her lower lip.

'Very well,' he continued, 'Mr Hayward had sewn this up,' rather crudely I might add, but his action undoubtedly saved your life considering the blood loss from the cranial damage beneath. A very resourceful man. When I lifted the skin I discovered a small depressed skull fracture in the shape of a horizontal groove, which had, when the wound was closed by Mr Hayward's er... sutures, caused a minor subdural hematoma, a blood clot, which I removed, and then cauterised the exposed blood vessels. I managed to reposition the two damaged splinters of bone, making an almost perfect closure that should knit up nicely in about a month.'

'So I will have no long-term damage?'

'We can never be absolutely certain,' he said, 'but I believe you can be reasonably confident of a full recovery. You will be left with significant permanent scarring but that will be concealed when your hair grows back.'

'When can I leave, Doctor?'

'The wound has healed nicely so you may leave this afternoon when nurse has removed the dressing. But you must have complete rest, at least one more week at the home of your friends.'

'When they take off the dressing, will you please arrange for someone to come with scissors and a razor? I want to shave off all my hair, otherwise I will look ridiculous.'

'I understand, yes of course. But you must wear a hat, for protection from the sun – your bare head, especially the wound, will be vulnerable.'

'Thank you doctor for everything.'

'It is my pleasure, Stella,' then his smile faded, and he grew serious.

'I am still unclear about what happened to you. Mr Hayward was very vague, and you have volunteered no explanation. Do you wish to share with me how this trauma occurred?'

She had been expecting this at some point.

'I was very stupid, I accidentally jibed my boat and the boom hit my head.'

He nodded. 'Thank you. That is what I will put in my report.'

She detected his scepticism and felt guilty about lying to this man who had done so much for her.

'But you do not believe it, do you?'

He glanced at the door, and then spoke in lowered tones.

'Stella, I have seen head trauma from such boating accidents many times, and I have seen bullet wounds. I am sure you have your reasons for covering this up, but if you are in trouble I advise you to go to the police.'

'I...'

He stopped her with a raised palm.

'No, do not tell me anything more, I have said my piece. I wish you good luck in whatever it is you are involved with.'

~ Chapter Twenty-Seven ~

It had been a long time since Stella had been in a motorcar and she felt lulled by the novel sensation of riding along the scenic coastline. She watched ramshackle fishing villages, roadside markets and banana plantations whiz past, letting the lush greenery of the surrounding hills on one side and the breath-taking colours of the shallow coral reefs on the other distract her troubled mind.

'You scar done look too bad, Boss, you jus need hair grow, den no one will ever know.'

'You are very kind, Thomas, but let us face it, I will not be entering any beauty contest, that is for certain.'

'No, I guess not.' he said glumly, turning his attention back to the road.

She removed the baseball cap Thomas had brought her and looked again in the vanity mirror, turned her head this way and that to check what it looked like from various angles. Without the unsightly contusion her shaved head would have looked impressive, she thought, in fact when she turned to show the left profile, it did.

The scar was a livid forward-pointing arrowhead crosshatched with thick suture marks painted on a garish background of purple and yellow bruising. However, she felt remarkably sanguine about the injury and its bizarre appearance.

'Maybe I take a picture and enter it for an art competition.'

Thomas laughed his braying laugh.

'Yeah man, you should do dat.'

Stella did not laugh. She had just reminded herself that her beloved Leica camera was on her hijacked boat.

Nevertheless, the gloomy thought did not linger; she could only focus on one thing, and she did so with a single-minded determination. The crimson arrow seemed somehow appropriate, pointing her inexorably forward until she recovered first her man, then the next most important thing in her life, her *Carriacou*.

'Did you manage to contact Hayward?' she said.

'Yeah man, he still in Vincy area, coming round to anchor in Gladstone Bay dis evening. Adhra invite he for dinner.'

'Good, I am looking forward to meeting him.'

Thomas's dive school lay in a picturesque little bay, where the couple also had their home, about a twenty-minute drive from Kingstown on the southern shore of the island.

~.~

Hayward cut an extraordinary figure; pale blue eyes that twinkled from deep laugh-lines in a cherry red face surrounded by a frazzle of straw-coloured hair.

'Glad to see you alive, Chickadee, you look a lot fucking better than last time I saw you.'

He took a closer look at her scar and shook his shaggy head sadly.

'Not a patch on my herringbone stitch. But at least you won't look like one of Frankenstein's creations.'

He followed this with a great, unreserved belly laugh as if he had just heard a hilarious joke. It was an odd trait of his which was to become all too familiar. He did not shake hands, just bumped fists Caribbean style and asked Thomas for a glass of rum. He followed this with another peel of laughter that shook the thickly carpeted paunch sticking out of his faded Hawaiian shirt, which he wore unselfconsciously, open.

Stella exchanged a bemused look with Adhra while a grinning Thomas twisted the cork out of a new bottle of Mount Gay Special Reserve and poured him a generous measure. Hayward took the glass from Thomas without a word and padded his way out onto the patio.

'I think I have just met *der nautischen Weihnachtsmann*,' Stella laughed, 'the nautical version of Santa Claus. This is truly the man who saved my life?'

Adhra grinned and nodded.

Stella and Thomas picked up their beers and went out to join him while Adhra went to prepare dinner.

They found him standing by the rail staring out over the bay.

'I am so happy to meet you, Hayward; I cannot begin to thank you for what you have done.'

'So those fucking spicks hijacked your boat and your fella' he said without looking round. 'Fucking piracy that is.'

'They also murdered those two Americans,' Stella reminded him, 'I am so worried for Patrick.'

'This is all McCredy's doing,' Hayward said, 'I always knew that fella was trouble, didn't realise he was such a bad bastard though.'

'You know of this policeman?' Stella said.

He turned to face her.

'Yeah, I know him, and he knows me. Knows that nobody fucks with Hayward, especially a fucking crooked local copper milking an island of badly educated fellow niggers of what little income they can scrape from fucking tourists - excuse my political incorrectness, Thomas.'

Thomas grinned good-naturedly.

'Hey, no problem, man, and you is exactly correct, Hayward, dat Sherwin McCredy is a piece o' prime nigger shit.'

Hayward let out another explosive laugh and clapped Thomas on the shoulder. To Stella he said, 'Sorry dear, I'm a real crude bastard with no manners - subtle as an atomic bomb,'

Another guffaw of unrestrained laughter ensued.

Stella was beginning to find it infectious, and could not help laughing along, despite not knowing what was so funny. It made her feel better, too.

'That bastard tried to board me when I left Pipah with you onboard. Claimed I was helping a fugitive murder suspect. Gave him both barrels of me shotgun, blew off his fucking outboard. He fell into the 'oggin, and him in full dress uniform, stupid cunt.'

This time when she joined in it was because she found his spontaneous banter genuinely hilarious.

'That's my boat down there,' he said, pointing to the bedraggled wooden boat in the bay, 'my old *Jupiter*, built her meself.'

Stella recognised the drunken masts and the tattered brown mizzen sail: not a schooner, but a gaff-rigged ketch.

'We saw you that morning in the bay at Pipah,' she said, 'you arrived in the night?'

'Yeah, I saw your sloop too, nice weatherly little boat, but plastic, and a bit modern for my tastes. Don't like all that new-fangled stuff, no place for it on my boat.'

While they watched the ketch, a small sticklike figure came up on deck, turned a pair of binoculars towards them and waved. Hayward held up a hand to acknowledge her.

'That's one of my brats, the one that found you in the woods. Name's Juanita, says she's fourteen but I think she's younger, named after her mother, apparently.'

'Apparently?' Stella said, 'You don't know?'

He buried thick calloused fingers into his beard and scratched thoughtfully.

'Well, there was a Juanita in Cuba, and that's where that one says she was born, so ipso facto…' he finished with a series of hoots.

'How many children do you have?' Stella said.

'Oh, fuck knows. Over the years, at least a dozen have caught up with me. They like to sail with me for a few months then go home again. I've got sprogs all over the fucking world, Indonesia, Philippines, Micronesia, here in the Caribbean, even got one in fucking Newfoundland. And I've just recently heard I've got a two-year old up in Barbuda. Don't think I'll be around when she wants to go sailing.'

He seemed even to find humour in his eventual demise.

'Anyway, you'll enjoy sailing on the old *Jupiter*, a proper sailboat, gaff-rigged and solid.'

He scratched in his beard and grew thoughtful again.

'Built her in Tasmania out of three-hundred year old Huon Pine.'

'You cut the trees yourself?' Stella said, incredulous but ready to believe anything of this man.

'Course not, that'd be impossible. That heavy wood has to dry out and weather for years before its ready for boatbuilding. No, what happened, they demolished this old wooden town hall to build a smart new one out of bricks. I asked them if they wanted me to dispose of the old timber and they agreed, even offered me money to do it, stupid bastards – I accepted it of course,' [prolonged laughter] 'that wood had been maturing nicely for seventy-five years, ideal for my new *Jupiter*. The old one got wrecked in a storm, smashed up on the reef, nearly lost me fucking life.'

Even shipwrecks were apparently hilarious.

As much as she was enjoying the eccentric banter, Stella was keen to move on to her own agenda. She had just realised what he had said a few sentences ago.

'You said I will enjoy sailing in your boat, what did you mean?'

He wiggled his empty glass at Thomas.

'Do the honours, there's a good chap.'

'I bring you de bottle,' Thomas grinned.

Hayward turned back to Stella. 'You want to get your fella back, don't you? And that plastic plaything, I presume?'

'Yes of course,' she said, 'you can help me?'

He wandered back to the patio chairs.

'Need to take the weight off me pins,' he said, sitting with a grunt, stretching out his legs and inspecting his gnarled feet with their crusty brown toenails.

'Come and sit down with your Uncle Hayward and we'll have a parley.'

Thomas came back with the rum bottle and two fresh beers.

Hayward refilled his glass then continued.

'It won't be easy, but I think I know their general direction, maybe even take a guess at their likely destination. When I left Pipah, with you in the saloon with your head shot apart, and me and the sprog thinking we'd have a corpse on our hands before morning, I think I saw your boat up near Union, lined up west through the gap on bare poles. I take it your fella can sail and navigate?'

'Yes, he is qualified Yachtmaster.'

'In that case we can assume these spicks don't know their butts from their backstay, so they need your man to get them to where they're going. To get a worthwhile price they'll need to shift it into US territory, that's where the cocaine market is. Trouble is, if it's Puerto Rico or US Virgin Islands they'll have landed days ago,' he turned to look into her face, 'but then you must have worked that out for yourself.'

She realised he was right, but she had been hiding behind a curtain of denial. Having her fears confirmed now swept that curtain aside – acceptance came as a blow. 'Yes,' she said weakly.

'Now I don't want to give you false hope, Chickadee, but there's another picture.'

She ignored the caveat and allowed herself a spark of hope.

'Once they've moved on the drugs they might not want to hang about, in which case they would need your fella, Patrick is it?'

She nodded.

'They'll need Patrick to take them wherever it is they want to go next. Maybe to sell the boat on somewhere it won't be checked.'

'But how can we know where they have gone, or where they will go next? And even if we did, we cannot possibly catch up with them in time, not in your boat.'

'Don't underestimate my old *Jupiter*; she's clocked seventeen knots before today, without any of that fancy rigging I might add. I doubt if your boat gets above nine on a good day.'

'I am sorry, I did not mean to offend you, but even with a speedboat we could not catch them in time.'

'Ah, things at sea are never that straightforward, my dear, you should know that – let us plan for the best outcome and see how far it gets us, agreed?'

'Yes, agreed' she said doubtfully.

'Cheer up, Chickadee, things are never as hopeless as they seem. In the morning we'll take one of Thomas's dive boats back down to Pipah and have a little chat with that twat McCredy – find out where they planned to offload that coke, and maybe shove a spike in his nasty little racket. That okay with you Thomas?'

'Dat okay by me, I drive us there.'

'Don't trust old Hayward with your boat eh?'

'No man, me does not!'

This kicked off another bout of helpless laughter from Hayward.

~.~

Thomas's dive boat, a powerful sixteen-foot rigid inflatable, departed the bay at sunrise, skimming the wave-tops under clear skies. With Thomas standing at the helm, Stella and Hayward weighing down the bow for stability, they scooted between Bequia and Mustique, passing countless lesser islands, leaving Canouan well to starboard, to reach the empty northern reaches of Pipah in a whisker under ninety minutes.

They tied the boat up to a handy mooring buoy close to shore.

'Do you know where to find him?' Stella said, as they waded ashore.

Hayward transferred his wrapped-up shotgun to his other shoulder and picked up Thomas's wrist to look at his watch.

'Still early, he'll either be in the Police House or having breakfast at Mollie's.'

~ Chapter Twenty-Eight ~

Police Sergeant Sherwin McCredy was thinking once more about moving on. This little backwater had served his purpose well enough while the business was running like clockwork, but now those two idiot Hispanics and their boat driver had fucked up it was only a matter of time before the boys from Grenada came sniffing round, especially now two Americans had been killed.

He knew the only reason it had not happened yet was the political situation that preoccupied everyone. The Rastafarians were kicking up shit again and that fool Bishop was losing it.

Besides, some of the parents here were starting to give him odd looks, and he wondered if those two schoolgirls had blabbed, despite his threats. This island was too small to keep his secret predilection concealed for long.

Yes, time for him to move on, get out of Grenada and up to Antigua or BVI. He would get good references from his contact in the Chief Constable's office in St Georges; the man owed him big time. He had done well from McCredy's business since he came to office after the Revolution. It would not be long before all the shit blew up again anyway. Time to get out before that happened.

'Lucinda,' he called, 'get your booty round here.'

The other two men at a table across the room sat with lowered heads spooning green calilou soup into their mouths, as if they couldn't wait to finish their breakfast and get out of there. They looked up briefly as the bead curtain behind the counter parted and a teenage girl slipped through and walked nervously around to McCredy's table.

'Ever ting okay wit you breakfas' Sar-gant?' she purred demurely, picking up his empty plate and coffee cup.

'More coffee, and make it stronger,' he said, slapping her tightly skirted behind, making the girl jump away from the table, 'black and strong, just like your sexy ass.'

'Hey, you lay off'n she Sherwin McCredy, her only sixteen, yanoo.'

The booming voice belonged to a heavy-set mama who had bustled through the beads and now stood glaring at McCredy, thick arms folded across an impressive bosom.

'Old enough in my book, Mollie,' McCredy said, 'and let us face it, I'm the law round here.'

'You bad man, Sherwin McCredy,' Mollie said, 'someday day de Good Lord gonna strike you down.'

Unfazed by the dire prophesy he turned back to the girl.

'What say Lucinda, you want some nice *bootoo* back in my place?' he leered, 'make it worth your while.'

He laughed evilly as she clonked the cup and plate on the counter and ran around the back in tears. The two men at the other table watched her leave then one of them glanced round at McCredy.

'What are you looking at Wilson?'

The man quickly turned back to his soup.

'Have I been to visit you for local tax this month, Wilson?'

'Yeamon Mr McCredy, you come last week, I pay.'

However, McCredy had lost interest; his attention was on the figure in the doorway. A honky woman leaning on the doorframe, casually swinging a baseball cap on her finger. Her pale blue eyes bored into him with a directness he would have found arousing under other circumstances.

However, this was a face he recognised, even with all the lush brown hair shaved off. The naked scalp exposed the arrow-shaped wound from the bullet that should have killed her. She had her head turned so that it pointed at him accusingly.

He gave an involuntary shudder, as if someone had just trickled iced water down his spine.

She smiled a cold mirthless smile. 'I smell the sweat of a crooked policeman,' she said calmly, 'it is sweat that smells like shit.'

Despite his shock at seeing her appear at the doorway and her confidently delivered broadside, McCredy had not maintained his dominance here for the past year by allowing himself to be cowed. She was alone, after all.

'You have made a serious mistake returning here, Miss Friedmann,' he said, letting his fingers creep slowly up the shiny leather holster at his belt, 'I will now have to arrest you for murder.'

His hand froze on the holster as another figure stepped in behind the woman and levelled a shotgun at him.

Hayward's presence changed everything. Only the previous week he had demonstrated the awesome power of the weapon he now held, blowing apart the engine of his boat. He still prickled with the humiliation of falling overboard.

'Both hands on the table McCredy,' Hayward growled, 'you two, fuck off.'

There was a sudden scramble for the far door of the café. McCredy hesitated a moment, wondering if the old man would have the audacity to kill a police officer. The steady eyes and the old man's reputation told him he would. He placed both hands on the table in front of him.

Mollie remained at her counter a moment, grinning. 'Ah tole you so, Sherwin, de Good Lord he come for you. You say you prayers good now.' She turned to the old man. 'Now Hayward, done you go messin' up me place.'

'Don't worry, Mollie, we'll deal with this piece of dog shit outside.'

Mollie withdrew through the beads into her kitchen, chuckling.

~ Chapter Twenty-Nine ~

Confronting McCredy had made Stella's blood run cold. It was just a piece of drama, true, but she had wanted to do it, glad she had, and was quite pleased with her performance. She let Thomas walk ahead behind Hayward as he marched the police sergeant out of the far door, followed them up the flagstone path around the back of the building to where the latrine and a chicken coop stood at the end of the yard.

When they reached the latrine wall Hayward ordered him to stop, turn around, back to the wall, and then shoved the twin shotgun muzzles up under his chin, forcing his head back.

'Thomas, take his gun.'

Thomas stepped up and flipped open the holster, withdrawing the weapon, then stood back.

'You are making a big mistake, Hayward; you will hang for this outrage.'

For an old man he moved very quickly, reversing the shotgun and whacking the butt into the police officer's stomach then stepping neatly back as McCredy doubled over, the wind knocked out of him, simultaneously retching and gasping for breath.

'That's just for fucking starters,' Hayward said calmly, 'now, I'll tell you what happens next. You will tell me the destination of your two spick fucking drug runners, where they were told to drop off the fucking cocaine, and where they would be likely to fucking go afterwards.' Then, incredibly, he gave one of his belly laughs, which in the present context sounded oddly sinister.

'Go and fuck yourself you fucking duppy.'

'Shoot him in the left knee, Thomas,' Hayward said, keeping his eyes fixed on the sergeant.

Thomas stared at Hayward in disbelief.

'Go on; shoot the bastard in the knee. If I do it with this it'll blow his fucking leg off.'

Thomas shrugged. 'May de Lord forgive me,' he murmured, lifting the gun, and fumbling off the safety. With long eyes, he pointed and fired, stunning a ragged tear into the immaculate uniform trousers.

McCredy screamed, clutched at the ruined knee and stared in disbelief at the spreading dark of blood soaking into the blue worsted.

Hearing a noise, Stella looked back down the path to where a group of children were staring wide eyed at the scene. She took a few steps towards them, shooing them away and they ran off chattering excitedly. The story would be all around the island in an hour.

'Feel like talking yet,' Hayward said, 'or shall we bust your other knee as well?'

'Puerto Rico,' McCredy grated, 'they took the stuff to Puerto Rico, a place called Guanica.'

Hayward glanced at Stella then turned back, pushing McCredy's head even further back with the shotgun, 'And how do you get paid? You trust those spicks to come back with the money?'

He did not reply.

'Thomas... the other leg.'

'No, no,' McCredy said, grimacing through his pain, 'alright, I'll tell you. It's a regular shipment, when the people there get the stuff they pay the money into a Cayman numbered account. I pay the runners when they get back. But it is all fucked up now, man, the regular boat driver got himself arrested, the boat is impounded in Grenada.'

'So that is why they took my boat.' Stella said, 'But they will want to come back for their money, surely?'

'Yes,' said McCredy, 'but they will keep away for a while, until I have dealt with the problem of those two fool Americans.'

Hayward said, 'What was the plan, McCredy, how did you mean to cover up the killings?'

McCredy looked at Stella. 'Your boyfriend, Redman,' he said, sneering through his agony, 'my investigation was going to point to you and he attempting to rob the Americans. It would have concluded that the robbery went wrong and you were shot by one of the victims, and Redman killed them both out of revenge.'

'That is reprehensible.' Stella said, 'and how could anybody believe it anyway?'

'Because it is white on white, more politically acceptable for the government, no come-back from the United States on our local unrest.'

Hayward said, 'And once the fucking story appears in the newspapers, your fucking hoodlums know they can return here and get paid, is that it?'

He nodded.

'So you fucked up,' Hayward said, 'you didn't check she was dead. I took her away and you were stuck with a possible live witness at large.'

He nodded again. 'I'm bleeding man; I need to stop this blood coming out of me. You got what you want, so let me go get fixed up.'

Hayward stood a long time looking down at him, alternately scratching and stroking his mass of facial hair in thought.

'What was the plan with the English fella? And be careful how you answer,' he winked at Stella, 'this little lady will happily blow your fucking evil head off if he comes to harm.'

'He will be okay, they have instructions to wait in Puerto Rico, and then bring the boat back here as soon as they see the news article. They will need him to sail the boat back for them.'

'And when they get back here? What happens to him then? Shot while resisting arrest?'

'There is no need; the evidence against him would have been conclusive. The court in Grenada will make sure the story runs as told. Politics, you know. He needs to be handed over alive to close the loop.'

'Corruption, more like,' Hayward said, 'but right now that works in our favour, and you've probably just saved your life. You got any medical kit in your cop shop?'

~.~

Stella found the shotgun surprisingly heavy.

'Keep it pointing at his head,' Hayward told her, 'if he moves anything except his writing hand, blow it off.

'Thomas, cover him from the front, same deal.'

When McCredy finished writing Hayward picked up the sheets and studied them a moment, scratching his beard. Then he shook his head.

'No, it's no good.'

'It is a complete statement, man,' McCredy said, 'it is all there, everything – you have not even read it, man.'

Hayward chuckled.

'No, I haven't, can't fucking read, that's why.'

He gave another of his belly laughs, took the shotgun back from Stella, and passed her the statement sheets.

'Here, Chickadee, cast your educated eyes over that and see if it's all kosher.'

She stared at him, incredulous.

'You can't read?'

'Can't read, except numbers, can't drive, either, except a boat. Never learned, never had need of either. Born at sea, been at sea all me life.'

Shaking her head in bemusement, she turned her attention to the hand-written notes. It was all there, the whole narrative of events, from the debacle of the boat driver's arrest, discovering that someone had found the cocaine, and eventually who had recovered it.

It told of the murdering of Frank and Martha in their home to protect the racket, the contingency plan when she and Patrick had gone back to the house and discovered the bodies. It was a strange moment reading about her own supposed death. She suppressed a giggle when she read the part about Hayward blasting his engine, then McCredy falling overboard.

'How did you discover I had been found and taken to Hayward's boat?' she said.

'I have my informants.' McCredy said, a shifty look coming into his eyes. 'When I heard Hayward and Lazy Lobster Kenny were carrying an injured woman to the boat I realised you had survived, so I intercepted his boat in the bay.'

She read on. The frank confession finished with their discussions to fake a cover story for the killings and to blame Patrick for them.

'Yes, it is written as he said,' she handed the sheets to Thomas, 'second opinion?'

He took them and began to read.

'Now, here's the deal again,' Hayward said, 'you file your report of the murder investigation, exactly as you originally planned it, you make sure the press gets the story. When those two twats get back here with Patrick you arrest them for the murders. It was all a big mistake; Patrick Redman is innocent after all. The bigwigs in St Georges get their result, Hispanic criminals, and not local villains. Everyone happy, comprende?'

'And my statement, you will destroy it?'

'Ah, that's the part I haven't mentioned. When all this has blown over you hand in your resignation and fuck off out of here, get lost and get out of these people's lives.'

McCredy nodded. 'I was planning to leave anyway. And then you will destroy the statement?'

'And then we burn it,' Hayward agreed.

'How can I trust you?'

'Well, my old matey, you can't, any more than we can trust you. Should of thought about that before you wrote the statement.'

'I didn't have a choice.'

'Exactly, at least this way you get to live.'

'That is if your leg does not go bad and poison you;' Stella added, 'now you have two reasons for going to Grenada. I have patched it as well as I can, but it needs proper treatment, in hospital.'

'Yeah it all look okay,' said Thomas, handing the statement back to Stella then turning a look of disgust on McCredy, 'you know man, I really ashamed you – you wicked man, you bring shame on all black man, you bring shame on Grenada police, an you bring shame on you country. I can't believe how anyone so wicked, man.'

Stella folded up the sheets and slipped them into a plastic envelope from the sergeant's desk.

~ Chapter Thirty ~

'So, Juanita, your Father told me you are from Cuba?'

'Sí, we have a pineapple plantation in the country. It is …' she glanced up at the mainsail, 'you sail too close, bear away a little.'

Stella eased the big wooden tiller and let her drift a fraction to leeward until the slight billow came out of the luff. She found it unsettling for this slip of a child to show her how to sail, but *Jupiter* was different to anything she had sailed before and she respected the advice.

'Sorry,' she said, 'my *Carriacou* can get a few degrees closer and I am not yet used to this rig.'

'Do not worry, you do well, obvious you are good sailor. Everybody have problems when first sail *Jupiter*.'

Yet Stella enjoyed the feel of the old ketch. She was heavy and sluggish to get going, but once she had her head she glided effortlessly along without fuss, stood unusually upright and never overpowered, even when close hauled as now, un-reefed in a moderate breeze.

She had been surprised the first time the log tipped twelve knots. However, for all the romantic appeal of this traditional rig she had soon discovered its pitfalls. For one thing, the main gaff with its heavy canvas sail permanently attached was a beast – it had taken her and Thomas all their combined weight and strength to hoist it while Hayward stood hooting uproariously from the stern sheets.

Another disadvantage was the cumbersome headsail arrangement, free from labour-saving winches or furlers. The bowsprit gib had its own sleeve cover strung fore and aft from the bowsprit, and the staysail attached to a heavy wooden boom. At least the mizzen was never a problem; Hayward kept it permanently up.

While Juanita explained how everything worked, Hayward merely responded to their frequent errors with his signature belly laugh, a background feature to which Stella was now becoming so accustomed she rarely registered it, like the hourly chimes of a night-time church clock.

Even the foresheets (which were secured to eyeplates either side of the mainmast), were heavy work when tacking, and then the big gib having to be dragged around the forestay.

'How on earth do you manage single handed?' she had asked him after they weighed anchor and stood calmly out of the narrow bay; sailing, engine off, something most skippers would have had cats about.

'Not sure,' he had grinned irascibly, 'it's a bit like asking someone how they ride a bike. Suppose the trick is never to show off, take it a step at a time and don't worry if the sails flog a bit. Not elegant, but safe and steady.'

There was a low rumble from below and then the steady thump of the diesel generator, its exhaust gurgling on the waterline below where she sat. The saloon lights came on and she saw Hayward and Thomas down there bustling about as they prepared the evening meal.

She looked again at the skinny little Cuban girl lounging comfortably on the bench beside her. 'So, you were telling me about your pineapple plantation.'

Juanita's eyes went dreamy as she thought of home.

'It is really beautiful, everything is green and many different crops grow, but only our family grow pineapples in our valley. From my house we see high *montañas* to the south and a big *laguna* to the north where I go swimming sometimes.'

Stella stood up to check up ahead, then ducked to look under the mainsail, shading her eyes against the setting sun, then out to starboard where the town of Kingstown drifted astern, a few early lights pinking through the settling twilight.

'It sounds wonderful, Juanita, and do you go to school?'

'Sure, I go to state school on bus each day, but at weekend I must help on the plantation.'

'Is it only you and your mother, running the plantation?'

'Oh no, we employ four workers,' she said, 'it is important business; our fruit is sold in the *supermercados* all over Cuba, even Habana.'

'Oh,' said Stella, 'so your family does well, with the business?'

Juanita looked surprised. 'Nobody has much money in Cuba, Stella, unless they are privileged few. If we make too much money, the government take more taxes. The money we make is enough to feed family and pay the workers, and one day for my education.'

'But isn't your education free?'

'Yes, in Cuba, but Hayward says I must go to University in England when I am old enough.'

'Really?' said Stella, genuinely shocked at this new revelation, 'and how do you feel about that?'

'I am very happy and excited to go – it will give me many opportunities I would not have if I stay in Cuba.'

'And your Mother, what does she say about this?'

'She is happy for me but says she will miss me. She is a little afraid for me I think. But it is Hayward's decision.'

'Why Hayward's?'

'Why, it is his business, of course, he own everything.'

Stella was silent for a long time, stunned by this new side to the man who only two days ago she had heard described as a penniless sea gypsy.

The old seaman himself came stumping up the ladder holding two glasses.

'Grub up for adults in fifteen minutes,' he announced, handing a glass to Stella, 'gin and tonic ok?'

'What a lovely surprise,' she said, holding up the glass in salute, '*Zum Wohl!*'

He returned the toast, holding up a glass brimming with what could only be rum, took a gulp then looked down proprietarily at his daughter.

'And you, my young lassie, your tea's ready down below, go and keep Thomas company.'

As Juanita padded away below he scanned around the horizon then checked the sails. 'Well, looks like you've mastered the black art of sailing a Hayward Ketch,' he said, 'but she'll manage quite well on autopilot now.'

'Autopilot?' Stella said, scanning the little cockpit for the least sign of any equipment from the current century, 'You have autopilot?'

'Of course we've got fucking autopilot.'

He reached down and tugged open a short, coiled rope attached to the windward guardrail and looped it over the tiller.

'There, autopilot.'

Her mouth made an O of amused surprise. She took her hand gingerly off the tiller while keeping a suspicious eye on the main luff.

'Don't worry, she's fine,' he chuckled, 'how do you think I get my fucking shut-eye when I'm single-handed?'

Impressed, she sipped her drink and watched the darkening coastline slipping by to starboard for a few moments, then turned back to him.

'Hayward, when you first told me of Juanita it sounded to me as if you hardly remembered her mother, and you were not even sure of your daughter's true age. Now she tells me that you are supporting her family and intend to see to her education. It is not my business, but I am curious to know why you wish people to think you are a heartless cavalier when you are really a father who cares. Can you tell me this or am I being too inquisitive?'

It was his turn for a moment's silent reflection, with his characteristic beard rubbing and scratching. She wondered when he had last washed with soap and fresh water.

Finally, he gave a deep sigh and began to speak.

'Built me first boat when I was twelve, called her *Jupiter* too. Crossed the Atlantic in her the following year, single-handed. Since then I've been shipwrecked six times, and each time I rebuilt the boat, I improved the design.

Eventually I realised I had something unique, a traditional gaffer ketch that was a dream to sail and nice to look at, but not falling apart like most of the hundred-year-old wrecks people were buying to fix up.

'So I bought the worldwide rights for the Hayward Ketch and started building boats for other people. But demand started outgrowing what I could deliver – it was taking up too much of me time, y'see. People wanted the Hayward design for their own boats, often people with a bit of *dinero*, but I hadn't the time or the inclination to build 'em, so now I sell 'em licences instead, to build it for themselves.

'I've been doing that for thirty-five years, so now you can find one of my boats at one time or other in every marina in the world. Earns me a fair amount of money, money I don't want and don't need. But I've got lots of women pregnant in lots of places, and they mostly do need money to support my illegitimate sprogs. So yes, I've got three pineapple plantations, one in Cuba, two in the Philippines. I've got a rubber plantation in Indonesia, and I've lost count of where all my banana plantations are. I've been buying plantations because they do the job, low technology businesses, easy to run, and don't need any input from me.

'And the only reason I do it is because I don't want people bad-mouthing me after I've shuffled off this mortal coil. Besides, I quite like my kids – haven't met one yet I didn't like.'

He raised his glass and drank down the remaining rum.

'So, there is your answer my dear, and thank you for asking, I didn't mind telling you, now shut the fuck up about it.'

He held her gaze with a serious expression for a few seconds then broke down in rip-roarious laughter.

~ Chapter Thirty-One ~

'This belongs in a museum,' Stella called down from the coach roof.

'Fine old instrument that, don't knock it.' Hayward lay flat out on his back in the narrow waist-deck where he had been since breakfast,

'Don't worry, I will not damage your old sextant.' she said. She was somewhat puzzled to see his recumbent belly wobble with silent laughter.

He had got drunk during the night, had sat at the helm singing bawdy songs to the stars, songs with obscure words but strikingly obvious connotations.

Thomas relieved her at two and she went gratefully below to the forward cabin she shared with Juanita. Even this far forward with the cabin door closed she had still heard the coarse tones of badly sung ballads drifting down; but amid the soft creaking of timbers, the gentle swish of water along the hull, his slurred tones gradually merged into the natural ambiance, and she'd slept properly for the first time since waking from her coma.

Lifting the sextant, she sighted once more, and called to Juanita. 'Stand by…mark! Eight three degrees, four eight minutes decimal one.'

'Your last two elevations were higher,' Juanita said, 'I think meridian is past.'

'Thank you darling,' Stella said, dropping lightly onto the deck. She stowed the ancient instrument in its box and took the little notebook from the child, glanced approvingly at the neat columns of figures, then swung down the ladder, careful not to wake Thomas, crashed out on the saloon cushions after his night watch.

'Zo,' she announced, returning on deck, 'we are one hundred twenty-eight miles west of Martinique and have three hundred thirty-seven miles to go to our destination.'

Hayward finally stirred, pulled himself up on a guardrail stanchion, stretched, and stepped down into the cockpit.

'About thirty hours at this rate,' he said, stifling a yawn, 'we need to talk about outcomes.'

'Outcomes?' Stella asked.

'Yeah, like what do you see happening when we find your boat and Patrick – assuming he's still alive? I know I'm a silly old fucker but I like to have an outline plan to work to, even if we need to change it later. Firstly, why did you browbeat me into taking you to Puerto Rico when we could just have waited for them to come to us, once McCredy's report has broken the news?'

'I see the outcome, as you put it,' Stella said, 'is that when we find these two murderers... when we find Patrick and my boat in the harbour of Guanica I go ashore somewhere and telephone to the San Juan police, to break this cocaine traffic of McCredy and tell them of the murder of two American citizens.'

'Fucking hell, Stella!' he said, 'you really want to stir things up that much?'

'Yes, of course, it is the best solution, and we use only one rock to kill two stones.'

'Ingenious!' he said, with a wasted trace of irony, 'and when, exactly, were you going to share this plan with me?'

'When you asked, of course.'

She had discussed it at length with Thomas who had agreed with her plan, and that was good enough for her. This was the first time Hayward had shown any interest.

Now he said, 'But why not just let it run the way we set it up?'

Although he'd capitulated without protest when she'd insisted they sail to Puerto Rico despite their agreement with McCredy, he had seemed lukewarm on the whole idea of pro-action, a far cry from his impressive performance on

Pipah just a few hours before. She found his ambivalence confusing and irritating.

'You trust McCredy? After what he has done?'

'Not as far as I could spit him, but we have his confession, and what we've told him to do was only what he planned anyway. We gave him an easy out; he'd be a fucking idiot to screw it up.'

'I have no doubt he would make the report happen,' Stella agreed, 'but I do not trust that he would turn against his two thugs once he has Patrick back. They know too much.'

'Ah yes, my dear, but will the police take the word of two murderers against one of their own?'

'And if we were able to show the police real evidence of McCredy's involvement…?'

He scratched his facial fuzz again. 'True, they might. I hate to repeat meself, but there's still McCredy's confession.'

She did not reply straight away, just looked into his wizened face and held his eyes.

'What happened to the boat driver, after he was arrested? Do we know?'

More beard scratching.

'Dunno, probably killed resisting arrest because he knew too much.'

'Exactly,' she said, 'if this man can have so much influence to arrange such a thing, then how can we feel safe in Grenada? Even with his confession?'

'Especially with his confession.' Hayward corrected.

~.~

Stella looked around and ahead, checked the sail trim, and then lay back down on the bench cushion looking up at tonight's spectacular show. The sky was moonless, and cloudless, so the stars were at their brightest, so bright it made her eyes water to look at them for more than a few moments. Low on the starboard beam was Vega, big and round as a near planet, a singular wink against a rare empty patch of black velvet. Further ahead, also low in the sky, stood Cassiopeia's wonky W, and there, much higher sat broody Andromeda, and mighty Pegasus straddled directly overhead.

She had the long night watch, two till six; the graveyard watch, Patrick called it. Except when it had been just the two of them, they had worked six-hour night watches: two till eight.

Now it was just Thomas and her on the night watches, with Juanita taking a day watch. Hayward? Well he was just there, not taking a watch at all, cooking, pottering about the boat re-splicing frayed rope-ends, cleaning and tidying, and getting drunk. Mostly getting drunk, or, as she had discovered last night, stoned.

She had smelled the marijuana as soon as she came up the ladder to relieve Thomas and had been pleased to see he was not stoned as well, though once he had been relieved he had accepted a few drags of Hayward's spliff.

'Help I sleep, Boss, yanoo.'

'You know it is not a problem for me, Thomas,' she'd said, 'when you are off watch.'

After Thomas had gone below Hayward had made her a cup of cocoa then took himself below to turn in. His was the after cabin immediately below the cockpit, and very soon, the sound of his soft snoring drifted up to merge with the other natural sounds of the boat.

She was worried about Hayward. Since leaving St Vincent he had been behaving increasing like a slob, letting Stella take charge and seemingly taking little interest either in her general running of his boat, or its progress across this exceptionally empty stretch of open sea to Puerto Rico.

She knew from personal experience that Thomas was a good man to have nearby when trouble came along, but she had also reckoned with the strong assertive Hayward she had seen on Pipah, not this drunken old half-wit.

When Juanita came up to relieve her at six Stella remained awhile to watch the sunrise.

'Is your father alright, Juanita?' she said, 'because he seems to be behaving very strangely these last two days.'

Juanita put a skinny hand over her mouth and giggled softly.

'It is like a holiday for him,' she said, 'having someone like you onboard. Believe me; Hayward is enjoying himself, Stella. Do not be afraid of the way he behaves. If something bad happens you will see a big change.'

Stella was not entirely convinced.

The sun's lower limn cleared the horizon and Stella stood to take a final look around before retiring below. As her eyes swept the distant reaches to port, she thought she noticed something.

Not sure what it was that had grabbed her attention, she slowly backtracked her eyes along the horizon to recapture that barely-noticed oddity. Then, there it was, a slight chip in the sun-sharpened margin of the sea, small, indistinct.

'Juanita, can you see something over there?' She pointed to where the object was. It was not always in sight, kept disappearing so she did not know exactly where it would appear again.

Juanita stood up to the waist deck and leaned on the guardrail staring out.

'No, I cannot see anything... no, wait, there is something, small and over the horizon, maybe the top of a ship?'

Stella went below and checked the chart, grabbed Hayward's binoculars and returned to the deck.

'There is an obstruction marked on the chart,' she said, scanning with the glasses, 'but nothing about it'

Hayward's charts were thirty years old... 'Ah, there it is. A small island I think.'

She handed the glasses to Juanita.

'I thought for a moment it might have been...'

'Yes, I know,' Juanita said, adjusting the glasses to her eyes, 'I heard in your voice, you thought it might be your boat, yes?'

Stella smiled and stroked Juanita's mousy hair.

'It is just wishful thinking,' she said sadly, 'I will turn in now.'

On impulse, she bent and kissed the little girl's cheek. 'Sleep well, Stella.' Juanita said.

~ Chapter Thirty-Two ~

Throughout the afternoon they had been crossing a busy shipping route, an exercise Stella always felt slightly nervous about, despite her many years at sea: an enormous tower suddenly appearing on the horizon, shockingly close, gradually revealing the great bulk of its hull beneath, finally its bow wave emerging, the great leviathan lumbering unstoppably closer. Tensely watching the oncoming vessel's relative drift – the frustrating wait between fixes – the hidden relief when the bearing change becomes apparent. It sometimes passes astern, but more often crosses ahead, causing everyone to brace against the boat's skittish tossing through multiple wakes.

As they cleared the shipping route, the island of Morillito appeared on the horizon to starboard and Stella took a bearing and estimated its range for a rough fix.

It was around six when she caught her first glimpse of Puerto Rico - the cranes and towers crowding the skyline of Ponce Harbour - and she told Juanita to bear away, to parallel the coast westward a good distance from shore. Meanwhile she laid off a track on the chart to take her into Guanica Bay some twenty miles to the west.

~.~

Another moonless night, but now a few broken clouds moved silently across a star-scape already dimmed by pollution from the shore lights. Stella was at the tiller, following a transit line between a chimney down on the harbour and a conspicuous mast on the hill above, both marked with red obstruction lights. She estimated around half a mile to the entrance. It looked very narrow, with waves breaking at the cliff bases on either side.

'I'll need the engine,' she told Hayward.

'Two reasons you can't,' he said, 'one, it'll be too noisy; don't want to draw attention cruising round the harbour looking at yachts.'

'That is a good point, but I think it is not safe with sails alone, there is a big swell in the entrance and the wind may be unpredictable. What else?'

'Eh?' he said.

'You said two reasons we could not use the engine.'

'Oh, yes, well it's fucked, prop shaft's busted. Hasn't worked for years.'

He stepped up to the tiller, 'No offence, chickadee, you're a fucking good skipper, but I'll take her from here if you don't mind.'

She was pleased to hand control back to him, even more pleased to have him back to his normal irascible self. As the dark coast loomed near, she could make out the shape of the wooded cliffs guarding the harbour entrance. She took the mainsheet in hand and sent Juanita forward to tend the two headsails in case of sudden wind shifts.

'Open the forward hatch,' Hayward called after her, 'if the shit hits the fan jump down below.'

Gliding silently through the entrance, Hayward said quietly, 'Thomas, nip below and bring up me shotgun, will ya?'

When the little harbour opened out, the breeze dropped to light airs, water like oil reflecting the harbour lights, ruffled only by the occasional zephyr of a breeze. The wind-ripples looked a little more pronounced on the western side, Stella noted with some relief. This man really did 'fly by the bottom of his trousers, as Patrick would say.

Hayward used the boat's heavy momentum to glide past the eastern pontoons and jetty berths, sails hanging worryingly slack and forlorn. Two white-hulled motor boats lay alongside the pontoons, and an ancient red ferry with a serious list sat tied at the jetty.

Hayward eased the tiller to starboard, letting the bow swing to port, gently to avoid taking off too much way. However, they were slowing now. Too soon, Stella thought, in a moment they would be stationary, adrift in a potentially hostile harbour and windless, no means of moving themselves.

Then a whisper reached the gib, and lazily it began to fill and draw. The stays'l soon followed and then they were picking up speed again, port tack as before. Stella eased out the main a little to trim to the quarter breeze.

'Oh ye of little faith!' she heard the old man murmur, then in a firmer voice, 'Just a couple o' stinkpots. Let's look over the other side.'

He steered the boat towards a small inlet in the southwest corner. Off to starboard, houses and industrial units lined the shore, a row of powerful sodium lamps illuminating the empty water in front of them. The inlet also proved clear of vessels.

'Going About!' Hayward warned, swinging the bow towards the narrow entrance.

~.~

They anchored in four metres, in the lee of one of several small islands, where the faint sounds of laughter and disco music drifted over the water from a lively hotel.

Stella said, 'Tomorrow I would like to have a look around these islands and resorts. Perhaps it was not in the harbour they were to rendezvous, but somewhere nearby.'

'Let's hope you're right,' Hayward said, 'we need to find out if that story's hit the news yet. If it has, they could be on their way back.'

'I go ashore,' said Thomas suddenly, 'listen to gossip, bring newspapers back.'

'Yes,' Stella said, 'good idea. Do you want me to come with you?'

'Naw, Boss, better on dis occasion I go by myself, less conspicuous alone, yanoo.' He turned to Hayward.

'You got dry bag, skipper?'

'I can do a bit better than that old son, what about a dingy?'

~.~

It took twenty minutes to drag Hayward's tiny inflatable out of the forward sail locker and ready it for use. Reasoning that it would be easier to propel the boat with two people paddling, Stella decided after all to accompany Thomas.

Her eyes widened when Hayward opened a locker and handed her one of a pair of portable VHF radios.

'Got to have 'em,' he explained, looking slightly embarrassed, 'otherwise the fucking coastguard kick up a fuss.

'Use channel thirty-seven. The battery's only good for a couple of hours, so keep it switched off unless you've got something to say. I'll keep this one on charge and switched on.'

She nodded thanks and turned to Thomas.

'We will split up when we get ashore, you go and mingle with the local people and see what you can learn. I will find newspapers. I will also telephone to the police in San Juan.'

'Is that wise?' said Hayward, 'it could jeopardise getting your man back alive.'

Stella frowned, 'This may be true, but they will have better means to deal with this than we, and they may also have information. What if they have already picked them up? We will need to involve the authorities at some stage, it may as well be now – later may be too late.'

He shrugged. 'Okay. Chickadee, it's your show. Good luck.'

She swung down into the dingy to join Thomas and they pushed off, sitting astride the tubes to get better position for paddling.

~.~

When they had dragged the dingy up onto the sand Thomas headed along to where lights glowed dimly among beached fishing boats and nets slung between palm trees.

'De font of all local wisdom, de rum shack yanoo.'

Meanwhile Stella stepped up onto the concrete patio that fronted a hotel swimming pool and cocktail lounge where groups of chattering guests gathered around the bar or sat on scattered settees and armchairs. The disco show of earlier now stood abandoned and silent in a corner, the small parquet dance floor deserted. Although some of the guests had dressed for dinner there were just as many still in their day swimwear, allowing Stella to pass unnoticed into the hotel foyer where various journals and newspapers were on display in a rack.

Disappointed not to find anything covering the Grenadines she settled for The Barbados Advocate, The Trinidad Guardian and The Virgin Islands Daily News, and sat down in the foyer to read them. Only the latter had any mention of the murders.

US Nationals Slain on Grenadian Island

18 Sept. Concern was growing last night at the US State Department when the Grenadian Government failed to give an adequate explanation of the deaths of Frank Cartwright and his Wife Martha on the island of Pipah. Despite assurances by the Grenadian Police that the investigation would be expedited local resources have so far failed to discover a motive for the murders, or any clues as to the perpetrators.

The couple, originally from Boston Ma, who for several years have been running a diving school on the island, were found brutally murdered in their home last Tuesday. A spokesman for The People's Republican Government said the deaths were not thought to be politically motivated.

However, this reporter has learned from local sources that anti-American feelings are running high in the Republic following Prime Minister Bishop's personal intervention over the alleged mistreatment by officials of Grenadian religious activist Suzanne Berkley during a visit to Puerto Rico last March.

She went to find a telephone.

The first person she got was the duty officer at San Juan Central, and when she'd outlined the story she was passed on to a sergeant to whom she had to explain the whole thing once more.

She was eventually connected to a different location where, after telling her story again, she was kept hanging on listening to background office babble long enough to use up most of her change.

She was about to hang up when a man's voice came on the line, an American accent. 'Hi there Miss Friedmann, my name is Tony Viteri, where are you right now?'

~.~

Thomas was waiting at the boat. He stank of rum.

'You ready go back now Boss?'

'I have to wait here for someone from the American drugs people. What did you find out?'

Thomas goggled. 'DEA coming here to see we?'

'He did not give me any choice. It was either wait here or he comes to the boat. Hayward may not have appreciated this. They want me to give them a statement and information to help find my boat.'

'We better keep dose guys away from *Jupiter*.'

'It is only one man, and he seemed very nice. I do not think he will be concerned with a little marijuana. What did you discover from the "fount of all wisdom"?'

'I tink we got someting. When I first axe, nobody seen any sailboats. None been in da harbour, and dey would ha notice cos is not a usual spot for dem. Dere no marina round here yanoo. When I mention coke dey all clam up like yanoo, and look at me scared like.'

'These men in the bar were frightened? Then you must have stroked a nerve, *nicht war*?'

He nodded, 'But when I come out, one man come after me and tell me sometime a motor boat come in dis bay and two men always go out from de harbour in tender to meet. He brudder work in de harbour, yanoo, an' he seen dese guys dat go out to meet de boat and coming back wid de merchandise.'

'They do it openly and no one reports them?'

'It organised, like syndicates, yanoo, dey control everywhere, and if you cross dem...' his eyes grew theatrically wide and he drew a finger across his throat. 'One ting more, Boss, and I tink dis de main point, yanoo. Dey white guys is American.'

~.~

Stella waited in the hotel lobby where she ordered a coffee and thought about the new information. Thomas had had no doubts about the Americans being McCredy's clients. He had explained that the nature of the drug syndicates made it highly improbable that more than one group operated at the same delivery point.

The crooked police officer had told them his contrabandistas regularly made the trip in a motor boat. However, the police from Grenada had arrested their boat driver and impounded the boat. That is why they had taken *Carriacou*, and Patrick to sail her.

She was therefore even more puzzled and worried that they did not seem to have turned up here in her boat. Had there been a change of plan? That seemed unlikely; since the rendezvous would have been due to occur well before their confrontation with McCredy.

Then there was the man she had spoken to on the telephone, the American from the Drugs Enforcement Agency. Although he had not said anything specifically, she got the impression he already knew something of the cocaine operation going on here. Not too surprising considering the apparently notorious reputation of the syndicates. She shuddered at the memory of Thomas' graphic sketch, thinking of Patrick.

However, if the authorities knew about it, why wait until now to make a move, when the criminals were not even here? It made no sense.

~ Chapter Thirty-Three ~

Viteri arrived at just after ten o clock when most of the hotel guests had trickled away. 'I need a beer,' he said to Stella, 'and then you can tell me your story.' He was a tall, gaunt man, around Patrick's age, she guessed, dressed casually in jeans and a denim jacket over a faded Miami Dolphins T-shirt.

She ordered a fruit cocktail and they took their drinks out onto the stone patio facing the darkened bay. Down in the gloom at the water's edge she saw that Thomas was still there guarding the boat, having ignored her suggestion he return to *Jupiter* without her and wait for her call on the radio.

'I do not wish to appear rude or ungrateful, Mr Viteri,' she said, 'but please can you show me some form of identification?'

Viteri hurriedly wiped away a frothy beer moustache. 'Call me Tony,' he said, and produced a leather cardholder, flipped it open to show the badge inside.

It held a gold circlet mounted with the eagle of the United States Government and the words Drug Enforcement Administration.

'Hmm, it says you are a Special Agent, should I feel impressed or threatened?'

She saw the slightly puzzled expression and smiled to emphasise she was teasing him. Whatever attributes Special Agent Tony Viteri had, subtle humour was not among them.

'I don't think you realise what kind of people you're mixed up with, Miss Friedmann.'

She let her face grow serious and removed her baseball cap, turning her head slightly to reveal the now purple arrow on her shaven skull. 'I know exactly the kind of people we are dealing with, Mr Viteri, so please do not patronise me. This was done by a bullet that was supposed to leave me dead with two other corpses.'

Viteri stared at the scar, his face, that a few moments ago had been a mask of supercilious blandness, slowly pinked with embarrassment.

'Jeeez!' he said, when he had found his voice.

She slid the copy of Daily News across the table to him, folded to show the murder story. He read it slowly, with a troubled frown that deepened perceptibly as he read. After a time she got the impression he was thinking, rather than reading.

Finally, he looked up and stared at her.

'You were there when these guys were killed?'

'Mr Viteri,' she said, feeling her good will slipping away, 'if we are to help each other, then may I request that you at least pay attention to what I tell you? I say again, what I told you on the telephone; it was my partner and I who discovered the bodies of Frank and Martha at their house. I was shot and left for dead; my partner, Patrick Redman, was taken, we presume in order to drive my boat for them – to bring them here with their contraband.'

She fought to control frustrated tears pricking at her eyes.

Viteri looked down at the low table that stood between them and ran the tip of his finger around the edge of his beer glass. Stella gave him a moment then broke into his embarrassed silence.

'Your insignia suggests that your primary concern is with the drug smuggling, and you must know that mine is the finding of Patrick and, of course my boat, but mainly my Patrick – the boat can be replaced.' She fell silent.

Though she realised the truth of this she nevertheless felt a deep undercurrent of regret for the boat that had been her home for so many years, and the last physical link with the deceased Nikkie - her lover for more than a third of her life.

Viteri looked up at her and nodded a deeply etched frown, discomfort, but also relief in his eyes.

'You're right ma'am, and I'm sorry for my insensitivity. Please forgive me.'

'So why are not the police investigating Patrick's abduction?'

His eyebrows raised, and he smiled sympathetically at her, but not before she noticed a flash of something else, irritation perhaps, or anger. However, it passed so fleetingly she thought she must have imagined it.

'Trust me on this, ma'am, the local bozzos here don't have the resources to deal with this kind of thing; bar-room combat and domestics are about their limit. And if we bring in the Feds then they and we will be stamping on each other's toes all the way. So we decided it best to have a single operation to recover your partner, your boat, and of course the illegal contraband. After all, we get one, we get all three.'

'Yes, I see this, but the priority must be to get Patrick alive. Your drugs must be a secondary concern.'

'Yes, Ma'am, I assure you we share that view.'

'Please call me Stella, as I will call you Tony. So Tony, what will you do now, to find them, I mean?'

'Well, M…, Stella, we figured that when Acosta and Figueroa lost their boat and her driver, and found themselves in charge of a million buck's worth of cocaine, on a sailboat with unlimited range, they decided to…'

He stopped speaking when he noticed she was gaping at him in astonishment.

'You mean you know these people,' she said, 'you actually know their names?'

He nodded apologetically.

'Yes, Ma'am: Felipe Rojaz, the boat driver, now deceased, having died in Grenadian police custody, Manuel Acosta and Elías Figueroa. This would have been their third delivery. We were waiting for this one to pick 'em all up together, along with the receivers at this end, and of course, the supplier. The drugs come out of Nicaragua so there ain't much we can do there. But it comes to us through Honduras and we've have some of our guys based there in Tegucigalpa. We were just about to smash up the supply ring here in the islands - the interference of the Grenadian Coastguard was a thing we didn't anticipate. To make things worse, we now figure the two guys that took your boat double-crossed their bosses and made off with the stuff to sell on for themselves.'

He held his hands apart in a show of helpless frustration.

Stella had caught little of what he told her; her mind was elsewhere, aglow with cautious happiness. He could still be alive.

Alive!

Because the smugglers, in betraying their paymasters, would surely need him to take *Carriacou* far, far away from the clutches of the drug barons. She allowed herself new hope, tenuous and optimistic perhaps, but more hope than she'd dared allow herself since she'd started out on this crazy chase.'

'You okay, Stella?'

'Yes,' she said, 'oh yes, I am very okay thank you. What are you going to do to find my boat?'

'There's a whole lot of things we'll be doing, starting with the US Coastguard. They have ships and P3's on constant patrol in these waters; and liaison with the military at Roosevelt Roads and the US Navy. There's a million square miles of ocean between here and Latin America, as I'm sure you appreciate, but once all these agencies are aware of an abduction in progress they'll pretty much work together and do their best to find your sailboat.'

'Pee threes?' said Stella.

'Sorry, ma'am, the P3 Orion: an airplane full of electronic stuff for surveillance and tracking. They're used by the Coastguard and the Navy.'

He took a notebook and pen from the pocket of his jacket.

'So, Stella, I'm going to need a real good description of your sailboat.'

~.~

Satisfied that the authorities in Puerto Rico were doing everything they could, Stella and Thomas spent the rest of October and into November sailing with Hayward around its coast, travelling clockwise and calling in at every tiny bay and inlet for signs or news of her boat. Whenever the opportunity arose she telephoned Tony Viteri for an update of progress, but it was always negative.

By the time they sailed into San Juan, Thomas was getting worried about leaving Adhra alone for so long and neglecting his business.

'We will both fly back to St Vincent, Thomas,' Stella said, 'I think it is about time I told the police there about what happened. They may have information… *Got*, I wish I had told them from the start – this is now so complicated.'

So they took a regular flight to St Vincent, and a week later, Stella flew back alone and re-joined Hayward and Juanita on Jupiter.

~.~

Before leaving San Juan, she phoned to arrange a final meeting with Tony. He suggested that they go to a restaurant in town for dinner and offered to pick her up from the marina.

'You know Stella,' Viteri said, 'we checked all those places around the coast, you and Hayward are wasting your time.'

She sat for a moment playing with her wine glass. When she looked up her eyes were shining with unshed tears.

'It is my time to waste, Tony; I will keep looking for Patrick until I find him, alive or… if it takes the rest of my life. What else can I do?'

He took the twiddling glass from her fingers and refilled it.

'I can see how much this means to you, and I'm really sorry we've got nothing more positive than a couple of false sightings. But really, honey, maybe you should think about waiting for news down in St Vincent. At least you'll be among friends there.'

She thought about that for a long moment, trying to draw comfort from his kindness.

'Perhaps I will,' she said, 'but Hayward is taking Juanita home in a few days, and I shall go with them. We can look for *Carriacou* along the way.'

He placed a gentle hand on hers and smiled.

'You are one helluva tenacious lady, Stella, Patrick is a lucky man.'

She knew she should remove her hand. But the gnawing loneliness that had been hovering at the edge of her emotions now began to assert itself. His hand felt warm and dry, comfortable on hers. She had never noticed before what nice hands he had, long straight fingers, neat manicured nails.

It had been a long time since she had felt like this. A warm glow was spreading up from down there, and she felt that old familiar tingling on her skin. She looked into his eyes, saw his desire there, felt her own need matching his. Her mind was in turmoil. She wanted so much for this man to sweep her up and take her to bed. He knew it as well; it was in his eyes, looking into her very…

Quickly she pulled her hand away. 'Please take me back to the marina now,' she said.

~ Part Five ~

November 1983

~ Chapter Thirty-Four ~

*Bleeding wounds repair, their injury heals,
then* vengeance *from the blood congeals.*

'She has never given up on you, Patrick. All this past year since her accident she has been pestering the authorities here, and the Americans in Puerto Rico.'

Patrick's mind was still reeling as he sat with the Governor General in the back of his limousine. He stared out unseeingly across the blue yellow reefs and out into a windswept sea dotted with myriad sails.

'She has spent months at sea searching for you, calling in every harbour, every little nook and cranny between here and Antigua. It is fortunate she happens to be here right now.'

Patrick turned to him.

'Has she got a new boat, then?'

'She sails with an Englishman called Hayward, and sometimes your friend Thomas goes with them.'

A pang of unreasonable jealousy struck him; a year was a long time.

'Hayward?'

'He owns the boat,' he let out a deep chuckle, 'do not worry my friend, when you meet him you will understand.'

'Did anyone investigate what happened on Pipah?'

Sir Reginald looked sorrowful, 'Ah, well unfortunately our police were unable to make much headway, there. McCredy seems to have disappeared. Our police handed the case over to the authorities in Grenada, since it is their jurisdiction. But then, with the troubles there, we were unable to get any further information. Perhaps when all this settles down…'

He was silent for a time, then said, 'I have briefed the Attorney General, who has taken a special interest in this case, and he is looking forward to any new evidence you have which may lead to the arrest of these barbarians. The American State Department are also watching developments. They still need answers about their two murdered people.'

Patrick had decided not to say anything about events in Grenada; didn't tell him the Americans had had the murderers and had let them go, and they were now dead. At this stage, it would just complicate matters. Right now, his stomach was in knots. He desperately wanted to see Stella, of course, but he was also strangely fearful of the coming reunion.

Could they just pick up where they had left off, after everything that had happened? Would they still feel the same about each other after more than a year of separate lives? Although the grief of her death had always remained with him, he had reconciled himself to it. The incredible truth was still hard to take in.

~.~

The limo pulled up at the bottom of a long flight of broad flagstone steps. Above stood Thomas and Adhra's house, a sprawling bungalow of dark polished wood and tinted glass.

Then he saw her, and his heart stopped.

She stood alone, at the top of the steps, grey shorts, white cotton shirt, knotted high in her usual fashion. She wore a white baseball cap, her brown hair cropped short like a tomboy. She stared down at him; even from here, he could see the suspended tears forming in her eyes. That first sight of her was a moment that would stay with him always.

She was beautiful.

He stepped out of the car, and they stared at each other without moving, her lovely smiling face creased with supressed excitement. All his earlier fears evaporated; he ran up the steps, and she ran down to meet him, squealing with unrestrained joy.

They came together laughing and crying at the same time, drawing apart to look at each other, touching faces, arms, shoulders, barely able to believe what was happening. Then they kissed a long passionate kiss that contained all the love Patrick thought he would never feel again.

Thomas and Adhra appeared at the top of their steps, hugging each other as they gazed down at the pair through tears of joy.

'Aw man,' Thomas said, 'me poor heart can hardly bear de happiness dis brings me.'

'Praise the Lord,' said Adhra. She took her husband's hand, and together they walked down to greet their long-lost friend.

~.~

Patrick and Stella sat close together on the rattan settee.

'Man, you is skinny,' Thomas said, handing Patrick a gin and tonic, 'and dat baldy head makes you look near old as me.'

Patrick held up his glass to chink with Thomas, bringing back the memory of those comradely sundowner evenings in Africa, when he and Thomas had often spent the night drinking themselves to a standstill.

'Now, on Stella de baldy look real good,' Thomas continued, 'me told her should keep shaved, but her tart de scar should be covered up yanoo, even after her disguised wid dat crazy tattoo.'

Patrick turned to Stella on the settee next to him. 'Can I see?'

She leaned over and let him brush his fingers through her short hair. He felt the ridges of her injury and winced at the thought of what she had suffered.

'I can see the blackness of the tattoo, but I can't make out the outline. What is it?'

'It is just an abstract design to hide the scar, darling. I have a picture; you can see later.' She snuggled up to him and kissed his cheek.

Adhra came in from the kitchen and picked up her drink.

'Sir Reginald,' she said, 'I want to thank you for bringing Patrick home to us. I hope you will join us for dinner? And your driver, of course.'

'That's very kind Mrs Dennie, but I have a meeting to attend this evening.'

The Governor General finished his drink, stood up, and walked over to Patrick and Stella.

'Patrick, I know you have much catching up to do. Take your time, but I would be grateful if you could come to my office in the next week or so, so a member of my staff can take your full statement.'

Patrick stood and shook his hand, 'Yes, Sir Reginald, of course, and thanks for everything.'

'Oh, I assure you it was my pleasure. Seeing the two of you reunited was the most joyful and inspiring sight I have witnessed in many years. Stella, I am so glad your long mission is fulfilled at last. We all at Government House have admired your tenacity over the past year. Now enjoy the fruits of your good fortune.'

He turned to face Thomas and Adhra.

'Mr and Mrs Dennie, I thank you most warmly for your hospitality but now I will leave you to enjoy the rest of the evening.'

He beamed around the room at everyone, 'Most gratifying. Truly most gratifying. Good evening.'

While Thomas and Adhra saw the Governor General to the door, Patrick and Stella took the opportunity for another long lingering kiss. When they came up for air she whispered, 'I long to get you in bed, do you think they will mind?'

'Tough if they do,' he said, 'let's go.'

~.~

Their first lovemaking was frenzied, desperate and noisy, with Stella almost screaming her way to their jolting climax. Afterwards they nestled close and speculated jokingly about what Thomas and Adhra must have made of her vocal performance. The second time was more deliberate, tender and considerate. More satisfying. They were back, a couple once more.

~ Chapter Thirty-Five ~

'Mornin' Captain, as you see we haul she out dis morning, and we done some inspec-*shan* already. Soon we start steam clean de hull.'

'Beeno,' said Patrick, 'this is Stella, she's the Captain now.'

The rigger looked first at Stella, then back to Patrick, a hurt expression in his face.

'You no say you sellin'she?'

'I didn't sell her, Beeno,' Patrick said, 'it's a long story, and complicated, but Stella owns the boat, okay?'

'I am very pleased to meet you, Beeno,' Stella said, and shook his hand, 'it looks like you have everything under control.' She walked over to the cradle, gazing up at *Carriacou* with misty eyes.

'She Swiss lady?' Beeno said quietly to Patrick, 'like da ensign?'

'She's German, the original owner was Swiss, but he's passed away.'

'Aw, me sorry to hear dat,' then he looked a little worried, 'so, dees jobs on me list, dey still on?'

'Yes, Beeno, everything is as I told you, except she might add a few things – she's in charge of the refit now.'

'And she will sign de work requisi-*shan*?'

'Yes, she will sign the work requisition.'

He brightened and hurried over to join Stella, his new customer, his "Captain". Patrick grinned and followed him.

'Her bottom has become extremely fouled,' Stella said to Beeno, 'tell me your work schedule for the hull.'

'When we finish steam clean we check for osmosis, but I tink you okay der, Captain, cos I look meself dis morning an find no blisters, yanoo. Den we rub down and apply gelcoat where needed. Two dees after, antifoul, two coat, den boot top, same colour red. Altogeder, one week, I would estimate.'

She nodded approval. 'I will go up,' she said, and mounted the ladder, 'are you coming Patrick?'

'Right behind you, Captain,' Patrick grinned.

She looked along the teak deck and wrinkled her nose. 'I can see green in the grain, and what are these brown stains?'

'Don't ask, I'll tell you later,' he said.

He hadn't told her anything about the firefight in Grenada yet, he wanted her to have the full story, not just snippets.

'Don't worry,' he said, 'Beeno assures me it will come up good as new.'

'*Ja,* but we lose two millimetres of teak in the sanding down.'

He didn't reply. She was right of course.

She looked at his face, and grimaced.

'Oh darling, I am so sorry,' she put her arms about him and kissed his mouth, 'I did not mean to be critical, I am just so upset to see her like this, you understand, don't you?'

'Of course, sweetheart, I understand. But you should have seen her when I found her. She looks like the Royal Yacht now, in comparison, which reminds me, I want to take you to meet the two medical students who helped me clean her up and get her here. They're great kids, you'll like them.'

He followed her down into the saloon. She stood and looked around, a delighted smile on her face, then twirled like a little girl.

'This is marvellous, darling, I really expected it to be filthy and damaged, but apart from the radios, everything is just as I last remember it.'

She went to him and hugged him again.

'I am so excited to have you both back,' she said, 'I cannot wait to get back to sea.'

He loved her most of all when she was happy and excited. He had forgotten how imperious she could get and it had thrown him a little to experience it again. However, he knew that was also part of her attraction – her independence and confidence to assume command.

Beeno waited at the bottom of the ladder with a clipboard and pen.

'If you can sign dis requisi-shan, Captain, we can commence work straightaway.'

Two men in coveralls were laying steam hoses around the cradle.

She read down the list of jobs, nodding approval at each item, then signed the form, handing it back to Beeno.

'You will rig awnings over the deck?'

'Yes, of course, Captain.'

'The men rubbing down the hull and sanding the decks must wear dust masks.'

'Yes Captain, no problem.'

'Very well, I will visit each morning for a progress report.'

'Yes Captain.'

Patrick grinned at Beeno. He had thought for a moment that the bosun-rigger was going to stand to attention and salute.

As she strode off, he gave Patrick a quizzical look. Patrick shrugged and smiled his sympathy then hurried after her.

Yes, definitely imperious. Some things never change.

~.~

Before they had parted yesterday, Patrick had arranged to meet Tim and Tracey at their hotel's beach bar. He hadn't spoken to them since so they were unaware of the extraordinary turn of events.

While they waited for the two med students, Patrick started filling Stella in on his abduction and his escape to Folly.

'Folly?'

'I called the island Redman's Folly, sounds stupid now, because that's what it turned out to be. With the portable shot to fuck, I had no way of getting rescued - until those Yanks started bombing me a year later.'

'But how on earth did you manage? What about food, fresh water? And there were some bad storms this last season. I want to know every detail, Patrick. I am very proud of you for surviving that horrible isolation.'

'It may take a long time to tell you everything.'

She smiled and kissed him.

'Darling, we have the rest of our lives together, so there is no rush.'

'Are we interrupting something?'

It was Tracey. The swelling of her lips had gone down but the bruising on her face had turned to a mottled purple and yellow. She sat down opposite and smiled politely, looked from one to the other, then raised an open hand towards Stella and lifted a quizzical eyebrow at Patrick. Her expression said 'are you going to introduce us'?

Tim took a seat next to her and mimicked her almost exactly. Patrick put his head back, laughed briefly, and blew into the air. How was he going to break this to them?

Before he could start however, Stella added further complications. She leaned over to Tracey.

'Darling, what on earth has happened to your face, did you have an accident?'

Patrick put his head in his hands and shook it. He didn't know whether to laugh or cry.

'Okay,' he said, looking up and taking a deep breath, 'here goes…'

First, he told Tim and Tracey who Stella was, and when they were over their shock, he spent another half hour answering their questions, with Stella filling in her side as they went along. Next, he told Stella about Elías and Manuel turning up at the boat, and the terrifying events that followed.

'But darling, why did you not inform Sir Reginald of this, because, apart from the missing policeman from Pipah, this case can now be closed?'

'I was about to tell him everything when I was in his office, but when he told me you were alive – and when I recovered from the shock – I decided not to. Because I thought he would have got the police involved straight away, and that would have involved endless questioning when I was just desperate to see you.'

'I understand, and I'm glad you did, but we must tell them today.'

'Looks like you can tell 'em now,' Tim said, nodding towards the bar entrance.

There were four of them, and they were not regular cops. Patrick's blood ran cold at the sight of the black-clad men walking purposefully towards him.

The Black Squad

Once again, he felt the fear of having a firearm aimed at him.

'Patrick Redman?'

'Yes?'

'Stand up please'

Patrick stood passively and let one of the squad frisk him. When the body search was finished the officer holstered his sidearm and said to him, 'Are you the owner of the yacht *Spirit of Carriacou*?'

'No he is not,' Stella said, 'I am.'

'And you are?'

'Stella Friedmann.'

'Madam, did you sail into Kingstown with Mr Redman yesterday?'

'No,' Stella said.

'Then our business is not with you, it is with Mr Redman.'

'But this is ridiculous,' Stella said, hot with indignation, 'what is Patrick charged with?'

He ignored her and turned to Patrick.

'Patrick Redman you are charged under the Contraband Act 1979, and the Possession of Illegal Substances Act 1980, namely, the landing a large quantity of cocaine into SVG territorial waters and the landing of said contraband into Kingstown, St Vincent on 7th November 1983.'

Before Patrick realised what was happening someone grabbed his arms from behind and snapped handcuffs on him.

The leader turned to the medical students. 'Tim Spender and Tracey Coldwell?'

'Yes, that's us,' Tim supplied.

He held up two passports. 'I have requisitioned your passports from the hotel manager. You will not be allowed to leave the island until further notice, and will make yourselves available for questioning if it is deemed necessary, is that clear?'

As they started to lead Patrick away, Stella jumped in front of them and tried to bar the way.

'You will take me as well; I want to be with him.'

'Please stand aside, madam, we have no business with you.'

'Then arrest me for obstruction.'

He swept her aside, but she clung onto his arm. 'Arrest me, you fascist pig, arrest me for assault,' she screamed, and swung a bunched fist at the officer.

He easily dodged the blow, but she hung on as they carried on out of the bar. Despite Patrick's pleading for her to go back, that he would be fine, she harried them all the way out to the carpark where a black van stood waiting.

'Please,' she pleaded finally, 'at least tell me where you are taking him?'

From inside the back of the van, with an officer either side of him, Patrick watched through the open side door as the officer turned round to her and spoke kindly but firmly.

'Miss Friedmann, please be calm. Mr Redman will be taken into Police custody and questioned. He will be allowed proper legal representation and of course, as a British subject, the Governor General will be informed of his arrest. He is quite safe, I assure you. Now please return to your friends.'

'I'll be alright, sweetheart,' Patrick called to her, 'this is a cock up. I'm sure it'll be sorted out soon.'

~ Chapter Thirty-Six ~

Ignoring Patrick's advice, Stella looked over the officer's uniform for some clue as to his identity. There was none; he just wore a plain black tunic, black trousers; only the badge on his beret showed who they were: it said SSU in bright silver letters.

'Why do you not dress as policemen?' she said, 'And what is SSU?'

The officer looked at her for a moment, then said, 'I realise this has frightened you, but please rest assured, we mean Mr Redman no harm. My name is Sergeant Purdy, and as you must be aware, I am a member of the Special Services Unit; our function is to clean up the evil of drugs trafficking that is bringing so much violence and calamity to these peaceful islands. I realise we have a certain reputation, and our methods are not always popular - but we normally deal with armed contrabandistas from the mainland. These are dangerous men and it is important for us to protect our anonymity…'

Stella tried to protest against Patrick being associated with such people, but he cut her off.

'…but as a British citizen, Mr Redman will be treated with all due courtesy and respect, and we will hand him over to the regular police just as soon as we have compiled our prima facie case.'

Stella allowed her anger to dissipate a little – the sergeant seemed a reasonable man and came across as genuine.

'Thank you, Sergeant. I assume you have found drugs in my boat?'

The sergeant looked exasperated by her tenacious questioning, but took a deep breath, then seemed to arrive at a decision.

'Look, Miss Friedmann, we are going to take Mr Redman to his boat…'

'My boat,' she corrected.

'Very well your boat, which is currently a crime scene, to confront him with the evidence. I will make an exception in this case and allow you to come along and see it for yourself. Is that fair?'

They would not let her sit in the back, so she spent the short drive smiling encouragement back at Patrick through the wire grill.

A barrier of yellow tape marked POLICE DO NOT ENTER had been erected around the cradle; the presence of three regular police officers who stood guarding it set her a little more at ease.

They removed Patrick's handcuffs to let him climb the ladder up to *Carriacou*'s deck. The sergeant went up first, then Patrick, followed by another SSU officer, and then Stella went up, followed by one of the uniformed police officers. The sergeant led the way down into the saloon and forward to the forepeak. The SSU sergeant invited Stella to come forward to stand with Patrick at the front. 'Do not touch anything,' he warned.

The two sole boards lay on the bunk above. She looked down and let out a gasp. Plastic bags of what appeared to be whitish powder packed the bilge space around the cylindrical log recorder. She looked at Patrick in disbelief. 'Tell me you did not know of this?' she demanded.

Patrick continued to stare down at the terrible cargo. He looked stunned.

'It was the only place I didn't look,' he said dully. After a long moment, he turned to her, 'that is why they came back: not for the boat, but for this lot.'

Suddenly his eyes widened, and he looked down again at the damning bags of coke.

'Look at that...' He moved aside to let the SSU sergeant see what had caught his attention, 'the stuff had to be packed in tight to get it all in, but there are two spaces there, where the bags are missing,' he looked up at the officer, 'did you remove them?'

'No, this is exactly how it was found. One of the boatyard workers discovered it, and two others were with him at the time. The indications are that there has been no disturbance for quite some time. I agree that two bags have been removed after the contraband was placed here, but they were not removed recently. Now if you have...'

'Did you take photographs, forensic examinations?' Patrick said.

'This is all work for the police, Mr Redman. SSU do not have these resources. Now, if you are satisfied we can pass you over to them to examine the evidence we have presented. Come. You too Miss Friedmann.'

Back down on the quay Stella stood outside the cordon and watched as the regular police officers led Patrick away to a police Landrover. At least he was out of the hands of those sinister people in black.

'Ah's so sorry, Captain,' Beeno wailed, 'dem boys lift de boards to service de log yanoo, an one of dem turn out Black Squad grass. He no work for me no more.'

'It is not your fault, Beeno, and it is not Patrick's either. He is not a drugs trafficker, just a victim.'

'Who put dat stuff in der, Captain?'

'It is a long story, Beeno, and I think I should not say too much,' she smiled at him with a confidence she did not feel, 'but if this mess is solved and Patrick is free by the time you have my boat ready for sea, I promise I will tell you everything.'

~.~

The Attorney General's Office was in Granby Street; Stella had been there many times over the past year and knew the man well. He agreed to see her immediately.

'So, Mr Redman killed these two men in Grenada, the men who he claims put the drugs in the vessel,' the

Attorney General said, 'and he freely admits the fact? This complicates matters substantially, I am afraid to say.'

'He was fighting for his life,' Stella pointed out heatedly, 'it was self-defence – there are two reliable witnesses.'

He removed his spectacles and started polishing them with a large handkerchief.

'As I have indicated many times, I cannot interfere with police investigations; I should not even be talking to you now about it, since it is I who will decide whether or not to bring a prosecution.'

He replaced his glasses and looked at her with a kindly expression. 'However, from what you have told me, and if Mr Redman's testimony can be substantiated, then I will probably decline to prosecute and order his release. In the meantime,' he handed her a business card, 'here is a good defence lawyer. His office is nearby – I suggest you go and instruct him immediately, so he can sit in and advise Mr Redman during his interviews.'

~ Chapter Thirty-Seven ~

Patrick lay on his back on the wooden bed board and stared at the bare concrete joists above, ruminating on his sudden change of fortune. The tiny cell smelled musty, with a hint of piss and stale cigarette smoke.

He had now worked out the probable scenario for how and why Elías and Manuel had landed in a Grenadian goal. Ever since his discovery of the boat's movements after his escape to Folly, he had been wondering how they had got the drugs off the boat and recognised the unlikelihood of them managing to smuggle such a large haul ashore from where they had grounded the boat. It had been stacked in the saloon, and it hadn't occurred to him they would stow it in the forward bilge.

However, they had, and had probably intended to sell it ashore in smaller quantities. It made sense now, in hindsight. They must have been caught with that first consignment, and then kept quiet about the rest of it, and the boat.

He sat up when he heard footsteps stop outside the door. A key turned in the lock and the door swung outwards.

'Visitor for you.'

The officer led Patrick along the corridor to a shabby interview room, sparsely furnished, just a tubular table and four chairs. He sat down facing the door.

A man entered.

'Good afternoon Mr Redman, my name is Gordon Howard. I have been instructed by Stella Friedmann to act on your behalf.'

Howard was a tall black man about Patrick's age, neat, close-cropped hair, gold-rimmed glasses, white open-neck shirt and grey chinos. He took the seat next to Patrick and opened a leather briefcase, took out a pad of foolscap and snapped the case closed.

'Miss Friedmann has filled me in on the main points, but I am going to need the full story from you.'

'How long have you got?' Patrick said.

'I'm afraid we are constrained for time; the police are waiting to interview you and they have given me an hour. So for now, let us just deal with how seventy-five kilos of high quality cocaine happened to be on your boat when you sailed into Kingstown.'

~.~

When Patrick had finished, the lawyer continued writing for a considerable time, every so often sucking the top of his pen and looking sideways in thought, then scribbling away once more as he answered his own question. He finally looked up and smiled somewhat ruefully.

'It is a plausible and convincing account; there is no question of that. But most of the possible corroboration we have so far is based on your own testimony, i.e. what you told others…'

'But what about…'

Howard stopped him with a raised hand.

'…with the following exceptions:' he counted the exceptions off on his fingers. 'One, Miss Friedmann was evidently shot, and we have her testimony of events leading up to that, including the presence of the drugs at the house of the American couple. Two, the two medical students who saw the two alleged perpetrators return to the vessel and they witnessed the altercation that led to their demise. Three, the boat owner, Hayward, who saw your boat being driven away from Pipah island by someone other than yourself, and we have an outline description of that person.

'But Hayward is quite an elusive fellow and we may have trouble locating him…'

'Stella says he's due back here next week.' Patrick interjected.

'That is good. And finally, the Captain of the American destroyer who rescued you more than one year later, though this adds very little of relevance. The most important testimony would be the confessions of the perpetrators, and they are both dead.'

'Except McCredy,' Patrick said.

'Except McCredy,' the lawyer agreed, 'but he has disappeared. Even if he is still in the Caribbean, he may be impossible to find if he does not want to be found. Against that the police have one tangible and incontrovertible fact, the drugs found in a vessel that you sailed into Kingstown.' He paused here to let Patrick absorb what he had heard.

'Apart from your own version of events,' he continued, 'there is one other, more sinister explanation that could fit all…'

At that moment, the door swung open and two men entered both wearing casual clothes. A young female constable followed them in carrying a chair and a notebook.

Howard leaned over and whispered in Patrick's ear. 'If I advise you not to answer a question then it will be for a good reason, please follow my advice.'

'I am Chief Inspector Stuart of the Serious Crimes Department, and this is my colleague Sergeant Ouelette. Constable Mara will take notes of proceedings.'

After advising Patrick he was under arrest and reciting a formal caution, the Chief Inspector went on to repeat the charges against him. He then placed two colour photographs in front of Patrick. One was of the interior of *Carriacou*, taken from the saloon facing forward. Patrick picked up the second one – it was still damp and flimsy from recent processing. It was a close-up of the open bilge and the incriminating contents packed inside.

'They showed me the real thing this morning,' Patrick said.

'But this was not the first time you have seen this shipment, Mr Redman. Do not expect us to believe that you were unaware of this substantial cargo packed in your vessel's bows.'

'Look, I have seen that stuff before, but then it was stacked on the saloon bench, and that was a year ago for heaven's sake. When I found the boat abandoned last week I naturally assumed it had all been taken ashore.'

The two officers exchanged a glance, and then the sergeant said, 'I have this morning interviewed Mr Spender and Miss Coldwell…'

'You haven't arrested them?' Patrick said, 'they had nothing to do with this, they're just students who came with me to get away from the war in Grenada.'

'They are not under arrest,' the sergeant assured him, 'I went to see them at their hotel. We will however retain their passports pending our investigations. After hearing what they had to say I am sure Mr Howard will agree it is in your interests they remain here.'

Howard nodded.

'So, Mr Redman,' said the Chief Inspector, 'how do you account for the cocaine found in your yacht? And I should remind you, you are under caution.'

They listened to his explanation in attentive silence, the only other sound, the rapid scribbling of shorthand from the uniformed woman at the end of the table.

Once, an officer at the door interrupted his flow.

'Stella Friedmann is here, Sir.'

'Stella is here?' Patrick said, 'can I see her?'

'Miss Friedmann is here voluntarily – she has agreed to make a statement,' said the Chief Inspector, 'there may be an opportunity for her to visit you later.' He twisted round to the door, 'Show her into Three, Constable.'

The sergeant said, 'Carry on with your account Mr Redman.'

~ Chapter Thirty-Eight ~

When Stella had finished speaking the Chief Inspector leaned back in his chair and stared thoughtfully at the ceiling for a few moments, then said to her, 'In your original statement of last year you say Police Sergeant McCredy was actually present when you were shot?'

'He was there.' she said exasperatedly. 'Of course he was there. He said he was assisting those... those two... those two *arschlöcher* to recover their property. I saw the big one raising the gun, and the sergeant just standing there, watching.'

She shook her head at the recollection. 'That is the last thing I remember, Chief Inspector - until I awoke here at the hospital.'

'And you did not report this to the police here at the time; it took another two months for you to bring it to our attention. Why was that?'

That was a good question, and she realised she did not have an adequate answer. In those first few bewildering days, she had considered approaching the police, and indeed, Adhra and Thomas had urged her to do so. But...

'I had already told the doctor my injury was from an accident on the boat. I do not know why I said that at the time, but I think at the back of my mind, I did not want to become delayed by bureaucracy, and I suppose I was worried about accusing one of their fellow... one of your fellow police officers – one never knows how deep these things go – do you understand what I mean?'

'You had no reason to think this way, Miss Friedmann – this is not Grenada. I assure you we here in St Vincent are a respectable force...' he paused and gave a cough.

If it was possible for a black face to turn red with embarrassment, Stella was sure she would have seen his do so. Even his sergeant looked uncomfortable.

'…at least the regular force is clean,' he finished, 'I cannot speak for everyone.'

'So you put your faith in this Mr Hayward,' the Chief Inspector continued, keen to move on, 'because you distrusted the Police.'

'Hayward,' Stella said, 'I do not know whether this is a first name or his last; he just calls himself Hayward.'

'Martin Hayward,' the sergeant said. He turned to his boss, 'I know him, Sir. His boat *Jupiter* is a regular visitor here.'

The Chief Inspector looked enigmatically at his sergeant for a moment, and then turned back to Stella with a quizzical eyebrow that looked almost comic.

Stifling an involuntary grin she said, 'That was part of it, as I have said. But also, I was in a panic to find Patrick who was out there somewhere in my boat, kidnapped by murderers. I had been in a coma for a week and it was most likely they were by then in open sea, international waters, so I thought it pointless to be held up here when I could be out there trying to find him. Eventually I knew I should report the whole thing to you here, and to the Governor General, especially because I had already told the people in Puerto Rico. After two months of searching I wanted everyone to know what happened on Pipah. I knew Patrick was still alive somewhere and I wanted him found.'

'Just one more question that has been puzzling me, Miss Friedmann, how did you know that your boat was heading for Puerto Rico?'

She did not reply immediately. She had not mentioned the trip to Pipah, and their confrontation with McCredy. Now she knew she had no choice.

So finally, she filled in the missing details. All except those of exactly how Hayward had forced McCredy's confession. She left that part to their imagination and refused to elaborate.

Just as she was finishing a sergeant came to the door and summoned the Chief Inspector, who returned ten minutes later wearing a worried frown.

'We have a report from the SSU that a Coastguard marine patrol intercepted your boat just a few miles west of here the day after you claim to have been shot.

'Mr Redman was at the helm and appeared to be sailing alone. When challenged, he reported he was on route to the Dominican Republic. Unfortunately Mr Redman failed to mention this in his statement.'

Stella was cautioned pending further enquiries but allowed to leave on condition she remained on the island. They did not permit her a visit with Patrick.

She drove to Tim and Tracey's hotel to update them on events. While she waited for them, she used the lobby telephone to make an international call, dialling the number from a card in her purse.

When she had finished she made another call, to Thomas and Adhra's number. She wanted to question Thomas.

'He is out on a dive with five students,' Adhra said, 'I expect he will return home around six. What is the matter, Stella, you sound stressed.'

Stella looked at her watch. It was four thirty.

'I need to know where Hayward is at this moment, and whether he can be reached.'

She told her what had happened this morning and subsequently.

'That poor boy!' Adhra said. 'Hasn't he been through enough? How do you think Hayward can help?'

'They do not believe me: that I was shot, because I did not report it straight away. *Verdammt*, I should have listened to you. Now I think they suspect me as well, that Patrick and I have been involved in the smuggling.'

After a moments silence, Adhra said, 'And Hayward will at least be able to testify that you were shot, yes I see. I can try him on the VHF, but you know what he is like – he rarely…'

Someone reached from behind, snatched the phone, and hung it up.

'Hey, what are you doing,' Stella shouted indignantly.

Before she had the chance to turn round, she felt her arms pulled roughly behind her back and handcuffs ratcheted tightly round both wrists.

~ Chapter Thirty-Nine ~

Patrick was back in the interview room, but this time the two coppers were not as friendly, nor as polite. The sergeant leaned on the wall by the door, staring down at him with mild hostility.

'Why did you not include this incident in your statement,' the Chief Inspector said, almost shouting as he paced the room, 'did you think we would not discover the connection?'

'I told you, it completely slipped my mind. It was a long time ago, and a lot has happened since. It just slipped my mind, why the big deal?'

The Chief Inspector leaned both hands on the table and glared at him.

'You know what I think, Patrick?'

'Go on, surprise me.'

Far from being intimidated, Patrick tried to keep the amusement from showing on his face. He wondered if they got The Sweeney on television here.

'I think you are lying. I do not think these two men were ever on Pipah. Do you know why I think that?'

'Don't be fucking ridiculous, what planet are you on?'

He felt Howard's hand on his shoulder, urging calm, and shrugged it off angrily.

Unmoved by Patrick's outburst the Chief Inspector went on, 'Because, as a result of our enquiries to Grenada we have just now received a fax from the police in St Georges,' he held up two printed sheets, 'their investigation of the double murder on Pipah concluded that the culprits were… Patrick Redman and Stella Friedmann.'

Howard held out a hand to him

'Let me see those please, Chief Inspector.'

While Howard studied the faxed report with an increasingly worried frown, the Chief Inspector continued, 'The report states, that the American couple discovered your cocaine smuggling operation, and you silenced them by cold blooded murder before sailing off to deliver your nasty cargo. Of course, they had no idea of your destination, but now we do know – it was Dominican Republic, as you told the Coastguard.'

'As I said, ridiculous, and how could Stella have been with me if she was in a coma in hospital here?'

'Patrick,' Howard said, looking up from his reading, 'I advise you to say no more for the time being.' and went back to reading the report.

The Chief Inspector, who seemed to be enjoying his role as Bad Cop, continued regardless of Howard's injunction: 'As you will see from the report, her statement has proved a blatant fabrication. There was no evidence of her having been shot, at least not in the house of the Americans. From all the hearsay, she was discovered in the woods quite a distance from the house, and I have no doubt this Hayward will confirm so in due course. I can only conclude that she was injured in some way during your return to your vessel, and you left her and made your escape alone. Is that what happened, Patrick?'

Patrick wanted desperately to rebut his vile suggestions, but Howard's raised finger warned him off.

'I also have obtained Miss Friedmann's medical report from the hospital, and it stated that she was treated for a head wound, sustained - she claimed at the time - not by a gunshot, but in a boating accident.'

'Chief Inspector,' Howard said, 'I would like to consult with my client in private.'

The two police officers exchanged glances.

'Very well, Mr Howard, fifteen minutes.'

He spun on his heel and they both left the room.

Patrick finished reading the faxed report and looked at the signature at the bottom.

Sherwin McCredy.

'Forgive me Patrick, but you don't seem very shocked by all this.'

'No, I'm not,' Patrick said, 'That was their plan, do you see? That was what Elías told me McCredy would put in his report, except for the bit about Stella – she was supposed to have been killed by Frank when we bungled a burglary of his house.

'It was to have been my motive for killing them – revenge for Stella. But when Stella disappeared, he had to modify it. The only surprising thing is that anyone still gave it credence when he did a bunk straight after.'

'Why did you tell the Coastguard you were bound for DR?' Howard said.

'Because that's what Elías told me to say – he was in the saloon with a gun pointed at me.'

'But why DR?'

'He said it was because it would be less suspicious than Puerto Rico, and he knew it was in the general direction we were heading. The chart was right there next to him.'

Howard wrote on his pad for a few minutes then looked up.

'Patrick, you might be thinking that the police version of events is so blatantly in error that it will not lead to a conviction, but I urge you to take it seriously, very seriously indeed. They have all the evidence, hard evidence, and I am afraid to say you have very little. The fact of McCredy's disappearance does not detract from the validity of his report. There was a revolution going on, all the islands down there in turmoil. When the paramilitaries started stalking the islands looking for opponents many people left their homes to go somewhere safer. As far as the authorities in St Georges were concerned, McCredy could have fled with them.'

Patrick was starting to get it, and he felt his earlier confidence starting to slip.

'What about when Elías and Manuel came back to the boat in Grenada? Tim and Tracey saw them; Tracey was beaten up for fucks sake, they were going to kill her.'

'But don't you see, Patrick, that doesn't link them to the events of a year earlier, and none of you were aware at the time that they came back for the cocaine.'

'No, well I didn't know it was still on the boat…'

'So the only evidence they can give is hearsay – what you told them afterwards. The police will say you lied to them to support your story, and that you killed those men so they couldn't deny the role you wanted for them.'

Patrick clapped his hands to the back of his head and bent forward.

'Jesus, this just gets worse and worse.'

He sat up abruptly.

'How did the boat get to Grenada when I was stuck on an island five hundred miles away for a whole year? The US Navy will back me up on that.'

'That is an inconsistency, I grant you, but it may not be enough. I will need to take specialist advice, but I suspect getting affidavits from the US Navy might not be easy.'

'So they could say I made the whole thing up, even my year on Folly?'

'Without any supporting evidence, Patrick, I am afraid we must face that possibility.'

Silence fell on them both. Howard frowned down at his notes.

'But don't give up;' he said brightly, 'I am sure we will find a way forward. I will ask the Governor General and the British High Commission in Barbados to help - with the US Navy I mean.'

'Supposing this goes to trial, and Stella and I get convicted, what could happen to us?'

Howard chewed his bottom lip, and for the first time since they had met, didn't meet Patrick's eyes.

'Let us take it one step at a time, Patrick. That scenario is not certain, and it is a long way down the line.'

'Tell me Gordon.' Patrick hissed.

Howard's smart city businessman persona abruptly fell away, and he reverted to island mannerisms - his eyes grew long and he spoke in gentle tones, kindly and with great empathy.

'If Stella is found guilty of drug trafficking and accessory to murder she will face between twenty and forty years in prison.'

'*Jesus!* And me?'

'Patrick, I know what you are thinking, but don't be afraid. Firstly, since Independence four years ago there have only been a couple of executions in SVG. The criteria set by the Constitution are very strict and the Privy Council in London must ratify a death sentence. Secondly, I don't believe that our Government would allow the death penalty for anyone from a country where it is abolished, though this has never been tested. I am certain you would both get custodial sentences, and I think that you could serve them in your respective countries.'

'So you think I'll get life?'

'If found guilty, yes, but we must not think like this. You are not guilty, Patrick, and we will prove it before it even comes to court… somehow.'

~ Chapter Forty ~

When she had been cautioned again and charged, Stella was led into the interview room, where to her surprise, waited Patrick and the lawyer, Mr Howard.

'Please sit down Miss Friedmann,' the Chief Inspector said.

She sat next to Patrick and gave him a quick hug.

'I have taken the unusual step of bringing you both together here because these are unusual circumstances for us. The normal procedure now would be to ferry you both to Barbados, as we have no detention facilities here.

'But the Attorney General has authorised your release, on Police Bail of ten thousand Dollars each, which Mr Dennie has agreed to stand. However, you must surrender your passports and remain at all times within the confines of Mr Dennie's home at Gladstone Bay.

'I must warn you both, should either of you be found outside the confines of Mr Dennie's property at any time, for any reason, you will both be taken back into custody to await the outcome of our investigations, at Glendairy Prison on Barbados. Is that clear?'

Patrick and Stella nodded in unison and tried to keep appropriately solemn. Despite the shocking events of the day – had it really all happened in one day? - being together again, and then told they were being released, had suddenly boosted both their morale and their innate sense of fun, so it wasn't easy to remain tight-lipped and serious.

'Mr Howard, I will leave you to stress to your clients the importance of following the rules, and I'm sure you can fill them in on the conditions they can expect at Glendairy. When you are ready come to the front lobby and complete the Conditions of Bail forms, then you may go.'

~.~

'I'm absolutely gobsmacked!' Patrick said, grinning like a coal scuttle.

Stella's eyes sparkled happily; like Patrick, she had pushed to the back of her mind the dreadful difficulties ahead to enjoy this oasis of good fortune.

'This is Sir Reginald's doing, I just know it. He is such a sweet man.'

'The Chief Inspector is right about Glendairy,' said Howard, cutting into her euphoria, 'you really don't want to be sent there.'

Howard gave them a lift down to Tim and Tracey's hotel where she had left Thomas' car, and then bade them goodnight, promising to drive over to Gladstone Bay in the morning to start planning their strategy.

The two students were out on the swimming pool patio and rushed over when they caught Stella's wave. They ordered drinks then found a table in a quiet alcove where Patrick filled in the tumultuous day's events.

'You must both be exhausted,' Tracey said.

'And scared.' Tim added, 'I know I would be. So what happens next?'

'Because whatever it is,' chirped Tracey, 'we want to help.'

'We can't go anywhere anyway,' Tim said, 'we might as well make ourselves useful.'

Stella laughed. They were like a double act. 'Let me go and call Adhra to check she is happy for you to come and stay. Then you can check out of this expensive place.'

'Does she have room?' asked Tracey.

'Darling, her house positively sprouts rooms,' Stella assured her, 'it is like the Doge's Palace.'

She took her drink with her out to the lobby.

'Maybe you could tell us a little about Thomas and Adhra,' Tim said to Patrick, 'I mean if we're going to stay there.'

'Tim! That's so rude!' said Tracey, 'I'm sorry Patrick. You just wouldn't believe he comes from such a nice family.'

Patrick laughed, 'It's alright, Tracey, I'll tell you some of it anyway. Stella and Thomas go back a long way, but the connection started even further back, around twenty years ago, when a young Swiss teenager called Niklas used to come here on sailing and diving holidays. Niklas learned to dive at Thomas' dive shack, which was in those days just a small live-in hut on the beach, not far from where his school is now.

'When Niklas left university he went to work in the family business, a firm of architects, but he hated it and sold his shares back to his Dad. He used the money to build the boat we came here on.'

'Hey, are you making this up?' Tim said.

'Ignore him,' said Tracey, 'go on, Patrick, I'm fascinated.'

'It gets better,' Patrick laughed, 'and I promise, Tim, every word is true. He had *Spirit of Carriacou* built in Malta and always intended to sail her to the island he'd named her after, the place the Yanks wouldn't let us land at day before yesterday. On the way he met Stella - Santorini, I think - and she crewed up with him. Anyway, when they eventually got to the Caribbean they decided after a year to carry on through the Panama and across the Pacific.'

He saw Stella making her way back, then changing her mind and going towards the bar.

'Anyway, cut a long story short, they eventually got to East Africa and Niklas decided he'd like to open a dive shack, like his old mate Thomas, but in Mombasa. He wrote to Thomas and asked him to join him in his new venture, which Thomas did. Stella started up a sail charter business with *Carriacou*, and business boomed. Eventually they had a string of holiday chalets as well. Thomas met Adhra and all was going swimmingly for everyone. Then it all went to hell in a handcart, and I'll tell you that story another time.'

'What story?' Stella said, sitting down.

'I was just telling them about Thomas and Adhra.'

She turned to the students: 'Adhra said she is delighted for you to come and stay, she is looking forward to meeting you.'

She turned to Patrick, 'Thomas has gone out somewhere to find out where Hayward has gone,' she chuckled, 'I think he is touring the Founts of all Knowledge.'

Patrick gave her a puzzled frown, 'Sorry?'

'That is what he calls the fishermen's rum shacks, the Founts of all Knowledge.'

'Oh, the Font of all Knowledge - I get it,' he beamed hugely then leaned over and kissed her.

'You see?' she said to Tracey, 'I teach him everything he knows, and he pays me back by patronising me. Do not let Tim treat you this way.'

'Oh, Tim and I are not an item,' Tracey said hurriedly, 'I should have told you earlier: we'll need separate sleeping arrangements.'

~ Chapter Forty-One ~

They arrived late at the house, but Thomas had not yet returned so Adhra had waited so they could all eat together.

'The dive class went fishing today,' she told the two students, 'so we have lobster for dinner, are you both alright with that?'

They both nodded enthusiastically, but Stella had noticed Patrick's face take on a sour look as he walked through to the Patio with his drink.

'I think Patrick is not so keen on the lobster,' she told Adhra when they alone, 'it reminds him too much of...'

Adhra's hand flew to her mouth, 'Of course, I am so stupid! ...I have a fresh chicken?'

'I am sure he will be delighted with anything that is not fish, or iguana.'

'There was a telephone call for you earlier this evening: Tony Viteri?'

'*Ah ja*, I was expecting this,' Stella said, 'did he leave a message?'

'Only that he would call back later.'

Just then, the front door opened, and Thomas came through to the kitchen. Adhra wrinkled up her nose after he kissed her, 'Pah! Rum and weed,' she said, wiping her hands on her apron, 'horrible. Go and wash your mouth at once – we have guests.'

He grinned sheepishly at Stella and turned back to his wife.

'Ah, woman, you got no soul, yanoo,' he said, shaking his head and walking unsteadily to the bathroom.

Thomas seemed to have sobered up by the time Stella and Patrick had filled them in on the day's events. They all sat out on the patio, where a thin breeze fanned in from the bay providing a little relief after the muggy heat of the day.

A necklace of bright lights marked the curve of the bay and faint voices drifted across the water, late night merrymakers just getting festivities under way.

'What did you find out, Thomas?' Stella said.

'De rumour mill say Hayward gone up to Cuba, but he due back next week, just as he told you, Boss.'

Yes, she thought, that makes sense. Hayward had mentioned several times he was going to take Juanita sailing once more before she went off to school in England.

'Thanks for posting our bail, Thomas,' Patrick said.

'My, friend,' he said, 'I tink after all we been tru together, you done need tank me for anyting, you know dat,' he waved a hand around the room, 'all dis, an' me business down der, is from de pure kind hearts of you an' Miss Stella, yanoo.'

Before Patrick could protest, Stella jumped in.

'Thomas, please understand about the money. I have told you before, the true reason for the payment was compensation for the way they treated us – and perhaps a bribe to keep us quiet. Half of it was yours by right.'

'Yes, Boss, I know dis, but…'

Stella held up a hand, 'Please, Thomas, no more about this.'

Taking Stella's cue Patrick altered the course of conversation.

'You found a great site to build your house; I'm surprised this land wasn't snapped up by some hotel chain. How did you get your hands on it?'

'It belong me family,' Thomas said, 'used be planta-*shan* estate in slave times, yanoo. When emancipa-*shan* came dis land was given to de slaves dat laboured here.'

He suddenly grinned brightly, 'I guess dat was compensa-*shan* too, eh?

'Dennie was de name of de planta-*shan* owner, yanoo,' he said, warming to his theme, 'so now we Dennie's all one big extended family, even if we not really all related by birt'. De family own all dis properties from de beach all de way back up de hill behind we. Some is houses where we live, some is hired out for vaca-*shan* homes, some permi-*nantly* to white folk who come here to retire, yanoo.'

Inside the house, the telephone rang, and Stella went to take it. As expected, it was Tony Viteri. She had not spoken to him for several months, and she had assumed by now he would have lost interest in the case, but she had promised to call him if there were ever any developments.

'Wow,' Tony said, when she had finished talking, 'you got your boat and your guy back. You say he took out Acosta and Figueroa?'

'I would not put it quite like that Tony, Patrick is not an assassin. He was lucky not to be killed himself.'

'No, sorry,' he said, and then, after a moment's hesitation, 'and the SSU have the cocaine now?'

'I do not know Tony, and I do not give a damn about these drugs. Because of this fucking cocaine Patrick and I are in trouble and we need to collect the evidence which proves we are telling the truth. Can you help us to get a… *Gott, was heißt es noch mal? Einen Versicherung… oh ja*, an affidavit from the Captain of this US warship?'

'An affidavit saying what exactly?'

'To testify that they have picked up Patrick from the island, that he could not have taken the boat to Grenada…'

'Stella, listen carefully. In order to get an affidavit from that Captain you will have to approach the US State Department, who will then eventually ask the Pentagon. The Pentagon will undoubtedly prevaricate until hostilities in Grenada are over, and even then, your petition will be very low on their list of priorities. Then there is the US Navy, older than *The Constitution*, semi-autonomous, a law unto itself, and protective of its personnel like no other service on Earth. It could take months I'm afraid, even years.'

Stella took the telephone from her ear and stared at it in tight-lipped frustration. She tried again. 'But, Tony, you have connections with the Navy, surely you could find an easier way through this... this bureaucracy?'

'Maybe, Stella, I'll try, but don't pin your hopes on it.'

'Thank you, I would be very grateful. But also I need you to tell the Police here that you... your administration, I mean, know of these two men, and you were expecting to arrest them with the shipment in Puerto Rico - because at the moment we have no evidence that they ever existed.'

'What about your friend, Hayward?' Viteri said, 'didn't he say he saw them driving the boat away from Pipah?'

'Yes, he saw one of them, but that is so little, Tony. I am hoping Hayward still has the written confession he took from McCredy, but we will not know until he returns...'

'Written confession?' Viteri interrupted, 'Hayward got a written confession?'

She realised she had never mentioned to Tony about the form of coercion they had used on McCredy. It had not seemed relevant when her only concern was to find Patrick.

'It was only to hold McCredy to his promise about his enquiry report – Hayward gave his word that it would be destroyed when it was all over. But it has never ended, you see, so I think perhaps Hayward still has it. If so it will prove our innocence.'

...

'Tony... are you still there?'

'Yeah, sure, I'm still here. So where is Hayward now, Stella?'

'We think he has been to Cuba to pick up his daughter, you remember Juanita? We expect him back in Vincy sometime next week. You will come here and testify for us, Tony?'

'I'll need to do it outside of work, but yeah, I'll take a few days off and come right down, but Stella, please don't tell anyone there I'm coming, especially the local cops, okay?'

'Alright,' said Stella, a little uncertainly, 'if that is what you want, but you will need to let them know you are here when you give them your evidence, *nicht var*?'

'It's complicated, leave it with me, Stella, I'll see you in a couple of days, meanwhile, give me your address down there.'

~ Chapter Forty-Two ~

Over the weekend, Stella took advantage of their house arrest to bring Patrick up to date on all the happenings of the past year. She painted him a verbal picture of the eccentric Hayward, his equally eccentric boat, *Jupiter*, and young Juanita, a girl wise and competent beyond her years.

She told him how Special Agent Viteri had supported her in those first weeks in Puerto Rico; updating her regularly on the progress of the US Coastguard planes that were searching the vast swathe of open sea to the southwest to try to locate *Carriacou*. Eventually though, he had given her the frustrating news that the search had been called off and she should assume the worst.

'They tell Tony I should go home and try to get over it, can you believe this? As if I could ever give up hope? Thomas had to fly home to take care of business, and I came with him. That was when I told the Police about what happened on Pipah. Afterwards I flew back, and in January I sailed to Cuba with Hayward to take Juanita home.

'Afterwards we make a brush to the south and came back here to Vincy. Then we check the islands to the north, as far as Anguilla, but in June there was a hurricane warning, so we returned here. I think by August even I was starting to doubt you were still alive, but I kept trying new strategies.'

She gave a sudden burst of laughter, 'I think I drove the people in Government House and the High Commission in Barbados crazy with my obsession. Everyone was extremely sympathetic, but really there was nothing anyone could do.'

'Thanks for not giving up on me,' Patrick said, 'I thought you were… you know. I kept seeing you dropping to the floor, and laying in that spreading pool of … I never dreamt for one moment...'

'We even sailed back down to Pipah,' Stella continued, 'but McCredy was gone. His police house was cleared out.

'We discussed going to the police in St Georges, but Lazy Lobster Kenny said it was too dangerous, with the revolution and all the shootings – he told us that Mr Bishop and his ministers had been put to death in Fort George. It was so tragic, those poor people…'

~.~

Monday morning arrived with no sign of Tony Viteri. Tim and Tracey had left early to spend the day on the beach, and Thomas was down at his shack taking his dive class for classroom teaching. Stella and Patrick spent the morning on the patio going over their options for proving their innocence while Adhra fussed over them with drinks and snacks.

Later that afternoon Thomas came running up to the house. '*Jupiter*, she come just now,' he said, pointing excitedly across the bay.

Adhra came onto the patio with a tray of coffee cups and together they watched the approaching ketch, her brown sails gliding above the palm trees towards the bay's entrance, hull still obscured behind the headland.

'*Fuck!*' Patrick cried, startling everyone. He clapped both hands on his shaved scalp and stared round at Stella. 'I've seen those sails. I tried to light the beacon, but my torch went out, and by then she was hull down and going away.'

Stella felt her stomach lurch. 'When was this?' she said.

'Not sure exactly, maybe ten days or so after my escape to Folly… *Was that you?*'

'My Gott, Patrick, I had forgotten about that. I was just handing the watch over to Juanita. We saw a tiny speck on the horizon and then it was gone. It was early, just after sunrise?'

Patrick nodded, mouth open in dumb amazement.

She felt as shocked as he obviously was.

'I thought at first it was the tip of a mast - that sea was so empty I hope for a second it is *Carriacou*, but then I look at the chart and it is marked as obstruction. I should have gone to check it out, what a fool I was.'

'You weren't to know I'd been marooned on the proverbial desert island.' he offered gently. 'But hey, just think, I was a whisker from getting rescued, and by you - how improbable would that have been?'

By the time *Jupiter* emerged from behind the land, the main gaff was down with its sail secured. She turned towards the anchorage with a jibe, and then the remaining headsail dropped as well.

Stella recognised the stocky figure of Hayward gathering up the sail. The gentle breeze now coaxed the heavy boat sedately forward under mizzen alone, the matchstick form of Juanita hovering over the tiller while Hayward waddled forward to prepare the anchor.

There was no finesse about the anchoring manoeuvre; Juanita simple hauled in the mizzen to power it down and Hayward slipped the big Bruce anchor with no brake, so the chain rattled noisily in the hawse. Finally, the boat came to an abrupt stop and then slewed round to point to windward.

'Not pretty, but effective,' remarked Patrick.

When they saw Hayward launch his dingy over the side and climb into it, Thomas left to drive down to the jetty to collect him.

'He reminds me of a Teddy Bear.' Patrick said, tracking the old sailor's progress to shore through a pair of binoculars. He swung the glasses back to the boat where Juanita was straddling the bowsprit, rigging a snubber on the anchor cable. 'Is he leaving that slip of a girl on the boat all alone?'

Stella almost guffawed into her coffee.

'Juanita has been sailing with her father for most of her life – *Jupiter* is her second home. You will not think she is such a slip when you meet her, Patrick, she is an extraordinary child.'

'Anyhow,' chipped in Adhra, 'the girl is kind of unofficial here: she has no visa, so she cannot book in.'

Patrick swung the glasses back to the old man, who was now tying up at the jetty astern of a smart-looking motor yacht. 'Hmm, that wasn't there yesterday,' he murmured, examining the vessel. '*Kilindini*. Road Town.' The British Virgin Islands Red Ensign fluttered at its staff. 'Long way from home for a private stinkpot,' he remarked.

Half an hour later they heard the front door open and everyone went through to the hall to greet the old mariner.

Thomas was at the door ushering Hayward ahead of him when two figures appeared behind them and pushed both men through the doorway.

'Hands on heads, everyone, and don't move!' American accent; a big bruiser of a man with an automatic pistol held two-handed at arm's length.

Stella thought he looked familiar, but right now her brain was too stunned to deal with it. His companion came around him and pointed his gun at Thomas's head, snatched the car keys from his raised hand and threw them out of the open door to someone out of sight, then slammed the door shut.

Stella's shock turned to horrified bewilderment as she immediately recognised the second man. '*Was zur Hölle?*' she gasped, 'Tony! What are you doing?'

'Collecting my retirement pension,' DEA Special Agent Viteri answered reasonably, 'now please everyone do as my friend here says and no one needs to die today.'

~ Chapter Forty-Three ~

'Tony, I do not understand...' Stella said.

'Understand this,' Viteri snarled, 'I'm with the bad guys, okay? Now shut the fuck up.'

More astonished by this sudden change of personality than cowed by his vitriol, Stella fell silent, casting her memory back over her previous encounters with this man, and trying to work out why she had placed so much trust in him. She had now remembered who the other man was: George something, Tony's work colleague. She had met him on a couple of occasions when Tony had come to update her on progress.

She remembered Tony telling her George owned a motor yacht that they used to take out for fishing trips.

Only Hayward seemed calm and indifferent to the danger confronting them.

'Always thought there was something fucking fishy about you, Viteri,' he said, looking him keenly in the eye, 'never fucking liked you, you smug cunt, never fucking trusted you neither. Only tolerated you 'cos my friend here needed your help,' he turned to Stella, 'some fucking help, eh?'

'Shut your fucking mouth you crazy old fool,' Viteri said, 'you should know that you're the reason we're here, and if you play ball these good folks might just get outa here alive.'

Hayward looked for a moment as if he was going to give him another stream of invective, but then closed his mouth and just glared at the agent. Stella admired the old man's defiance but now found she missed the spontaneous belly laughs.

Viteri turned to Patrick and sneered, 'I assume...'

'Who do you think you are?' Adhra interrupted, bristling with indignation. Indifferent to the weapons they held she took a step towards the two men, her face distorted with anger, 'Coming bursting in here like this? Get out of my house at…'

But she didn't get chance to finish: Viteri swung a swift backhander, a violent blow that caught her squarely on the side of her face and sent her sprawling to the floor.

Thomas' response was immediate and instinctive: snarling with outrage, he charged at Viteri and made a grab for the gun, almost wresting it from his hand before the other man's pistol made sickening contact with his forehead, felling him to the floor.

Before Patrick could stop her, Stella was down by Thomas' side. However, when Viteri took a step towards her Patrick glared furiously at him.

'Touch her and you're dead, and trust me on this you bastard, I don't give a monkey's fuck if you shoot me, I'll just keep on coming.'

The vehemence in Patrick's reckless challenge must have struck home, because Viteri backed off.

'Everyone just calm down.' he said with forced composure, face pale with adrenalin rush. The unexpected show of resistance had shaken him. 'Co-operate with us and no one else needs to get hurt.'

Despite her anguish, Stella felt a surge of pride in Patrick's show of bravado. She kept her face averted downwards to hide her grin as she checked Thomas' over, and then examined the swelling rising on his forehead.

'Who the fuck are you?'

She looked up to see Hayward staring at Patrick, as close to perplexity as Stella had ever seen him.

Before Patrick could respond, Viteri motioned to him. 'Help her to pick him up, and then I want everyone into the house. Our business won't take long.'

'What is your business, exactly?' Patrick said with the defiant edge still in his voice and demeanour.

Hayward looked at Stella quizzically and jerked a thumb at Patrick. 'Who the fuck is this?'

Patrick once more opened his mouth to enlighten him, but...

'You heard the man, PICK HIM UP,' the big American cut in, clearly exasperated by the dissent they were encountering, 'and no more fuckin' questions, *comprende*?'

With Hayward's help, Adhra had now regained her feet and stood leaning with her back to the wall, staring listlessly at her husband, who was coming round as Stella and Patrick helped him to his feet. The two men hustled everyone into the lounge, where Viteri attended them in turn, binding their wrists behind them with cable ties, while the big one covered them with his gun. When he had them all trussed tightly he ordered them all to sit on the floor in a line facing the entrance hall.

Stella was scarcely aware of the ties chafing her wrists; such was her confusion at her erstwhile friend's sudden betrayal. She felt sick with revulsion, and stupid for having been so thoroughly deceived.

'You Patrick are the cause of all this,' Viteri said, 'for all these months...'

'Fucking hell!' said Hayward, still seemingly oblivious to their dire situation, 'so you're the long-lost Patrick. Where have you been hiding for the past year? You've been driving this woman of yours...'

'Shut the fuck up, old man' Viteri snarled, and then turned back to Patrick, 'I thought those two numbskulls had killed you and made off with our shipment.'

'*Your* shipment?' Stella said, 'they were bringing it to you?'

Viteri ignored her and continued, 'But it wasn't like that, was it? When your girlfriend here told me what really happened I figured they had intended to complete the delivery all along – why else would they have been headed for PR?

'But you, Patrick, fucked up the boat and left them helpless. Once they got it back under control they were so late and so far away, it was a no brainer to make off with it, 'cos the Big Guy doesn't tolerate mistakes.'

'I haven't met him yet and like him already.' Hayward said, beaming at Patrick.

Viteri turned to Stella and smiled evilly. 'Yeah, you guessed it. See, me and George here have been doing a little moonlighting. The deal was, we would help the Syndicate land three shipments on PR and keep our DEA boys off his back. And here's the Big One: when the last shipment is delivered we get paid off, a cool million bucks. That's a big incentive for two underpaid special agents.'

'So you lost your last fucking shipment,' said Hayward, 'and now you're both up shit creek without a paddle. I fucking like it. Nice one Patrick.'

And there it was: the explosive belly laugh, drawing a startled look from Patrick, but which Stella found oddly comforting.

'No, old man,' Viteri smirked, 'we have our paddle back. Now we just need to tie up the loose ends.'

'You got the drugs back?' Patrick said in disbelief, 'from the Police? How?'

'Well that's the thing, the SSU didn't hand the stuff over, knowing it would just end up on the streets of Kingstown. So I called in a few DEA favours from the boys in black, and they were only too happy to oblige.'

Patrick was now looking at Stella with that strange expression he had worn just before Manuel had shot her. He looked back up to where Viteri stood. 'And you're telling us all this because…?'

'All this is going to just go away,' Viteri told him, 'the cocaine will disappear just as if it had never happened, which is great for you, because you'll be off the hook - at least as far as the drug trafficking charges are concerned.'

'And you expect us just to keep quiet about all this?' said Patrick incredulously, 'or are we going to "just go away" as well?' He looked back at Stella, his face grey with apprehension.

Just then, the front door opened and something heavy clunked onto stone floor tiles in the hallway. Stella's brief second of hope faded as Viteri grinned at whoever was at the door.

'Come on in Sherwin and say hi to your old friends.'

~ Chapter Forty Four ~

Dripping from her swim in the bay, Juanita climbed up the ladder and stepped onto the deck. She cursed herself for not reminding Papa to get her some of those tins of baked beans she liked and could not get in Cuba. As she stood drying herself with the towel, she looked up toward Thomas' house to see if Stella was on the patio, so she could wave to her. But the patio was empty and the sliding glass doors to the house were shut. There was definitely *somebody* there because she caught a quick flash of movement in the room beyond.

Strange that they had closed the doors on such a nice day, and the movement she had seen had looked somehow irregular. Sensing something was not quite right she dropped the towel and fetched the binoculars from the cockpit. She adjusted the focus until she had a relatively clear view into the room beyond the glass. At first, she could not see anyone at all; the upward angle was too steep to see fully into the room. Then she gave a little cry of alarm as she glimpsed the top half of a man crossing the room. It was not that the man was a stranger to her that had scared her; it was the gun he held, pointing at somewhere out of vision.

Undecided what to do she continued studying the house for further clues. Then another man with a gun came into view, facing towards her but looking down at something she could not see, and this was a man she recognised. It was the American called Tony from Puerto Rico, whom Papa had told her he did not like very much. What was he doing here? What was happening up there? No sign of Papa, none of Stella or Adhra, or Thomas either - just two men pointing guns. Scared and confused, and not knowing what else to do, she went below and got dressed.

The idea came to her while she pulled the comb through her wet hair. She stopped combing and stared at herself in the mirror. 'You are not allowed to go ashore,' she said to her reflection.

'But Papa may be in trouble and needs your help.

'But he might not be, and then it is you who will be in trouble, and if he is, then it will be dangerous. Look at you, just *una pequeña chica flaca*, what do you think you can do?

'Now you sound like Papa.' She started combing again, and then stopped. 'You could call the police on channel sixteen?'

'But what if Papa is just buying some marijuana? He will get arrested again.

'Why would marijuana dealers have guns? And there is that *sospechoso* American there.'

Her Papa was usually a good judge of character. She put down the comb and pulled a funny face. Her reflection laughed back at her. She knew what she had to do.

She swam to the little pontoon jetty because it was nearest, and then, keeping under the cover of the bushes, made her way around the sandy shore to where Thomas' dive shack stood set back from the beach beneath the house, locked up and deserted. Ignoring the flagged footpath up to the house, she climbed up through the tall charianthus shrubs that festooned the rocky slope; the dense bushes provided her diminutive form with continuous cover all the way up to the concrete columns that supported Thomas' patio.

Looking up she saw that the grassy bank on the east side of the house was slightly higher than the patio and jutted out a little way in front of the house wall. That grass was just tall enough to hide her, she thought, and if she crawled to the very end, she should be able to see right into that room.

Treading carefully to avoid cracking the twigs that lay scattered about, she made her way around the side of the house. When she was out of view from the patio doors, she scrambled quickly up the bank. As she reached the plateau, she heard muffled voices from inside the house, indistinct, but definitely not friendly voices.

Going down on her belly, she crept forward through foot-high grass. 'Don't make so much noise.' she whispered to the lizards scuttling away through the grass at her approach. She reached the corner where the bank sloped steeply down almost to the base of the nearest column where she had stood a moment ago.

Before she could get her first look into the room, dust from the dry grass made her want to sneeze; she squeezed her nose until the urge subsided and then snorted out the offending debris. Then she heard Papa's voice, and he did not sound happy. Slowly she reached forward and pressed down some of the grass that obscured her view.

~ Chapter Forty-Five ~

'McCredy!' Hayward spat, 'might a known you'd be in on this little charade – shit attracts shit, after all.'

McCredy stood in the lounge doorway looking down at Hayward, his face a mask of hatred. The discredited policeman looked different out of uniform: his shabby appearance seemed to Stella more appropriate, more faithful to his true character.

He limped into the room towards Hayward, head bent down in vengeful purpose.

'No, Sherwin, I don't want them touched,' said Viteri, '...for now, anyway. You'll get your revenge soon enough.'

'I see that knee's still bothering you,' taunted Hayward, 'shame that.' His laugh boomed out defiantly, causing McCredy to clench and unclench his fists in impotent rage.

'What Sherwin really needs from you, Hayward, is that confession you forced him to sign. Ain't that right, Sherwin?'

McCredy nodded stiffly. 'And his fuckin' liver,' he added vehemently. His eyes swung on Patrick. 'I should a let dose pricks kill you,' he hissed.

'But those "pricks" couldn't take a sailboat to Puerto Rico without him.' Hayward pointed out gleefully, then turned in an aside to his companions on the floor: 'Show me a man who can't sail, and I'll show you a man with a fucking hole in his soul.'

'Should a nicked them a stinkpot,' he told McCredy, 'more in your league. By the way, tell me McCredy, did you have the other guy, the boat driver, murdered while in police custody?'

'Naturally man, there was no way I could risk him talkin.'

'Course you couldn't,' agreed Hayward, 'you're a real piece of work – I should a blown yer fuckin' head off when I had the chance.'

'Enough!' said Viteri. 'Where is that confession, old man?'

'Yeah, thought that's what you were after, soon as I clapped eyes on this shit. Well, I don't have it, and even if I did, you wouldn't get your fucking sticky mitts on it.'

'Now let me see,' Viteri said, 'you came straight here from your boat, so it's either somewhere on you right now, or on that old wreck down there.' He moved close to Hayward and gazed coolly into his face. 'Your daughter's down there ain't she? Want Sherwin to go down and ask her? He's quite partial to young girls.'

McCredy looked suddenly hungry at the suggestion and glanced out of the window to where *Jupiter* sat at anchor.

'Fuck off, yank. You can kiss my bony, salt-lined arse.'

Stella could not believe Hayward would sacrifice his daughter. Surely, he was bluffing?

Viteri swung around on his heal and nodded to McCredy, who positively drooled as he headed for the front door.

Stella was about to intervene when Adhra beat her to it. 'Hayward! You cannot let him.'

McCredy stopped and turned a quizzical eye on Viteri.

'I agree,' Stella told Hayward, 'you must not let him go near her.'

Viteri flicked a finger to McCredy who turned back to the front door.

'Wait!' called Hayward, stopping McCredy in his tracks again, just as he reached the outer doorway.

'Don't panic, ladies,' he said, 'I just like a bit of brinkmanship, good for the old nerves.'

He looked up at Viteri. 'Call your fucking pervert back; I'll give you the document. The fucking thing's not on the boat.'

McCredy sauntered back into the room, a look of grave disappointment etched on his face.

'Now,' said Hayward, 'I'll tell you where it is, but I promise you McCredy - and you know how well connected I am - if anything happens to that brat of mine, anything at all, I'll hunt you down like the fucking animal you are, and they'll hear your screams in fucking China.'

'Okay, spare us the dramatics,' Viteri said, 'just tell us.'

'It's here in the house,' Hayward sighed resignedly, his game over, 'stowed it here for safe keeping, same day that cunt writ it.'

'You left it in my house?' said Thomas. 'Why you never tell me?'

Hayward tapped the side of his nose and winked at Thomas. 'Sorry old son, but he who doesn't know, doesn't tell. And you, Thomas, are a terrible liar – someday I'll teach you how to be more convincing.' He nodded to the main bathroom door at the back of the lounge. 'In there, there's a hatch into the roof space, between the second pair of rafters on the far side.'

'Go check it out George,' Viteri said, 'if the old bastard's lying I swear I'll let McCredy loose on him.'

'And George,' Hayward called, 'don't forget to disarm the booby trap.'

The big man stopped and looked round uncertainly.

'Go on, George,' said Viteri, 'the old fucker's just screwing with your brain.'

'What fucking brain?' Hayward said, feigning pain in his wobbling belly.

A few minutes later George came out of the bathroom grinning triumphantly and handed the clear plastic envelope, that Stella recognised, to Tony.

Viteri removed the sheets of foolscap and sat down on the settee to read McCredy's confession.

Patrick, whom Stella had noticed kept glancing down the hall, looked round at her again, that same meaningful glance. She smiled back an encouragement she did not feel.

'Jesus, Sherwin,' said Viteri, slipping the sheets back into the envelope, 'you sure spilled your guts for the old bastard.' He stood up and looked at Thomas. 'Key to the front door.' he demanded.

Thomas kept defiantly silent, staring up at him with long resentful eyes.

Viteri swung his gun on Adhra, aiming at her head. 'Your front door key, where is it?'

'In de kitchen,' Thomas said dully, 'on dah hook by de door.'

'Right,' Viteri said, 'let's get this fuckin' show on the road.'

~ Chapter Forty-Six ~

As evening fast approached, Juanita tried to ignore the bugs biting and stinging her bare legs and arms, keeping perfectly still for fear of being spotted by the bad men now moving purposefully about inside the house.

She pressed her face closer into the ground when one of them came right up to the patio doors. She could not see now but she heard the doors slide open and then close again with a loud clunk. Then she heard the locking bolts slam shut.

Carefully she lifted her head. Only the five captives were there now, sitting together on the floor. The armed men were elsewhere in the house. Then she heard the windows being closed from within.

One of the men returned to the room from the hallway, bent under the weight of something heavy that he seemed to be swinging back and forth. When she realised what he was doing she stifled a cry, and now she could hear the angry shouts of protest from the five inside, then a scream, Adhra, maybe. The man continued slopping what she guessed was gasoline on the walls and furniture. He disappeared into one of the back rooms, still pouring and splashing.

She fought down her terror, remembering the coaching of Papa for dealing with dangers at sea: *if there is nothing you can do then stay calm and think, because an opportunity will always come. If you panic, you might miss it.* She hoped desperately that rule applied to the horrors unfolding before her now.

When she looked again, the armed men had disappeared, and an ominous stillness had settled on the room. The light was fading fast, but she could still see the outlines of the five people sitting on the floor, heads moving in animated talk that she could not hear. She had somehow to get into the house and free Papa and her friends. With the patio doors now locked, she would need to enter from the front. Hesitantly she got up on her knees.

Then she dropped flat again at the sound of voices. They had come from the front of the house. Perhaps they were leaving. She did not understand about the gasoline, if that is what it was. As she waited for her chance she looked once more into the room. One of the huddled shapes sagged onto the floor, and one by one, the rest toppled over and lay still. Perhaps it wasn't gasoline, poison maybe?

But that was just too dreadful to contemplate. She wanted to go to them now, but she still heard snatches of conversation from the front of the house, and so forced herself to stay put. After what seemed to her an eternity, the voices ceased, and it went quiet. There was just the soft ticking of insects in the nearby shrubs.

The time for caution was over – Papa needed her. She sprang up; long bounding strides on silent bare feet, sprinting along the bank until it joined the level ground at the front. She skipped lightly to the corner of the building and peered round it to the front entrance.

The first thing that drew her attention was Thomas' car on the driveway at the bottom of the steps. In the dim light leaking down from the porch, she made out two men sitting in the front seats looking up to the house. She looked to where they looked and dodged back in fright. What she had seen was a third man approaching the front door. Despite the porch light, she had not been able to see his face because he was wearing a gas mask.

She stood with her back pressed against the wall and silently recited her times table to calm the thumping in her chest. After a few seconds of this she could stand it no longer and ran along the side veranda to the rear of the house.

She stopped on the corner again and peered around. Soft light from the room fell on the patio. Seeing it clear she moved round with her back to the wall and edged along towards the glass doors.

When she reached the doorframe, she stopped to listen. Now she could smell the gasoline. Someone was moving around inside, a faint shadow flitting across the pool of light, footsteps and shuffling noises, dragging something or someone along the floor. She took a deep breath and risked a peek through the edge of the window. The light came from a table lamp and there was a pall of yellow haze in the room. The man in the gas mask had his back to the window, lifting the recumbent form of Adhra onto the settee.

She stooped to look further into the room and located Papa, seated in one of the rattan armchairs, his head tilted to one side, arms hanging loose down the sides. She quickly ducked back as the man started to turn around. Her heart was pounding in her ears and she fought once more to push back the black fear that was telling her to run, to get as far away from this terrifying place as possible.

She pressed against the wall and recited her Hail Mary, mouthing the words in Spanish. Slowly she felt calmness return as she drew strength from the familiar litany.

Then there came a dull roar from inside and a flare of bright orange light spilled onto the patio floor. She turned to look again through the glass and froze in terror. Flames licked up the walls all around the room, fire and smoke billowed from the doors off to other rooms. In the fierce light, she saw the five bodies seated around the room as if snoozing peacefully after too much to drink.

She heard the car start up at the front of the house and drive off with a squeal of tyres. She dragged at the door handles in feverish panic, but it was pointless: they were locked fast, as she knew they would be. She looked around the patio and saw a heavy cast iron table.

Strengthened by fright she lifted it and charged at one of the glass door panels, closing her eyes at the moment of impact. The glass shattered instantly; dropping the table she jumped back to avoid the falling shards.

But something was wrong; the fire still flickered behind unbroken glass. Then she realised the panel was double-glazed and only the outer sheet had smashed: the inner one stood stubbornly intact. Summoning her strength, she picked up the table and charged again at the panel.

This time her momentum carried her on through the exploding glass and she sprawled headlong into the blazing room. She could feel the stinging of sliced skin on her arms and legs, but more terrifying was the searing heat from the blanket of flame that roared across the ceiling as new oxygen fed the fires around the room.

The awful stink of burning filled her nostrils and made her eyes water; the hot gases burned her throat, her lungs. She stopped breathing and closed her eyes.

When the heat subsided a little she jumped to her feet, then instinctively closed her eyes as she felt her eyebrows and lashes frazzle. Ignoring the sharp sting of glass cutting into her bare soles, ignoring the pain and dread that threatened to overwhelm her, fighting the urge to take a breath of the deadly hot gases, and groping blindly through the fiery smoke, she found her Papa.

All too aware she lacked the strength to carry him, she tipped the rattan chair onto its back legs and dragged it to the doorway, where she opened the locking bolts and threw both doors fully open, ducking the secondary flashover that caused.

She dragged Papa's chair onto the doorsill and tipped it backwards, spilling his limp body out onto the patio. Pushing the chair aside, she took a deep breath and re-entered, groping through the burgeoning smoke barrage until she found another occupied chair.

Gulping back the appealing reflex to breathe, eyes streaming and stinging from the smoke and heat she repeated the chair manoeuvre. She tripped the chair, and Stella rolled out and slapped onto the stone tiles. Then she noticed a steaming towel lying next to her, and with no time to wonder how it got there, she picked it up and draped it round her shoulders.

Fatigue now started to slow her efforts, but she managed once more to enter. She was so desperate for air she found it impossible to hold her breath and took in a lungful of the cloying black smoke. Her face was burning and she closed her eyes once more, memorising her path to the doorway. Coughing and choking, she dragged Adhra from the settee and along the floor by the folds of her kanga. Near to collapse with exhaustion, with a last big effort she rolled the woman's limp body unceremoniously over the doorsill, and then sank down to her knees, unable to do more.

She sobbed helplessly between fits of coughing, her exhausted body unable to respond to the awful knowledge of two more people in there. She had used up every gram of strength her slight frame possessed. Gasping and hawking up sooty mucous, she stared frantically into the billows of black smoke and flame in that hellish room, willing her spent body to do more.

Then, out of the swirling black cloud, a horror from her worst nightmares: a pair of legs without a torso came lurching towards her out of the flames. Frozen to the spot she screamed with terror.

Then realization dawned as she saw above the disembodied limbs the outline of a pair of buttocks silhouetted against a burst of bright flame: someone shuffling out backwards and dragging a body along the floor. Somehow, then, perhaps spawned by the comedy of the moment, she found that extra fuel she needed and staggered to her feet, running forward to help him.

Emerging for the final time from the inferno she helped the unknown man drag who she now saw was Thomas over the door sill, staggered to the far handrail and stood heaving in great lungful's of sweet air between bouts of coughing and vomiting.

As soon as she felt able to move again she went to the man she had helped, who was down on all fours coughing and retching loudly. The house was now well ablaze with flames licking out of the broken doorway

She wanted to go to Hayward now, but instead, coaxed the stranger to stand up and together they managed to drag the unconscious bodies away from the burning house.

The moment everyone was clear, she went to Hayward and sank to her knees by his side, looking down at him through stinging, streaming eyes. The tiles beneath her legs felt slick and sticky. Uncomprehendingly she ran a finger through it.

Blood! Then she looked at her folded legs and understood. The blood was hers. She touched Hayward's craggy smoke-blackened face, and then felt under the singed pillow of matted beard for his neck. The pulse was strong, and she whispered her thanks to Santa Maria. She looked again at her Papa's unconscious face. As she looked, it appeared to float away from her. She reeled, and then sank to the floor and her universe turned black.

~ . ~

Juanita awoke in the back of a swaying vehicle. It was dark, completely dark. There was something over her mouth and nose – a mask, letting her breathe cool oxygen; it felt sharp on her tortured throat. Somewhere a two-tone siren was going off. She was hurting everywhere. It was so dark – had the fire blinded her?

'Papa!' she cried out.

Then someone was holding her hand.

'Hi, Juanita, I'm Tracey, and I'm a doctor, well nearly. Your Papa is here in the ambulance with us, he's going to be fine. You're both going to be fine.'

She tried to feel her eyes, but she could not raise her arm, something was holding both arms down. Panic rose in her and she struggled to get free.

'It's alright, Juanita,' the lady doctor said softly, 'the straps are just for your safety while you were unconscious. Wait, I'll take them off for you.'

She felt the straps loosened. It scared her that she still could not see. '*No puedo ver nada,*' she said, '*No puedo ver nada!*'

'You can't see because your eyes are bandaged,' the lady doctor said, then, '*Er... sus ... ojos están... vendados.*'

Despite her increasing pain Juanita calmed a little and smiled – her world had just become a little more normal. 'Your Spanish need's a little practice but thank you for trying. I think it may be easier if you speak English.'

The doctor gave her hand a little squeeze. 'Yes, you're right; maybe you can help me with it when you're better. We will remove the bandage at the hospital, you will see then.'

'Stella... is she...?'

'Stella is doing just fine,' the kind doctor said, 'so don't you worry about a thing, just rest. We'll soon be at the hospital.'

She breathed in sharply as her pain intensified. It was as if she was in the fire again, burning, burning everywhere, and now she relived the broken glass entering her flesh as well. Through her torment floated a new voice, vague and distant.

'Am I going to die? Oahu! I hurt so much...' she broke off with a scream as another wave of agony struck.

Then the doctor's voice, close to her ear. 'We're giving you something, Juanita; it will make you sleep.'

Then all the horrid sensations faded, as if someone had just turned off the pain tap: she was no longer scared, just felt magically relaxed and happy. Someone was holding her hand.

'What is your name?' she murmured.

'It's Tracey, I'm a friend of Patrick's.'

'Patrick...' she said, starting to feel very heavy - she was sinking into the bed. 'I know of someone called Patrick, he is lost...' She wanted to ask about Thomas and Adhra. And who was that other man...?

She drifted off into the blissful nothingness.

~ Chapter Forty-Seven ~

As Stella awoke, she was aware of a tingling sensation all over her face and body, her skin felt tight and raw. She opened her eyes and what she saw was Patrick's crimson face hovering above her.

'Welcome back,' he said, smiling and stroking her cheek, 'how are you feeling?'

'I am having a wonderful dream,' Stella said, smiling drowsily, 'I am dreaming that my boyfriend has come to see me in heaven.'

'Well I'm afraid that's only a dream, because they sent me instead.'

'Oh well, I suppose you will have to do.'

'And I'm afraid you're out of luck with heaven as well: this is Kingstown Hospital, which must be feeling a bit like your second home by now.'

She gradually came fully awake and realised she did not know how she came to be here.

'I suppose you have an explanation for this? And why is your face that colour? … and your arms. Oh! You are hurt. Patrick, what happened to you… to us?'

He glanced down at his bandaged forearms and then smiled at her.

'Later. What's the last thing you remember?'

She considered this, but her mind was a blank. She patted her face and winced.

'Did I fall asleep in the sun? Am I here for sunstroke?'

'Eighty percent first degree burns, the doctor tells me; just like sunburn, but that's not what happened. You really don't remember anything about yesterday?'

'Patrick, I... wait, yes,' the memories returned like a speeded-up movie show. She started up from the bed. '*Herrgott noch mal*, Patrick, is everyone alright?'

'Oh good, so you do remember. I thought for a minute...'

'Thomas, and Adhra, are they safe? and Hayward? Hayward was there as well. Is he alright?'

'Shhhh,' said Patrick, putting a finger to her lips, 'everyone's alive. Hayward got out first, the fire hardly touched him. He's up and about now, fussing over that amazing kid of his.'

'There was a fire? That I do not remember.'

'No, you wouldn't' Patrick said, 'you were out cold. But you do remember the petrol the big guy splashed all over the place?'

'Yes, of course I remember that. We all shouted at once, Adhra was screaming. I think we all knew they were going to burn us alive.'

'Right,' Patrick said, 'alive, but not awake.'

'The yellow gas, yes. You were the first to become unconscious. That is when I realised what it was... but why gas us first?'

'Because it had to look like an accident. We were tied up, remember?

'The gas was APCI. I think I was the only one in a position to look down the hallway. I saw that bloke George come in with a gasmask on and activate it. With all the petrol he'd just splashed about everywhere, it wasn't hard to work out what came next.'

'APCI?'

'A chemical agent, designed to incapacitate enemy troops... knock-out gas, basically.'

Stella kept silent, piecing together these new facts. From where she had been sitting, she had not seen any of what Patrick saw. So, he had worked out a plan to save himself. She felt betrayed but did not say so. Not yet. 'You must tell me exactly what happened in there, Patrick,' she said, coldly, 'step by step.'

He had caught her tone and looked at her aghast. 'Stella, you don't think I…?'

'Never mind what I think, just tell me what happened.'

'Come on, Stella, think about it…' he saw the look she gave him and stopped. 'Okay,' he said, 'I didn't know exactly what was going on until he came in with the gas canister – I've seen APCI before and I recognised it straight away - if I'd tried to warn you and the others what was about to happen, he'd have seen it and known I was faking it when I went down. What do you think he would have done then?'

She thought about that for a moment, then admitted to herself that she was being unreasonable, but she needed to hear the rest of it. 'Yes, I see, please go on?'

'I realised that their plan to untie us was our chance to get out after they lit the fire and skedaddled. Only, if everyone was unconscious…'

'So someone had to stay awake, but only you knew about the gas, so it had to be you… Patrick, I am so sorry. Now I think I understand.'

'Consider yourself forgiven, Skipper,' then he grinned mischievously, 'but you owe me big time now, and I'll be collecting as soon as we get you out of here.'

'You will be careful with my first-degree burns?'

He bent down and kissed her. 'Darling, by the time I've finished with you; first degree burns will be the least of your worries.'

'Ooooh, I cannot wait. So tell me the rest of it.'

'Well, first I'll remove all your clothes…'

'Patrick!' she laughed, slapping at him playfully, 'You know what I mean.'

'Oh, you mean…? Okay, so when the yellow cloud got close I keeled over. That's rule number one with that stuff, get as close to the ground as possible. That way you minimise the inhalation. The gas itself, not the colouring agent, is similar density to air…'

'Patrick, please don't be technical, I get the photo. So you stayed awake.'

'No, not exactly, I took shallow breaths to reduce the intake, but eventually I dozed off. By then I think you'd all zonked. When I came to, the fire was well under way and I was sitting in a chair. Either the fire burned off the gas or the smoke displaced it. Anyway, I woke up coughing my guts up. The fire was everywhere by then and because you were all sitting dispersed around the room I saw there was no way I could get you all out without some of you getting fatally burned or suffocated.

'So I ran to the bathroom and threw all the towels I could find under the shower. Then I heard the patio door shatter – I panicked then 'cos I thought the fire had done it. That would've meant it was too hot to survive.

'When I came out with the soaked towels I couldn't see a fucking thing for black smoke. And Jesus, it was hot. I found you and covered you up. Then I heard another pane shattering and felt the air whistling in. 'I knew there'd be a flashover, so I ducked down and threw the bunch of towels over my head. But I didn't get my arms under it, so...' He held up the bandaged arms. 'Second degree, *nah-nah*. Anyway, when it passed I went to where I thought the old man was, but he'd gone, chair and all. That's when I realised someone else was in the room, because I'd heard the chair legs dragging across the floor but hadn't made the connection, what with the noise of everything burning.

'I went to get Adhra, but I tripped over Thomas and went flying. He was flat out on the deck, must've fallen off his chair. Anyway, I was in a bad way by then from the smoke and stayed down to get some air for a few seconds... maybe longer. When I got to Adhra she was gone as well, so I went to get you, and fuck me, you'd gone too.

'I thought then it must have been George, come back 'cos his conscience got the better of him. Stupid, I know, but by then I wasn't thinking straight. Anyway, I thought it must have been a big strong man to have got the three people out so quick.

'I was just dragging Thomas out when I heard this almighty scream – nearly shit myself. Next thing I know there's this skinny kid helping me. When I got outside I just collapsed in a big heap, throwing up and coughing at the same time. I was out of it. But then this kid's telling me to get up because we had to get everyone away from the house – I'd have died of shame if I hadn't been so knackered and dozy.

'It all went a bit wonky after that. I think I must have flaked out for a bit. The next thing I remember was Tim and Tracey coming round the side of the house. They only just made it as well, 'cos that side wall crashed out onto the railing straight afterwards. The other side had gone as well, so we were stuck there until the fire fighters got to us.

'I tell you Stella, the saddest thing was seeing that poor kid lying there next to her Dad.'

Stella gaped. Realization had just struck her like a slapped face.

'It was Juanita, the girl that helped you?'

'Stella, weren't you listening? It was her that smashed in the door and got everybody out. That girl was star of the show!'

She sat staring at him, her eyes filled with tears that wouldn't fall. She felt sick with dread for the next answer she would get.

'She was hurt?'

He took her gently by the shoulders.

'Out of all of us, she came out the worst,' he shook his head sadly, 'kid's in a bad way in intensive care. Hayward's with her now.'

~ Chapter Forty-Eight ~

Three days after leaving St Vincent, as the sun's dying rays cast the craggy cliffs into sharp relief, the motor yacht *Kilindini* reached the Guanica fairway buoy where George throttled back the big Volvo engine and turned towards the gap that marked the narrow harbour entrance. As her bow dropped and the speed fell away he picked up the handmade cigarette he had been saving for now and lit it up with his zippo. He had been trying to kick the habit, but right now, he needed it to calm his frayed nerves.

Not having the range to make the passage in one hop, they had routed around the string of islands, as they had on the outbound trip, stopping off at various quiet fuelling jetties along the way, avoiding the popular marinas where their presence might have been noticed. The two off-duty Special Agents were keen for anyone seeing their return to assume it had been just another local fishing trip, thereby not attracting a random customs check.

'Hey, Tony,' he called, now the rumble of the engine had died down, 'that German chick, you ever get round to screwing her?'

Tony Viteri came up the steps out of the cabin and joined him at the control station. 'Oh, almost home.' he said, gazing ahead where the wooded clifftops overhung the entrance.

'Well?' George insisted, 'did you?'

Viteri shook his head wistfully. 'Tried, a coupla times, but she was all messed up about her missing limey boyfriend. Now I seen him, I can't imagine what the fuck she saw in him.'

George didn't say anything, just stared ahead grim-faced.

After a time Tony said: 'Hey, let's have a beer to celebrate a successful mission.'

He went below and came back with two opened bottles. George accepted the beer in silence and took a long drink, but the glum expression persisted.

'What's the matter, Buddy,' Tony said, 'conscience trouble?'

'Not really,' George said, then, after a long pause, 'all the same, shame we had to waste 'em.'

'Forget it, George, what's done is done. Just keep thinking about a million smackeroos and our early retirement to Mexico.'

George lapsed back into morose silence.

'Look, George, those people knew where the consignment was headed, even knew the landing spot, for Christ's sake. It was only a matter of time before someone from the Administration came sniffing round wondering what we were doing here. How do you think it would have looked, eh, two DEA agents going out on regular fishing trips while cocaine was being trafficked right under their goddamn noses?

'Besides, we needed the stuff back to appease Gonzales, otherwise, instead of early retirement on the playa, it'd have been early concrete caskets for George and Tony. You can see that, can't you?'

'Yeah, I see that, and you're right. I just worry, that's all. I'll be okay when we get paid off and out a here.'

Tony patted his friend on the shoulder. 'Well, don't worry, Buddy, we covered our tracks pretty good. The only ones that knew we were ever on that island were those people in the house and the two SSU guys that got us the coke back. And the way those Boys in Black operate nobody's going to be shocked that two of 'em got killed in the line of duty.'

'They weren't the only ones that knew, Tony, you're forgetting McCredy.'

'Don't worry about that asshole, George, when Gonzales reads that confession of his, he'll track him down wherever he's holed up. There's no hiding place now for Sherwin.'

As the entrance approached, George gradually emerged from his black mood, so by the time they glided between the two rock walls he was back to his cheerful self. 'So, back to work tomorrow,' he said, 'we act normal and wait for our money.'

'You got it, Buddy,' said Tony, 'I'll get a message to Gonzales and he can pick the stuff up from the boat whenever he likes. Then, Mexico here we come.'

Darkness had settled on the little harbour as George nudged the jetty for Tony to step ashore with the bow line. He gave her a short burst of astern to bring the boat neatly alongside, then stepped ashore with the stern line.

Across the harbour, the sodium lights of the commercial port sent bright yellow shafts across the oily water, but solemn shadow pervaded the buildings along the quay where *Kilindini* lay.

With everything now shut down and secured, George locked the cabin door and put the key in its usual hiding place where Gonzales' boys would find it. He then joined Tony on the quay, and together they walked to the security gate.

When George had locked the gate behind him the two men continued towards where Tony had left his car, at the parking lot under the thickly wooded hill that overlooked the harbour.

The few businesses and workshops along the port approach road had locked up for the night, so the place was quiet and deserted. In the pool of light from the last street lamp, before the darker area beyond, George stopped to roll a cigarette, letting Tony saunter on ahead. When he looked up again he couldn't see Tony because the flare of his zippo had ruined his night vision, so he hurried to catch up.

As he entered the dark, he spotted his friend standing waiting for him beside one of the blacked-out buildings.

'What's up, Buddy,' George said, when he came up and Tony didn't move on, 'seen a ghost?'

He turned to where Tony was looking and froze.

~.~

Up on the hill, in the trees overlooking the harbour the man with the night-vision binoculars gave a grunt.

'Any second now, Boss.'

Then the view through the lenses clouded over with a bright flare and six rapid gunshots shattered the evening silence. When the view cleared, he saw two glowing bodies sprawled on the pavement. As the killers' car drove off, he continued to watch the two bodies for a couple of minutes. Slowly the glow from the corpses started to fade, and he turned to the man next to him.

'Okay, Boss?'

'Yeah, let's go, we'll pick up Gonzales and company in the morning. And then get a team down to that boat, I want every trace of what those idiots have been doing cleaned up.'

They walked along the trail that led down the back of the hill.

'You know Chuck, I always liked those two guys: time was, they were one of my best teams. It's such a shame when good agents turn bad.'

~ Chapter Forty-Nine ~

'I don't suppose we can charge you with breach of bail conditions, Mr Redman, under the circumstances.'

Before Patrick could reply, Howard put a restraining hand on his shoulder and said to the Chief Inspector, 'I am surprised you even consid...'

'Relax Mr Howard, I'm joking, you will be pleased to know the charges against both your clients have been dropped.'

He turned to Patrick with a grave frown. 'How is the little girl?'

'Apparently the burns aren't too serious, but she'll be badly scarred from the cuts on her arms and legs. Apart from that the doctor's say she should make a complete recovery.'

'You must find her a good cosmetic surgeon,' the Chief Inspector said, 'possibly from the United States – they are expensive, but it is amazing what they can achieve nowadays.'

Patrick didn't reply. He was thinking.

'But a traumatic experience for a fourteen-year-old,' the Chief Inspector went on, 'such a courageous child. She is from Cuba, I understand?'

'Yes...' Patrick said no more - his mind had been elsewhere, but now he thought he knew where this was going.

'Ah, I see you misunderstand my intention, Mr Redman, I am merely concerned that she should be returned to her family. After what she has been through that is only proper, do you agree?'

'Hayward is her father.' Patrick said.

'Yes, I am aware of that, but the child needs her mother right now. Mr Hayward is a somewhat, shall we say, unusual father, and his boat is hardly a fit place for her right now.'

'And Juanita's an unusual child, Chief Inspector,' Patrick said, 'and *Jupiter* is a kind of home to her. But, yes, I agree with you, and we'll get her back to her mother just as soon as she's fit to leave hospital.'

'Very well, let us leave that there for now. What I called you here for is… well there have been developments.'

'*You've caught the bastards?*'

The Chief Inspector looked uncomfortable.

'Er, no, not exactly. As you know, the Governor General has been in contact with the American authorities in Puerto Rico, and this morning he had a communication back from them. Apparently, two men have been found murdered there, and they have been identified as DEA Special Agents Anthony Viteri and George Bannermann.'

'Murdered?' said Patrick. 'Who by?'

'Apparently they were killed in the line of duty while investigating a drugs ring. Their killers have been apprehended and charged.'

Patrick felt cheated and outraged.

'So, a cover-up to protect reputations,' he said, 'fucking typical.'

'I should not really comment, Mr Redman, but I believe Sir Reginald is of a similar opinion. However, let us be thankful this messy business has now concluded.

'Apparently the drugs shipment is in the hands of the DEA, and I cannot say that displeases me. Having such a large quantity of cocaine impounded here on this island would have been, shall we say, a liability.

'On the positive side, there is no longer any evidence to implicate you and Miss Friedmann, and we have avoided an expensive and time-consuming inquiry, and not to say embarrassment in some quarters.'

'What about McCredy?' Patrick said.

'Ah, the illusive Sherwin McCredy. No, I am afraid not. But I am sure he will turn up, dead or alive. There is a general notice for him throughout the Caribbean. It is only a matter of time.'

'He was on the loose for a year, what makes you think you'll find him now?'

'We must live in hope, Mr Redman, we must live in hope.'

~ Epilogue ~

Hayward stood on *Jupiter*'s short bowsprit and watched her anchor chain rattle out of its hawse, the heavy Bruce sinking down into glass-clear water then kicking up a white cloud as it buried itself in soft coral sand.

'Fucking crap holding ground, old girl,' he muttered, looking up at the sky, then around the horizon, 'should be okay if this weather holds though. Fuck-all choice I'm afraid. We'll give you all eight fathoms, just in case, eh?'

Hayward was sailing single-handed once again. He had been sailing up and down the islands for almost four months, following rumours and whispers he had picked up in rum shacks, yacht marinas, and from fellow seafarers.

He watched as *Jupiter*'s slight sternway dragged out the cable, counting the marker links. When the eighth one appeared he jammed on the clutch, nodding with satisfaction as the weight of the cable slowed her gently to a stop then tugged her forward again as it settled back on the seabed.

Ever since the fire, an irresistible desire to fulfil the unfulfilled was driving him. He couldn't clear his mind of the image of his favourite brat lying there in a hospital bed suffering what no child of her years should suffer.

He had a promise to keep.

His current location was a small island off French Guadalupe. It was one of the few he had never visited.

He waddled aft along the deck and swung down into the saloon to kill the engine. That had been her doing, Stella, bossy miss that she was. She wouldn't let him sail without getting that prop shaft fixed, arranged the haul out behind his back and got the old donkey serviced: it hadn't run for… he couldn't remember when he had last started it. Insisted on paying for it herself too. Cocky bitch. Still, it had come in handy, he had to admit, and now he had kind of got used to having it.

He paddled towards a huddle of small fishing boats hauled up on the beach. Behind them in the trees, he'd spotted a couple of buildings, smoke from a cooking fire, and one or two gracile black figures wandering around. Even if he drew a blank here, he was getting low on weed, so the visit wouldn't be entirely wasted.

'Hey, welcome, oleman, come an' join we for some grag.' He was a long-limbed man of indeterminate age, with prominent brown-stained teeth and an impressive bundle of dreadlocks piled into a woollen basket hat. Hayward had met plenty like him over the years. Some could be quite capricious, even dangerous.

However, this one had a wide friendly smile and an honest look about him. Hayward decided to give him the benefit of the doubt.

'Thanks I will,' he said, following him up to a driftwood shack crooked among giant almond trees.

'Ma neem Hiron.' he called back. 'You want some weed?'

'Later, perhaps, Hiron. Let's have that drink and I'll tell you why I'm here.'

'Some a me buddies hee jusnow, but all friendly yanoo, no trouble, done worry.'

It was the kind of rum shack found all over the islands: chunky driftwood, pieces of old wooden boats and odd planks ingeniously nailed together and anchored to the trunks of trees to make a functioning bar, with improvised tables and chairs scattered around. Behind the bar stood an enormous rusty fridge that rattled and shook when the thermostat cut in and out.

Hayward turned to his host.

'Pleased to meet ya, Hiron, I'm Hayward.'

With a grin like a forest of trees, Hiron bumped fists with him and squealed with pleasure.

'We glad to meet you too, Hayward, dees me buddies.'

Hayward turned to the half dozen or so bony black men idling on the tree-stump chairs and benches and nodded to each one as Hiron introduced them. He knew he wasn't expected to remember any of their names and he didn't try. One or two asked him pointed questions as islanders often did, but generally, he felt accepted by the group, at home with their simple and non-judgemental outlook on life.

The rum was raw and fiery, even to Hayward, and he tried to squeeze back the tears it forced to his eyes when he took his first, overly large gulp. When a spliff the size of a Cuban cigar started doing the rounds, he decided he had better start asking his questions while someone was still capable of answering them. He described the man he was looking for.

'Yeahman,' Hiron said, 'der somebody like dat here, but he aint called McCredy. He neem Thompson.'

'Yey, dat right,' called someone else, 'Narain Thompson, he a fuckin bad piece doe, you done wanna go near dat mudder.'

'He own music bar in da village,' another added, "and he walk with a limp."

Hayward, who hadn't really expected a result here, felt his interest cautiously pricked.

'How long has he been here?

'Bout treemont, ah feel,' Hiron said.

'No, dat not right, man, he come jus' before *J'ouvert*,' said one of his buddies, 'de carnival, yanoo. Ah remember cos dat when his place open. Dat only two montago.'

'Where can I find this man, Hiron?'

~.~

The dense bushes along the beach came almost down to the water's edge, forcing him to slosh a mile through wave-sodden sand in which he sank to his ankles at every step. When he got to the clearing, he gratefully turned inland onto a hard-packed soil track, where he dropped his sandals and stepped back into them.

Transferring the heavy bundle to his other arm, he marched on up the slope where there stood a row of low adobe-clad buildings with signs outside offering a variety of goods. He soon located the source of the reggae music he had been hearing for most of the walk here, now blarting out with teeth-rattling determination. It emanated from a wooden building on stilts, a sign sporting the name "Narain's Place" in lurid colours above the open front entrance. Even now, he wasn't really expecting a result. He had felt this close to success a few times before, only to be disappointed.

Then, there he was, looking much the same as when he had last seen him, coming out of the bar and down the wide wooden steps with a pronounced limp; the man who had caused so much pain to so many people.

McCredy!

McCredy, multiple murderer, abuser of children; McCredy, bent copper turned cocaine trafficker,

Hayward unwrapped his shotgun and stepped out into the street.

The End

About the Author

Inveterate sailor and novelist Mike Rothery was born in Yorkshire, England in 1949. He went away to sea at the age of fifteen and served twenty-five years in the Royal Navy. He then went on to run a software company for another twenty years. More recently he has toured Africa, crossed the Atlantic in sailboats, and explored islands in the Mediterranean and Caribbean. Mike now lives on his boat, Island Spirit, sailing and writing wherever the wind and his adventurous spirit takes him.

Other books by this Author

Please visit Amazon to discover other books by Mike Rothery

The Patrick Redman Thriller Series
Return to Africa
Intervention

The Underworld Series
The Incomer
Bicentenary

Short Stories
The Balsam Children

Books by Amanda Wheelhouse
Girl on a Boat

Printed in Poland
by Amazon Fulfillment
Poland Sp. z o.o., Wrocław